STEVEN FELT NO EMOTION as Carson Hill's six-seater Piper Cub barely escaped crashing into the hill below him. He simply watched as the plane drifted silently down the valley. Carson was full of all kinds of surprises. He shouldn't have been able to make that turn, not with his engine gone and his controls damaged in the small explosion Steven had set off in the plane's engine compartment.

The hillside below Steven had been the intended crash sight. More than likely the crash would still kill Carson, but it wasn't going to be close enough for Steven to retrieve Carson's key.

Steven shrugged. That was only a slight glitch in his plans. Too bad. He had wanted to take the key from Carson's dead, mangled body. There would have been a nice justice to that. But there would be other keys to give him that pleasure. There had been ten players in that poker game. Nine keys.

Carson's key would survive the crash, and even with Carson dead, someone would have the key very shortly, then take Carson's position in the game.

If Steven had to kill that person, as well, so be it.

Also by

Dean Wesley Smith

The Cold Poker Gang Mysteries:

Kill Game
Cold Call
Calling Dead

Doc Hill:

"The Road Back"

DEAD MONEY

MONEY

A DOC HILL THRILLER

DEAN WESLEY SMITH

*wmg*PUBLISHING

Dead Money

Published 2015 by WMG Publishing
www.wmgpublishing.com
Cover and layout copyright © 2015 by WMG Publishing
Cover design by Allyson Longueira/WMG Publishing
Cover art copyright © Superherotm/Dreamstime,
Adam Vilimek/Dreamstime
ISBN-13: 978-0-615-82490-1
ISBN-10: 0-615-82490-0

For Kris
Who never should have been forced to go through this book with me.
Thank you.

DEAD MONEY

A DOC HILL THRILLER

Dead Money:
A poker term referring to a player who has paid an entry fee into a tournament in which he has no real chance of winning.

SECTION ONE

THE GAME BEGINS

Poker is not a game of cards. It is a game of people.

PROLOGUE

CENTRAL IDAHO MOUNTAINS. AUGUST 17, 2009

SILENCE.

Silence, the absolute worst thing a pilot can experience at seven thousand feet in a single-engine Piper 6XT. A moment before, the engine had filled the cockpit with a solid rumbling, a vibration-filled sound that Carson Hill knew from hundreds of hours of flight time.

The engine-monitoring system panel hadn't given him a warning. The plane had shaken with what had felt like a small explosion. Then everything on the control board had just snapped down to zero. Black smoke had poured out of the engine compartment, covering the front windows with a thin, black film.

Now the smoke was gone and through the film he could see the tree-covered ridgeline directly ahead.

The slight creaking of metal, the faint sound of the wind rushing past the six-seater's windows. Nothing else broke the deadly quiet.

He forced down the panic threatening to overwhelm him.

"Goddammit! What the hell happened?" His voice seemed extra loud.

He took a deep breath. Losing control now would just make sure he died.

In his hands, the plane's controls felt heavy, unresponsive. His dead-stick training was from a book and a few sentences from his original flight instructor over three decades ago. He had never actually flown a plane without a working engine.

Around him, the dark blue September sky contrasted with the green forests and brown rocks of the Idaho wilderness below. Normally, he loved this easy flight. He'd done it every year at the same time for longer than he wanted to admit. Now everything below him looked like a nightmare in the making, ready to reach out and tear him apart.

The ridgeline loomed ahead, a wall of death. He wasn't clearing that ridge.

He forced himself to take a deep breath. Then, with shaking hands, he fought to get the plane into a very slow turn.

Nothing wanted to move.

The trees ahead filled everything in his sight.

He kept fighting the controls, forcing the plane to turn by almost sheer will. It took every bit of his strength, as if the plane had a mind of its own and actually wanted to crash into the trees and rocks.

Everything seemed to slow down.

Finally, the trees were no longer growing threats filling his vision, but instead were flashing past the wing's tip.

He bet he didn't miss the tops of the pines by more than a few feet.

Somehow, between deep, sobbing breaths of oil-tainted air, he got the plane leveled and back over the deep valley, headed downstream. Sweat ran down his face and into his eyes as he tried the restart sequence.

Nothing.

With almost no control, no engine, no place to land but into trees and rocks, he was as good as dead.

He pushed that thought away and grabbed the radio mike. "Mayday! Mayday!"

4

Silence.

No response from either the McCall or Cascade, Idaho airports.

He clicked on the global positioning emergency beacon. At least Search and Rescue would find him quickly.

Ahead, the narrow valley floor closed down tighter and tighter. He couldn't be more than a thousand feet above the stream and dropping faster than he wanted to think about. It was taking every bit of his strength to keep the plane flying and not stalling.

He wiped the sweat off his face with his sleeve and tried to get a good look at what lay ahead through the oil-smeared window. Sharp rocks and thick forests covered everything. At this speed, and without any real control, the plane would be torn apart on impact.

"Need an opening," he said. "Just give me an opening." His voice sounded loud and strained in the silence of the cockpit.

The valley narrowed ahead into a rock canyon, but over the edges of the rocks he could see a meadow beyond. If he could make the meadow, he might have a chance.

He tried to focus on the open area where the sun was shining, pushing the plane past the dark shadows of the rock canyon and into the light.

But he was dropping far too fast.

He tried feathering the controls to keep the plane up, but nothing seemed to work. Instead of something responsive in his hand, it felt like he was pushing against a stuck handle and pedals.

The rock walls now loomed ahead, a tiny opening leading to the sunshine beyond.

It was going to take a lot of luck to fit the plane through that narrow canyon opening. And after thirty-three years of playing professional poker, he didn't much believe in luck.

Then, quicker than he realized possible, he was in the canyon, the rocks flashing past. Ahead, the meadow seemed to call to him, the bright sunshine a beacon.

A tip of one wing caught the rock cliff face.

Before Carson had time to react or even cover his head and face, the small plane slammed into the rock wall.

***

STEVEN LEANED against a tall pine in the shade, trying to stay cool, watching impassively as Carson Hill's plane struggled to stay in the air.

From Steven's position on the top of the major ridgeline dividing the Cascade Valley from the central Idaho primitive area, he could see clear to the Middle Fork of the Salmon over thirty miles away. He had picked the spot just for that reason.

The day had turned beautiful, almost hot. He had waited patiently for six hours, slowly drinking bottles of water, until the signal had come in from the device he had planted in Carson's plane that told him Carson had started up his engine at the Scott airstrip deep inside the primitive area.

Steven felt no emotion as Carson Hill's six-seater Piper Cub barely escaped crashing into the hill below him. He simply watched as the plane drifted silently down the valley. Carson was full of all kinds of surprises. He shouldn't have been able to make that turn, not with his engine gone and his controls damaged in the small explosion Steven had set off in the plane's engine compartment.

The hillside below Steven had been the intended crash sight. More than likely the crash would still kill Carson, but it wasn't going to be close enough for Steven to retrieve Carson's key.

Steven shrugged. That was only a slight glitch in his plans. Too bad. He had wanted to take the key from Carson's dead, mangled body. There would have been a nice justice to that. But there would be other keys to give him that pleasure. There had been ten players in that poker game. Nine keys.

Steven dropped the small remote detonation device he had used to set off the explosion in Carson's plane into a three-foot-deep hole he had dug while waiting, then quickly filled the hole back up, covering it with pine needles. No point in carrying the device back down the mountain with him. No one would find it here, and even if they did, it couldn't be traced to him. He had left no detail to chance.

He trusted no one.

He had learned that lesson well.

Carson's key would survive the crash, and even with Carson dead, someone would have the key very shortly, then take Carson's position in the game.

If Steven had to kill that person, as well, so be it.

CHAPTER ONE

RIVER OF NO RETURN CANYON, CENTRAL IDAHO. AUGUST 18

I COULD HEAR the shouts of excitement from the raft behind us over the roar of the churning white water.

I had just come through the Elkhorn Rapids like water down a new drain, giving my three passengers a thrill without ever nearing trouble. Elkhorn was one of the toughest runs on the entire Main Salmon River during low water, and I loved the challenge of it, especially early in the morning.

We had broken camp right above the rapids and the sun had just colored the tops of the mountains on both sides of the river with reds and oranges, promising another wonderful, warm day on the River of No Return. The air was still crisp with that morning bite of freshness. My life jacket didn't provide much warmth, but I didn't care. I loved these cool mountain mornings. They did wonders to clear out all the nights I spent at poker tables in the nasty, smoke-filled air of casinos.

"Doc!" Hank shouted, pointing behind me. "Look!"

I spun around in time to see the next raft in line behind me hit a rock, get shoved sideways into a standing wave, and flip over like a pancake, dumping Terry, the guide, and his three passengers into water so cold it shriveled parts men didn't want shriveled.

All four of the red life jackets disappeared into the churning white water.

"Oh, shit! Hold on!" I shouted to my passengers. I got set, my feet planted, then pulled hard and fast on my two oars, shoving my raft back toward the base of the rapids, fighting the strong current. I had to get into position below the white water.

"Grab the extra life jackets," I shouted to Hank and my other two passengers without looking. "Rope them!"

Every passenger had been given training the first day on what to do when another raft turned over. I had no doubt that Hank, a short, stocky accountant from Seattle, would do just fine, but I wasn't sure about Ben and Julie, newlyweds from San Francisco. But it didn't matter at the moment, since I didn't have time to supervise them. Right now my focus was on the appearing and disappearing heads in the white water.

One man came up, tried to shout, got a mouthful of water, and was yanked under again through the next standing wave.

"That doesn't look good."

Carl and Kenyon, in the remaining two rafts above the rapids, were pulling hard toward the right bank, just as I would do in their situation. The last thing anyone needed was two rafts over at the same time in the same rapid. Especially Elkhorn.

Of the four rafts in our party, I was the only one in the calm water below the run. It was my responsibility to get to the four people when the churning white water spit them out like a half-used cough drop.

Between two standing waves, Terry levered himself up and onto the base of the overturned raft, holding on like a cowboy riding bareback on a bucking horse. Then, with one hand, Terry reached out and yanked one of his passengers out of the water and onto the raft with him, a fraction of a second before the raft vanished under angry water.

In thirteen years on the river, I had turned over five rafts. I knew exactly what Terry was going through, and it wasn't fun. Especially this early in the morning.

"Two out, two to go," I shouted, glancing at my three passengers. Hank, bless his heart, had grabbed an emergency oar and was working hard to help me shove the raft against the current and closer to the rapids. Ben and Julie both had life jackets attached to ropes and seemed ready to throw. I knew this would be the story of their lives.

If no one died. Otherwise, it was going to ruin a perfectly good honeymoon.

A woman in a red life jacket appeared out of the lowest wave not more than fifty feet away, coming fast on the current. She was floating on her back and looked a little shocked at the sudden violence she had just been put through. I didn't blame her a bit. Riding a class III rapid without a boat can beat you up something awful.

I pulled on the oars as hard as I could, moving toward her. "Throw it over her head!" I shouted to Ben when I got a little closer.

The life jacket hit the water two feet beyond the woman and the rope smacked her in the face.

Perfect shot. First try. Maybe there was hope for young Ben after all.

"Julie, has he been practicing that at night?" I asked, giving Ben a smile and wink as I kept rowing.

Ben just smiled and Julie, bless her, laughed.

The woman in the water grabbed onto the rope and all three of my passengers pulled her with enough force to get her skimming on the water.

The man who had taken the mouthful appeared a dozen feet behind her, face down. I shook my head. The dumb idiot couldn't even figure out a way to get on his back and ride out the rapids on his life jacket.

There was no way I was going to get the raft over to him before he went past on the current.

"Take these!" I shouted to Hank over the roar of the rapids. I shoved the handles of my oars forward just as Ben and Julie hauled the woman from the water.

"Pull for the right bank as fast as you can!"

"Got it!" Hank shouted to me.

With that, I did a shallow dive into the cold water.

Even after thirteen summers of working part-time on the river, I was still not used to the breathtaking cold of the water, and that first contact with what had been snow not many days before. I doubted I was ever going to get used to it, to be honest. The sensation could suck the breath right out of you. And on top of that, the sun wasn't even up yet.

I aimed at a point I knew the current would take the man in just a few seconds, then put my head down and swam as hard and as fast as I could. Considering I was in top shape for my thirty-one years and was certified as a top scuba instructor, that was pretty darned fast, if I do say so myself, even with the drag from my life jacket trying to slow me down.

I timed it right and got to the floating body before it went past. I grabbed the guy first by the right arm, then by the shoulder. With a little leverage, I flipped him over so that his face was out of the water.

His name was Bob. He was an overweight, ex-football player who sold insurance and had hit on every woman in the entire party, even when his wife was watching. I considered for a half second doing the world a favor and letting him slip from my grasp. But only a half second. He wasn't worth the nightmares I'd have.

Just above me, Terry and the other passenger broke out of the white water on the overturned raft. They both looked shaken, but fine for the ride.

"Now let's try some breathing," I said to the limp body of Bob in my arms as we floated into the calmer water. He didn't seem to have any injuries, so more than likely he had just swallowed a bunch of the river.

I put him in a Heimlich-like hug and then squeezed, doing my best to not break any ribs, while at the same time giving him enough force to shove the water from his lungs.

Once.

Nothing.

Twice.

Still nothing.

"Don't be playing with me now, Bob. I'm not giving you mouth-to-mouth."

On the third shove, it finally worked.

Bob coughed, blinked, looked at me, then coughed some more, water pouring from his lips like a drunk trying to talk and drink at the same time.

"You're welcome," I said, letting Bob float on his back so his life jacket would hold him up and keep his head out of the water. "Now relax. You and I just got our evening dips into the river a little early today. Actually, way early."

I gave Bob credit for managing to nod and smile a sickly looking smile. I turned around to see how far my raft had made it toward shore. To be damned honest, I wasn't looking forward to towing dear old Bob to the riverbank like so much whale blubber.

Hank was pulling hard on my oars, doing a fairly good job, actually. Julie and Ben had the emergency oars out and were managing not to hit each other with them as they tried to help Hank. They were coming for me and my tow, not heading to the shore as I had ordered them to do.

I smiled at them. Thank heavens they hadn't listened to me. But I was going to have to talk to them tonight around the fire about following orders next time.

The woman they had pulled out of the water had a life jacket on a rope ready to throw, but she was shivering so hard, I doubted she was going to be a very good shot.

"Doc! You all right?" Terry shouted as his overturned raft drifted past about twenty feet away.

I gave Terry a thumb's up. "I got hot, decided to go for a swim."

Terry laughed. "Glad I could give you an excuse."

Everyone helping everyone, trusting each other, working together. True frontier spirit.

I had to admit, it felt damned good.

Of course, right at that moment, I didn't know everything about my life was about to change.

Chapter Two

River of No Return Canyon, Central Idaho. August 18

I LEANED against the gear stored in the back of the four-man raft, my feet stretched out down the middle, my hands holding my two oars, letting one act as a sort of rudder working against the current to keep the raft drifting toward the bank.

Ben, Julie, and Hank sat talking, the excitement, the shouting, the adrenaline rush of Growler rapids a quarter mile behind them. The craziness of the start through the Elkhorn run was now just a distant memory of a long-ago morning. I loved how the river did that, changing one moment of thrills and replacing it thirty minutes later with another, and then another.

Terry dumping his raft had given everyone a little excitement to start the day, that was for sure. Even good old Bob seemed to be a nicer person at lunch after his near-death experience.

Now I sat in what I called a beer-commercial moment. *It just didn't get any better than this.* I sighed and leaned back, enjoying everything around me.

A fish rippled the smooth surface and swallows darted in low, swooping back and forth in their late afternoon routines. Not a breath of wind stirred the dry grass and brush of the lower mountain slopes. A perfect day.

Actually, it had been a perfect summer. I'd been on the river four different times between poker tournaments, once in the spring run-off before the World Series of Poker and three times after the World Series in the calmer, late-summer waters. No passengers seriously hurt, no trip washed out due to weather. Not even a single snakebite in any of my groups. And best of all, I hadn't turned over one raft. It really didn't get any better.

In a few days, I would be heading back to the casinos and poker tournaments, and this wonderful river would be behind me for another summer. I loved my dual life of playing professional poker and being a part-time rafting guide on the Salmon in the summer. When someone asked me what I did for a living, I usually just said, "I risk money in the winter, lives in the summer."

A couple trips on the river, a week out here in the clear mountain air, and I always felt ready to get back to the poker tournaments. This time was no exception. And coming fresh off the river, I sometimes played my best cards.

Actually, the river often reminded me of the ebbs and flows of a poker tournament. The calm drifting was exactly like the early rounds in a big tournament, when I usually sat back, doing nothing, watching the flow of the tournament and studying the other players. Then, like rapids in the river, there would be hands where everything was often risked, my very survival in the tournament at risk. Those were usually followed by calm periods again.

Someone once described professional-level poker tournaments as hours of boredom punctuated by moments of terror.

That sounded like the River of No Return to me on a warm summer day.

I stared up at the towering mountains on both sides of us as the river lazily took us into sight of the night's camp on a sandy beach just above MacKay Bar.

Finally, I pulled my attention from the towering mountains around us and glanced ahead. The camp crew worked as they always did to set things up for the night. But an extra person stood above them, near the cars.

My business partner and best friend since childhood, Fleetwood Korte, saw me and waved.

Not possible. I was seeing things.

Fleet moved away from what looked like his new Lexus SUV to stand on a slight rock ledge. My stomach twisted into a tight knot. Fleet never came into the wilderness like this.

Ever. But there he was, big as life.

Not a good sign at all.

CHAPTER THREE

THREE DAYS AGO was the last time I had talked to Fleet, and the biggest problem he'd had with our business was getting a local fund-raising group for breast cancer research to sign a non-disclosure agreement to keep secret who was giving them the money. On Fleet's suggestion, we had decided to just put the donation under my mother's name to skip the problems.

I stared at my friend, still stunned that I was seeing him there.

And scared to death at the same time.

At six-two, Fleet stood a couple inches taller than I did, and weighed a good fifty pounds more, all carried around his stomach. His hair had thinned since our college days, but he had made up for it with a long, handlebar moustache.

Fleet's normal dress slacks, expensive black dress shoes, and silk shirt looked very out of place in the Idaho wilderness. He had taken off his jacket and actually loosened his tie, but that was all. This had to be the first time a shirt and tie had ever been seen this close to the Idaho primitive area.

I sat up straight, feet braced, hands on the oars, as if I were about to take the raft into a dangerous stretch of white water. "Hang on," I warned my three passengers.

When they were set, I pulled hard twice on the oars, sending the raft pushing through the shallow water.

A catered dinner waited, along with sun-warmed showers and fresh clothes. The three-person ground crew from the company already had the campfires going. The smell of wood smoke filled the valley, greeting the rafters like a good host smiling at the door of a party.

Another hard pull on the two oars and the raft banged into smooth rocks on the bottom of the shallows. Two of the ground crew quickly waded into the water to help.

"Oars stored," I said, repeating what I had said a dozen times over the past few days to make sure I didn't bang someone. I quickly secured the oars, then said, "Everyone out. Let's get the raft on shore and tied down."

I hoped the urgency in my voice didn't show too much.

Laughing and talking, clearly excited about the coming dinner and shower, the tourists splashed into the shallow water, going through the basic routine that made them feel like they were actually out there playing a part in their own survival on the dangerous River of No Return.

I made sure they were all ashore and the raft lashed down for the night. Then, with a glance back at the other three rafts moving slowly toward the bank, I turned and climbed up the rocky slope toward my best friend.

"Looks like fun," Fleet said, trying to smile.

There was trouble. I could always read Fleet's emotions like he had them printed on his forehead.

"Actually it is. You finally come to take me up on a ride? We only have one more day on this trip down to Riggins. I bet we can find a spot for you and come back for your car."

"Oh, boy, do I wish."

Big trouble. The kind that had my stomach twisting.

I made sure my footing was secure on the stones and stared into the dark eyes of my best friend, trying to get a read on him and the news he was carrying. "So what's happened? Is Mom all right? Ace?"

"Both are fine."

"Carrie? The boys?" Fleet was married to a real sweetheart of a woman and had two boys, ages four and six. "She finally come to her senses and kick you out into the street?"

"No. And they're all fine as well."

I relaxed a little. If my mother and grandfather and Fleet's family were all fine, then this had to be a business problem. "So spit it out. You're here for a reason and your tie is starting to scare the fish."

Fleet didn't even smile. "Your mom sent me up here to get you. Your dad was in a plane crash outside of Cascade."

"Is he all right?"

"Killed instantly."

It felt as if someone had kicked me squarely in the stomach.

My father couldn't be dead.

Nothing could kill that son-of-a-bitch.

I forced myself to take a deep breath and look out over the calmness of the water, to the tree- and rock-covered valley wall on the far side.

I didn't know what to think. How often as a kid had I wished my father would just die? Too many times to count.

Now Carson was actually dead.

Carson and I had been what some would call estranged, even though both of us were professional poker players. He mostly stayed in the big live-money games, I tended to stay in the tournaments.

Actually, *estranged* didn't describe my relationship with my father. Cold, angry, and pissed-off fit it better, and that was just my side of things. I hadn't said more than a dozen sentences to my father in twenty-seven years, even though we were often in the same casino. I had no idea how Carson had felt about me.

And didn't much care.

He had left my mother while I was in the first grade. The selfish bastard had never come back, had seemed to make it a point to avoid me and Mom. As far as I was concerned, Carson had died a long time ago. My mother and Ace, my grandfather, were now my concern. For some reason, they both still cared about Carson. Always had, no matter how much of an ass the man was to them.

"Does Ace know?"

Fleet shook his head. "That's why I'm here. Your mom thinks it would be best if you told him. She's pretty upset."

"Someday, someone's going to have to explain that to me."

Fleet shrugged. "Yeah, me too. You'd think she'd have gotten over the jerk by now."

Fleet and I had been friends since the first grade, the year my father had left. Sometimes, I wasn't sure which one of us hated Carson more.

"Anything on the news yet?"

Fleet shook his head. "The Valley County sheriff promised me he won't release Carson's name until tomorrow."

"Thanks."

So my father was dead.

I honestly didn't much care, beyond not having someone to hate all the time. Actually, it surprised me that I had any reaction at all. If I were alone in life at this moment, I would just go on and finish the trip. But I had an obligation to my grandfather, the man who had become my father when Carson left. Mom had been right to send Fleet for me. It was better that I tell Ace the bad news.

"I appreciate you coming and getting me."

"Wanted to give the new wheels a little spin. You need some time?"

"Five minutes. Let me tell my boss what's happened, make sure he's got someone to take the raft the rest of the way to Riggins, say goodbye to my passengers, and then we'll head back."

"Anything I can do?" Fleet asked.

"Try not to get your tie dirty."

I turned and was halfway down the rock-covered slope, my wet tennis shoes squeaking in the dust, when one of the details Fleet had told me sank in. I stopped and faced my business partner.

"Plane crash outside of Cascade? Right?"

"Right. Carson was the only one on board. A small plane, registered to him, from what the sheriff told me."

I nodded and kept on going toward where my boss stood beside one campfire.

Strange. I didn't know much about my father, but I did know that Carson lived in a huge home in Las Vegas and believed that roughing it was taking a cab instead of a limo.

So what the hell was Carson Hill doing in a small plane by himself in the Idaho mountains?

CHAPTER FOUR

WHITE HOUSE, WASHINGTON, D.C. AUGUST 18

PRESIDENT DOLAN CHASE took one longing glance at the pair of kings in his hand, then flipped the two cards facedown into the muck.

The game tonight was Texas hold'em, as it usually was. He had raised with the kings before the flop and been called by both his wife, Penny, and the attorney general. After an ace hit the board, Penny had led out with a fifty dollar bet, and the attorney general had raised her another one hundred.

Dolan didn't have to be a professional poker player to know those two bets made his pair of kings as worthless as an umbrella in a hurricane. Penny seldom played a hand without an ace in it, and the attorney general was known as El-Rock-O, for never playing anything but quality hands.

Still, laying down pocket kings was never easy. Dolan felt a little proud that he was able to do so and not waste any more money on them.

He glanced at his stack of chips. Down only two hundred for the evening. Not bad, actually. If he could get one good hand to hold up, he'd be ahead again.

He leaned back and watched the play, enjoying the peaceful moment. Penny had some jazz piece playing so softly he could barely hear it, and outside, the Washington, D.C., night was hot, humid, and unusually silent.

Somehow, even though Penny had left most of the furnishings in the residence like she had found them, she managed to make the place feel like a home to him. She had brought in their reading recliners from Seattle, and the custom-built poker table that converted to a regular table during the day. Unlike most presidents of the past, he didn't mind hanging around the White House and had only been to Camp David once, just to see what the place looked like.

They played poker every week he was in town, and always on Sunday evening. He'd been an avid poker player before his long-ago first election to the Senate, and he still liked the game more than any other sport. It helped him stay balanced and relaxed, as much as the President of the United States could be relaxed.

The regular players were Penny, Attorney General Donald Pearce, and FBI Director Taylor Smith. Three or four others on his staff joined in, depending on who was available. Tonight it was the assistant attorney general and one of Dolan's top speech writers. All were pretty good poker players; all were sworn to not tell anyone about the game.

Even though Truman had played poker with his press corps, Nixon had won the money for his first try at Congress by playing poker, and Clinton had a monthly card game with his old college buddies the entire time he was in office, there was just no point in letting the American public know its president played cards every week.

Dolan had no doubt most people wouldn't give a damn, but what his enemies could do with the spin made him shudder. Better to just keep the game secret until after he got out of office.

As the attorney general flipped over his ace-queen to beat Penny's ace-ten, there was a single knock on the door and Paul Hanson stepped into the room.

Paul always looked perfectly put together, no matter what time of the day or night, or what crisis was going on. His tie was never out of place, his dark hair always combed. In all the years that they had worked together, Paul had never changed what Dolan called his accountant look.

At six feet, Dolan was a giant compared to Paul's five-foot-two. Even in the Oval Office, Dolan seldom wore ties and his suit coat unless required to by a meeting. Half the time Paul or a secretary had to chase him down the hall to remind him to even put on a coat. Tonight Dolan wore what he called his lucky poker clothes—a University of Washington sweatshirt and gray sweat pants over his slippers.

"Here comes bad news," Penny said, smiling at him.

The smile didn't reach the look of worry in her green eyes. Paul never interrupted the game unless there was a problem.

"Pull up a chair," the attorney general said to Paul. "The picking is easy tonight."

Penny just glared at the attorney general, but said nothing.

"Wish I could, sir," Paul said, "but I'm just not up to your level."

"Yeah, right," the attorney general said, laughing. He was one of the few people who knew that Dolan and Paul had made some of their early business start-up money playing poker. In fact, that was how they had acquired the grocery chain, which ended up earning them millions and launching them into the Senate.

"Mr. President, can I talk with you for a moment?"

Dolan pushed his chair back and stood. "Save some of that money for me."

"Oh," Penny said, sitting forward, her small frame on the edge of her chair, "he won't have it for long. Deal those cards."

Dolan knew that look in his wife. Focused and a little angry. The attorney general was in trouble if she caught any cards at all.

Dolan turned his back on the table and moved with his chief of staff toward a private corner of the room. "What's the problem?"

Paul glanced around to make sure that no one could hear. "Carson was killed in a plane crash. He was flying out of the Big Game, headed for Cascade, when his plane went down."

Dolan forced himself to take a deep breath as his stomach twisted into a knot. He turned his back to the card game and lowered his voice. "Do they know what happened yet?"

"Too soon. Local police are at the scene, NTSB will be there tomorrow."

Dolan made himself take another long, deep breath. Just the mention of Carson's name brought back way too many memories he would rather just forget.

"What are we going to do?" Paul asked, the stress in his voice clear.

Dolan felt annoyed at his friend. "Hell, I don't know. Start by sending flowers. Some people are going to remember we were friends. Might as well not hide that fact."

"I'll do that, sir. From both you and Penny and me. Anything else?"

"I'll think about it." That was a key phrase they had set up long ago to stop discussion on a topic until later.

"Yes, Mr. President," Paul said, and left.

Dolan stood there for a moment, listening to the banter among the players. Then he put on his best public face and went back to the game. But his mind just wasn't on the cards. He ended up six hundred down for the night, his worst loss since he started the game the month after coming into office.

CHAPTER FIVE

BOISE, IDAHO. AUGUST 18

I CLICKED OFF Fleet's cell phone and slipped it back into its hands-free slot on the dashboard. "Mom said Ace is at the Club. You got an extra tie I could wear with my tee shirt and cutoffs?"

Fleet laughed. "Actually, I might. But I'd be afraid to let you use it. You might start a new fashion trend."

"Yeah, river formal."

Fleet laughed. He had just turned off of Highway 55 and had the Lexus headed down State Street and into the downtown area of Boise. The roads were still busy with evening traffic.

I felt like I was in some weird *Twilight Zone* movie, with everything clear, yet feeling out of focus. Since waking up in a tent on the river at sunup, this had been a damned long day, and it didn't look like it was going to end any time soon. It felt a lot later than only eight.

"God, I hate the Club," Fleet said. "Too snooty for my blood."

"No argument from me."

Actually, I didn't hate the Club as much as Fleet did. I just found it a little too highbrow.

The Club catered to the rich and powerful in Idaho, from the governor to the corporate presidents. A limited membership of three hundred kept a long waiting list active and political. It took ninety percent of the members voting to allow in a new member when an opening happened, due to death. Ace got voted in when I was still a kid, right after he won his second World Series of Poker Championship. I had always figured they wanted him for the poker action.

Ace just looked at the place as easy money.

The Club filled the top two floors of a downtown office building. As a kid, I thought it was really cool that the elevator only said it went to the eleventh floor. But magically, Ace, with a key, could get me to the secret floors above.

"Is your mom all right?" Fleet asked.

"Upset. Very upset."

Fleet just shook his head. "So how are you going to handle telling Ace?"

"There's no good way that I can see to tell him his only child was killed. I suppose just get him into a private area in the Club and tell him."

"How about we call him, get him to meet us at his house?"

"He'd want to know why I was pulling him from a game, and he'd argue with me. I don't want to have to tell him on the phone."

Fleet pulled onto Main Street and then, in one block, turned again onto Capitol Boulevard. The Club's building, called the Hoff Building, towered beside the Capitol Building. The top two floors used to be a restaurant and bar before the Club bought them and moved there.

When home from college, Ace had let me sit in on a few of the poker games at the Club. Ace had always offered to cover my poker losses during those games, but I had never taken him up on it. Instead, I usually went home thousands ahead. Some of that money helped me and Fleet become two of the only people I knew to go into college flat broke and come out rich—from my ability to make money at a poker table, and Fleet's ability to have the money make even more money in real estate and investments.

We were the perfect team.

"You want me along to talk to Ace?" Fleet asked.

"Damn right I do. I don't want to do this alone."

"Figured."

"Would you in my spot?" I asked, turning to stare at my best friend.

Fleet shook his head. "Not with *your* grandfather. Ace comes up to my chest when he's standing up straight, and he still scares the hell out of me. He could intimidate a lamppost into bending over."

"Only if there was a good bet riding on it," I said.

"No kidding."

A minute later, Fleet found a parking spot in the building's garage and we got on the elevator. I pushed a small, unmarked blue button on the top of the elevator panel. Ace had pointed out the official guest button before I was tall enough to reach it, and warned me that the button was only to be used in emergencies. This was the first time I had used it.

"Yes?" a voice asked as the elevator doors closed and we started up out of the parking garage without pushing any floor buttons.

"Jonathan 'Doc' Hill and Fleetwood Korte, guests of Raybourne 'Ace' Hill. He should be in the card room."

"One moment, please," the voice said.

The elevator stopped at the first floor and the door opened, revealing a woman wearing a purple pants suit. She had a stern, take-no-prisoners look on her over-made-up face. Her dark hair was stuck up in a bun so tight, it looked like her eyebrows were trying to make an escape into her hairline.

"Oh, oh, trouble," I whispered to Fleet.

The woman stepped on, pushing a wave of lilac perfume ahead of her. She nodded to Fleet, then gave my shorts, tee shirt, and water-stained tennis shoes a dirty, once-over look, as if I had shown up at a formal dance in my underwear.

With what sounded a little like an actual "huff," she turned her back and pushed the tenth floor button. Then she must have noticed that we hadn't pushed a floor button.

"Which floor would you like?" she asked, not even glancing at us, her voice sounding like it was just *too* much trouble for her to stoop to help.

I hated people with this woman's attitude. Just because I wasn't dressed the way she thought I should be, I wasn't worth anything. I didn't get this attitude either on the river or in casinos. Money talked in casinos, and the cards didn't care how a player was dressed.

"None, thank you," Fleet said. "We're going to the Club."

"Of *course* you are," she said.

I could hear the slight laughter in her voice. I was annoyed enough that I had been forced to come off the river early because of my father. I didn't need to deal with people like this woman.

"Actually," I said in a loud whisper, right to the back of her head, "if you must know the truth, we just enjoy riding elevators."

For some reason, I just couldn't leave people like this woman alone. I was like a kid with a stick staring at a beehive. I had to poke. It had been a habit that had gotten me into my share of problems.

"Yeah, we really love it," Fleet said, following my lead. "A different building every day."

"Three hours a night. It gets us *hot*." With the last word, my breath actually loosened a hair in her bun.

"The short buildings are the hardest," Fleet said, managing to keep a pretty decent poker face. "Up and down. Up and down. All too fast."

"Yeah," I said, "slow is better. Longer is better. Slow. Longer. Don't you think?"

I stared at the back of the woman's head. Her shoulders had hunched up by her ears and she looked like she was about to explode.

"I sure do," Fleet said, pretending excitement. "Longer is *always* better." He stretched the word "always" out to the length of a normal sentence.

The doors opened at the tenth floor and the woman fled into the hallway, not even looking back at us.

"Nice meeting you," I said as the door closed.

"Too bad we have to continue to live with her smell." Fleet waved his hand in front of his face as if it would help clear out the thick lilac perfume that hung in the elevator like a purple cloud from a bad horror movie.

The elevator started up.

"Mr. Hill will meet you in the lobby," the speaker voice said.

"Thank you," I said.

"You are welcome," the speaker voice said. "I hope you *enjoy* the rest of your ride. I'm afraid it's not very *long*."

Fleet snorted, and I could feel my face turn red. Caught once again with the stick in my hand.

CHAPTER SIX

BOISE, IDAHO. AUGUST 18

AS THE ELEVATOR DOORS opened onto the twelfth floor, Ace stormed into the marble-covered foyer like a bull entering a ring. His gold sweater, white shirt, and brown slacks made him look like a shrunken golf pro. More than likely, he had played golf earlier in the day. Like my passions were poker and the mountains, Ace's passions were poker and golf. Ace's nickname came not from cards, but from making two holes-in-one on the same day at the Dunes in Las Vegas back before I was born.

I loved the way my grandfather never did anything half-heartedly, even walking. When Ace entered a room, everyone knew he was there. His attitude was that you either pushed every moment of life to the fullest, or you didn't belong on the planet. I couldn't count the times my grandfather had said to me, *Move it! You're wasting space.*

"Good seeing you again, kid," Ace said, sticking out his hand.

Same greeting, no matter how long we had been apart. I wanted to give the short, bald man a hug, but instead settled for our standard handshake. The routine handshake and greeting started back when I was a kid and my father had just left.

"Good seeing you again, Fleet," Ace said. "How's that wonderful family of yours?"

"Healthy and growing taller by the day."

"As they should," Ace said. "Get worried when they start shrinking."

With a large gesture with his arm, he indicated we follow him through the ornately carved lobby doors and into the club bar area. The low lighting and fantastic evening view of the city made it feel as if we were walking out onto a rooftop. Only without the wind and the city noise.

"So, what's the bad news?" Ace asked as we entered the bar. "It's got to be something to bring you off the river early and both of you here. And it's not your mother, since she just called a while back to see if I was here."

"Let's get settled first," I said.

"Kid, you're scaring me."

Ace pointed to a table near a window looking down over the state capitol building.

"View always gets me up here," Fleet said.

Ace snorted. "What would you expect in a playhouse for the state's richest people? A view of Denny's? You two ready for me to put you up for membership yet?"

"You're kidding?" Fleet asked.

"You see me laughing?" Ace asked, staring at Fleet until Fleet shook his head no. "You know enough people, have enough money, are swinging some pretty good power with those businesses and land holdings, not to mention all that money you keep giving to charities. Who knows, you might just get in sometime in the next decade."

I noticed that Fleet actually shuddered.

"Thanks," I said, "I think we'll wait a while."

"Just give me the word."

Fleet slid in beside the window and I sat beside him, letting Ace have the other side of the table. A waitress arrived before I had my chair up to the table.

"Glass of Chablis, Debbie," Ace said. "Ice teas for both these light-weights. Bring the pink sugar stuff with you. They can't handle *real* sugar."

Ace had many tricks he'd learned over the years. He never forgot a name, even of a waitress, and he remembered what people drank, even if he hadn't seen them in years. He got a lot of mileage out of those two details.

When Debbie finished putting down the drink napkins and left, Ace focused on me, leaning forward. That laser look could get to the core of a regular card player, see their intentions, sometimes it seemed, their very thoughts. That ability to read other players had made Ace one of the most respected and feared card players in the world, both in tournaments and big-money games.

"Spit it out, kid. What happened? What the hell are you doing here?"

I forced myself to take a deep breath and then just blurted it out. "Carson was in a plane crash outside of Cascade."

Ace's eyes seemed to sink into his skull. He sat back like someone had shoved him.

"The one on the news this morning?" he asked softly. "I was afraid it was his plane."

Ace's voice was barely a whisper. In all my life, I had never heard my grandfather whisper anything.

"I'm sorry, Ace. He was killed instantly."

Right at that moment, I hated my father even more for making me hurt my grandfather. That son-of-a-bitch Carson couldn't go into the ground fast enough as far as I was concerned.

Ace sat there, his eyes blank.

The soft sounds of people talking at other tables, the clinking of glassware, seemed to grow in volume. I wanted to move around to the other side of the table and just hold him. For the first time, my powerful grandfather looked small and weak and old.

Debbie finally brought our drinks, and Ace seemed to come back into his eyes. "Thank you, darlin'."

After she left, he asked, "Do you know where they took his body?"

"Cascade," Fleet said. "Along with the money he had in the plane with him."

"How much?" Ace asked. "You know?"

"Three-point-six million in a suitcase," Fleet said.

I glanced at Fleet. He hadn't told me that little detail. Suddenly, Carson being in a small plane in Idaho made sense to me. A private game players called the Big Game was held at the R.A. Scott ranch on the upper Middle Fork of the Salmon. The ranch had its own airstrip, and the game was a weekend-long event held in the late summer every year.

Ace nodded and sat back again. "He at least had a good last weekend. He would have wanted to go out that way."

Fleet whistled softly. "Three-point-six million. I guess you could say he had a good weekend. What was his buy-in? What kind of game was it?"

"One million buy-in," I said, letting my grandfather have a little more time for the news to sink in. "R.A. Scott started the Big Game a long time ago, holding it on his ranch. Ten players, half businessmen, half top poker players. The rich guys love to say that they sat down in a game with the well-known poker players. The players go for the easy pickings."

"I don't remember you playing in it," Fleet said.

"I'm usually still on the river every year."

At that moment, I didn't want to say I didn't play because Carson was always there. Seemed wrong.

Fleet nodded.

"So what happens next?" Ace asked.

"NTSB investigation unit will go to the scene," I said, "to determine the cause. At some point they'll release everything and we can make plans then."

"You've worked with the NTSB before?" Ace asked, staring at me again.

"Sure. A number of times."

Actually, the last time I had gone out with an NTSB team was on a search and rescue dive. Three of us had ended up scuba diving in a muddy pond looking for a kid's body from a small plane crash.

Just the thought of having that child's bloated face appear out of the muddy water inches from my face mask had given me nightmares for a month afterwards. Thank God, I hadn't been the one to find the body.

"Kid," Ace said, the intensity back in his eyes as he stared at me. "I need you to do me a favor."

"Anything."

"I need you to stay on top of every detail of Carson's death."

"Why?" Ace's favor actually surprised me. "The authorities are investigating. There's nothing more I can do. They won't even let me on the crash site."

"I need it for me. From you. I trust you. I don't trust *authorities*."

I stared at my grandfather's wrinkled face and his intense dark eyes. The old man never did anything without a reason. Especially something like this.

"How far do you want me to go with this?"

"All the way. Every detail. Doc, I know how you felt about your father, but do this for me."

"What aren't you telling me?"

Ace glared at me. "Kid, do it for me, as a favor, or don't do it. Up to you."

"Dammit, Ace. You're dealing me half a hand here. You think something more might have happened to Carson, don't you?"

"I honestly don't know," Ace said, leaning forward, his voice intense and powerful. "That's what I want you to be god-damned sure of. You've been on these sorts of investigations before, right? Worked with these people. Just bring me the damned answers about the death of my son."

I leaned back from the power in my grandfather's words.

No matter how much I wanted to just wash my hands of Carson's death, it seemed my grandfather wasn't going to let me. I owed Carson nothing. I owed Ace everything.

"All right. I'll head up to the crash scene tomorrow morning."

"I'll go with you," Fleet said.

"Thank you," Ace said. "Both of you."

The old man again seemed to vanish from his eyes. He sat back, the glass of wine in his hands, his head turned to look over the city.

The three of us sat there for a half hour in silence.

Then we took Ace home.

CHAPTER SEVEN

LAS VEGAS, NEVADA. AUGUST 19

AS GROVE PRIED open the top half of the casket lid, the stench of rotted human flesh hit him in the face and knocked him against the dirt wall of the newly opened grave.

"Holy Christ!"

He scrambled out of the hole, moving behind the backhoe. As soon as he was far enough away, he gulped huge breaths of the warm, fresh morning air, trying to clear his nose and the rotten taste in his mouth. It helped, but not much.

The son-of-a-bitch who hired him to do this should have warned him about the smell.

Grove leaned against the shoulder-high wheel of the machine and struggled to settle his stomach. The early morning traffic on the other side of the cemetery gave the place a distinct background rumble. It felt damn weird doing a robbery in the middle of a graveyard, with people going by on their way to work. But the guy had assured him that it wouldn't be a problem. If Grove wore a cemetery maintenance suit and used cemetery equipment, no one would notice. It was normal for the cemetery crew to dig new graves early in the morning.

So far, the man had been right, and this job had been a drop-kick. Except for the damn smell.

Grove took a couple more deep breaths and moved back to the edge of the hole, peering in as if the dead guy might jump out at any moment. The cover of the concrete liner was hanging where Grove had left it, on a chain attached to the back-hoe bucket. The top half of the lid to the casket was flipped up against the dirt.

He stared at the guy in the casket, surprised. He expected bones or something wrinkled and dried like a mummy. This guy looked like he was sleeping in a hooker's bed, like he had been buried yesterday.

"Oh, hell, did I get the wrong grave?" He moved around the pile of dirt and checked the stone at the head of the grave.

Jeff Taylor.

Right name, right death date. The guy has been down there for over twelve years. In his day, he'd been one of the best poker players around. He'd won the main event at the World Series of Poker three years before he had been killed.

"Man, they're cremating my ass," Grove said, staring at Taylor's body. "No way am I going to end up like that."

He glanced around, then checked his watch. Six-thirty in the morning. He needed to get the hell out of the cemetery in the next fifteen minutes. Besides, the smell was bad enough. He couldn't imagine what it was going to be like when the hot desert sun hit the body.

Grove stared at the dead guy again. He had already made some good money on this job, and was going to get a bunch more if he went down into that hole one more time. He had done a lot of stupid things over the years, for a lot less money. He could do this.

He took a few more deep breaths of the fresh morning air, then covered his nose with the sleeve of the maintenance suit and slid back down the slope of dirt and into the hole.

Trying to hold his breath, he knelt on the edge of the casket and liner and opened the guy's suit coat. At first it didn't want to come loose, sticking as he pulled.

"Oh, man, that's gross."

The odor thickened, smelling like rotted fruit left in a dirty outhouse on a hot summer day.

"No amount of money is worth this."

He tried to keep his head turned away while at the same time working to unbutton the man's shirt.

The cloth had stuck to the dead guy's chest like a bandage soaked in blood. Through his gloves, he could feel the guy's skin where the fluids trapped by the shirt and coat had turned it to jelly. He hoped that by opening the shirt the guy was not going to just melt and run like Jell-O left in the sun.

Grove finally managed to get two buttons open and the shirt pealed back enough to see the key he was after. It looked like a stupid bank key. For some reason, after all this, he expected it to look special.

He scooped the key off the guy's chest, tape and all, trying not to take too much of the guy with it. He tucked the key into a plastic bag and stuck the bag in his pocket.

Then he climbed out of the hole and walked away. He had no doubt he was going to have nightmares about this for months.

CHAPTER EIGHT

LAS VEGAS, NEVADA. AUGUST 19

"GUN!"

The shout echoed down the hall from the Las Vegas Police main precinct room.

Uniformed officers and plainclothes detectives dove for cover behind whatever they could find, pulling suspects and others to the ground with them.

Detective Annie Lott had just stepped off the elevator coming up from the photo lab and was headed for her desk. She had on a jogging suit and tennis shoes, and had her long brown hair pulled back into a ponytail. In her hand were pictures of what twelve years of being buried had done to professional poker player Jeff Taylor.

As she ducked for cover near a short, metal drinking fountain tucked between the two restroom doors, she realized that the man in the middle of the hallway a few steps in front of her was the one with the gun. He was twisting from side to side, the gun waving in the air as everyone scrambled for cover.

He was clearly focused on the men and women in the big room in front of him and not looking around at all.

Annie's gun, along with her street clothes, was in her locker downstairs. In fact, most of the police in the big room had checked their guns when they came in. It was standard policy.

From behind, the guy appeared huge, with linebacker shoulders and no neck showing above his tee shirt. The gun looked small in his hand. From his movement, she could tell he was panicked and angry.

Without really having a plan, she took three quick and silent steps toward him. Then, as his hand came around with the gun, she used her forward motion and did her best impression of a field-goal kicker, keeping her attention focused completely on the gun.

The top of her foot caught the guy's lower arm, right above his wrist, and she could feel and hear the bone in his arm snap.

The impact jarred her foot and leg, but not enough to hurt her.

The gun went flying toward the main room. She just hoped like hell it wouldn't go off when it landed.

It didn't. It bounced twice and then smashed into a chair leg and stopped.

She caught her balance as the guy, holding his wrist, spun around to face her.

There was a craziness in his eyes. And a ton of anger. Someone was going to have to shoot this bastard to stop him, that was for sure. More than likely, he was on some sort of drug. And now he was going to take out his anger on her. Smart thinking on her part.

He was far too big and wired to let him even have an instant to come at her. She kicked again, this time right between his legs, trying to drive his family jewels right up and out of his mouth.

Direct hit.

And with a lot of force.

The crazed idiot's eyes went wide, like he was some sort of poorly drawn cartoon character, then he went to his knees as the shock hit him. He tried to grab his crotch with both hands, including his broken arm, and managed a pitiful choked sound of pain.

"Pulling a gun in a police station is damn stupid," she said to him.

Then, as he bent forward, she planted one more solid kick to his nose, heel first this time.

He went over backwards, his nose crushed.

The back of his head hit the tile floor hard and bounced.

He was out like a light.

She was panting. And her heart was racing as she stood over him. What a morning this had turned out to be. Staring at an open grave and taking down a lunatic wasn't the way she had hoped to start the day.

"Clear!" someone shouted.

Then the round of applause started, along with the cheering, as everyone climbed to their feet.

She just smiled as two uniforms grabbed the guy, flipped him over onto his bleeding nose, and roughly put handcuffs on him. She was going to have to soak her foot for a few hours tonight, but otherwise, she wasn't any worse for the event.

By the time the congratulations, back-patting, and jokes about her soccer ability for kicking two balls at once had stopped, she had made her way to her desk.

She still had the folder of pictures from the cemetery in her hand.

She put it on her desk, then took off her shoe and rubbed her foot. It was going to be bruised, but at least nothing was broken. That was a hell of a lot better than she could say for the guy they were hauling out on a stretcher. Served the bastard right.

Thank heavens she made it a habit to stay in shape. At thirty-four, she had no intention of stopping the running and sessions in the gym just yet. They kept her at her desired 140 pounds, which for her five-ten frame was perfect. And allowed for her to be able to deal with events like crazed gunmen.

She left her shoe off and forced herself to focus on the pictures of the grave robbery.

The *Las Vegas Sun* would have a field day with this. The captain wanted it solved, and solved quickly, before it started hitting every national poker broadcast. She had no doubt it already would. It wasn't often that a former World Series of Poker champion had his grave robbed.

From what she could tell, twelve years hadn't done much to Jeff Taylor. The embalming must have been done correctly and the casket and concrete liner must have remained sealed fairly tight. That often wasn't the case, but with this body, it clearly was.

As she studied the pictures, everything around her went back to normal as street patrolmen, detectives, and brass came and went, sometimes with civilians, sometimes alone. After six years with full detective rank, she was used to it.

She had been called in on this case because of who Jeff Taylor had been while alive. At the time of his murder, he was considered one of the best poker players in the world, if not the best. The case was still unsolved, but almost everyone figured it had been a robbery gone bad, one of those types of cases that took luck or a confession to solve.

She tucked a few errant strands of hair that had escaped from her ponytail behind her ear, a gesture that her father always told her meant she was stressed.

Hell, she *was* stressed, both because of the idiot with the gun and this case.

As a kid, she had idolized Jeff Taylor and a bunch of the other poker players of that time. It had been her dream to play full-time professional poker, and she was moving closer and closer to the dream with each day.

Before this case had come up, she had asked for some time off during the next week to play in a few poker tournaments at the Bellagio. And grave robbery or no grave robbery, she was still going to be there.

Six months ago, she had gone half-time with the force, working almost on a case-by-case basis, spending her free days playing ring games and smaller poker tournaments around town. She had enough of a bank built up that poker would soon be her life full-time, and she couldn't wait. She would miss the police work at times. But not that often.

She glanced again at the pictures. She hated the smell of a long-buried body. It was enough to make any hardened cop head for the nearest bush.

That key must have been damned important for someone to fight through that sickening odor, crawl down in that newly dug hole, shove open the casket, and take the key from the decomposing skin and chest fluids trapped by Taylor's shirt and suit jacket.

Really important. And that was what was going to lead her to the solution to who opened the grave.

And with luck, maybe even solve the cold case of Jeff Taylor's murder along the way.

CHAPTER NINE

Las Vegas, Nevada. August 19

IN THE HALLWAY, the elevator signal dinged.

Grove was coming.

With a glance, Steven made sure everything was as he needed it to be in the huge Monte Carlo penthouse suite. The marble floors and columns shined in the recessed lighting. Lush couches and chairs filled one section in front of a huge stone fireplace. A dining table with a dozen chairs around it was slightly elevated to one side of the big room. Heavy drapes shaped the fifteen-foot-high windows that looked out over the Strip and downtown Vegas beyond.

A towel blocked open the door leading to the elevator. He adjusted the room service uniform, then stepped back into the shadows toward one bedroom, out of sight.

He could hear as Grove pushed open the door, kicked the towel away, and let the door close behind him.

"Yo," Grove shouted, his voice echoing through the five rooms. "Anyone home?"

Steven put a hand-held voice-changer to his mouth. "Do you have the key?" The words sounded low and powerful and echoed in the big suite.

"Of course I do. And let me tell you, opening that casket was one smell I ain't gonna soon forget."

"Just place the key on the dining table."

Grove's footsteps clicked on the marble floor as he moved toward the table. Steven wanted to peek out at the man he had hired, but restrained himself, instead trusting his ears. So far Grove couldn't identify him, and that's the way it needed to stay if Grove was going to live. Steven hadn't decided yet if that would be the case. One moment he planned on killing the man, the next he decided it was just too much of a problem.

He had found Grove by listening to a conversation between two off-duty cops in a poker game down at the Golden Nugget. He had called Grove, who had not been interested in the job until he understood that it paid one hundred thousand dollars.

Grove put the key on the hard table of the penthouse suite with a click. "Okay, where's my money?"

"Describe the key."

"It's just a damn key. Looks like it belongs to a bank. Long and thin, has a three etched on the side of it."

Steven's heart skipped, and he wanted to race out there and pick the key off the table. *Taylor's key.* It was actually here, in the suite with him.

"Good," he said, keeping his voice level and powerful-sounding. "Look on the second chair on the window side of the table." Again his altered voice seemed to echo in the huge suite like a bad movie character.

Grove's heels clicked on the tile as he moved around and pulled the chair out with a scraping sound. There was a rustling of paper and then a gasp.

Grove *should* gasp. There really was seventy-five thousand in the bag. But the price was worth it, especially for Taylor's key.

Steven shook his head. Wait. Now that he thought about it, seventy-five thousand was too much to waste on a petty thief.

"Thanks," Grove said. "Man, you need anything else, you just call me."

"I have your number. I know where you live. I know more about you than you want me to know."

Steven stepped out of hiding and walked toward Grove, putting the voice device in his uniform pocket as he did.

Grove looked shocked to see him. He studied Steven's room service uniform. "Tips must be good," he said, holding up the bag.

"Not that good," Steven said. He pulled out a pistol and shot Grove in the chest before the man could even move.

The loud explosion echoed around the room, but Grove knew these suites were very soundproof. And at the moment, there was no one else on this floor.

Grove went over the dining room railing backward, landing face-down on the white carpet. Blood splattered against the window and over the couch.

Steven took a deep breath and enjoyed the smell of cordite mixed with the copper-smell of blood. By the time this game was over, he might come to love that smell.

He walked down the few tile steps and shot Grove through the side of the head.

The paper bag full of money had fallen near the couch. Using a plastic bag he had brought, Steven picked it up, wrapped it tight and put it in his pocket, making sure that as little as possible of Grove's blood got on his gloves or uniform.

Then he put the gun beside Grove on the coffee table. It was untraceable, from a robbery in Salt Lake City five years ago.

Steven then moved back up to the dining table, putting the chair Grove had moved back into place. Then he picked up the key in his white-gloved hands and studied it for a moment, like he was studying a great piece of art.

Jeff Taylor's key.

He actually had it.

The thrill of success cut through him like an expensive scotch whiskey, warming him.

He put the key inside his vest pocket, then moved over and picked up the towel beside the door. He hung it back on the towel rack in the bathroom, then walked slowly through the suite, making sure nothing was out of place. A whale from Japan would arrive in twenty minutes and find Grove's body.

When Steven was satisfied that he had missed nothing, he stepped out of the door and into the corridor, moving like an employee toward the service area, his head down, his face hidden, just in case the camera in the corridor had been brought back online sooner than he had expected.

One key down.

Eight players with keys remaining.

This game was going to be more fun than he had imagined.

CHAPTER TEN

CENTRAL IDAHO MOUNTAINS, AUGUST 19

"MAN, I STILL can't believe Carson left you everything," Fleet said as he took the SUV off the comfort of Idaho's main north-south Highway 55, turned east and headed away from the small crossroads called Banks.

I had been stunned as well. We had stopped by to see if Ace was all right. Without even a good morning, or asking if we needed a cup of coffee, the old man had tossed me Carson's will. "Wanted you to know this before you got started. He left everything to you."

"I don't want it," I had said, tossing the paper back at my grandfather like it was on fire and about to burn me.

"Too damn bad," Ace had said, smacking me in the chest with the will. Fleet had taken it from me before I could toss it back once again.

I actually felt insulted, and damned angry, that my father might think that giving me a bunch of money might make up for leaving and never coming back. Nothing made up for that cold, cruel act. Certainly not money.

I took a deep breath and forced myself to calm down. Just thinking about it made me mad.

"There," I said, pointing to a gravel road on the left heading north up a wide valley. "The Middle Fork Road."

Fleet left the pavement and hit the gravel going a little too fast. The first chatter bumps forced him to slow down. Behind us, a cloud of dust billowed in the warm morning air.

"How far do we have to go?" Fleet asked. "This is going to jar my fillings loose."

"Until it ends, actually," I said. "Thirty-five miles, maybe forty. I've never been up this way."

"Wonderful," he said, as he unsuccessfully tried to dodge a series of chatter bumps that looked like standing waves across the road. "You bring a map?"

"Who needs a map? We're guys, remember?"

Fleet only snorted.

I glanced at my watch, twisting it on my wrist to a normal, more comfortable position. It always felt odd putting the watch back on after coming off the river. Out there, I didn't have to worry about time. Everyone lived by the rise and fall of the sun.

Eleven-thirty.

The NTSB team wasn't due to be on-site until two. We were ahead of schedule. Amazing for two guys who never seemed to make a class on time in college.

"You get some sleep last night?" Fleet asked. "I'd suggest you doze now, but no one could sleep on this bump-fest."

"Doing fine."

Actually, I had managed a really hot shower and three hours of sleep after spending time consoling my mother and getting her to go to bed after taking a couple of sleeping pills. Carson had left her twenty-five years ago, divorced her, flat walked out of her life. And mine. How could she be so upset at his death? She had never even been angry at Carson for leaving, and had never allowed me to speak poorly of the man in her presence. Maybe she thought he was coming back at any moment and was just away on a very long poker jaunt.

She had never remarried, never even dated. I had tried to get her to date when I was in college, at one point even signing her up for a singles weekend dance. She had flatly refused to go. For decades, my mother had to be in the worse case of denial in modern record, and it wasn't anything that could be changed without a whole lot of counseling, something else she refused to do.

Maybe, now that the bastard was dead, she could move on. More than likely, she was going to just be waiting for him to return, like she had done for years.

"How's your mother doing?" Fleet asked as he cut to the right along the gravel road, avoiding the biggest of a dozen potholes.

"As expected for a woman who just lost her husband instead of one who left her over a quarter of a century ago."

Fleet shook his head. "Maybe now we'll find out why he left. There's bound to be something in his old papers."

"Not sure I really want to know," I said.

"Well I do," Fleet said. "Just call it lawyer curiosity."

"I thought that was called voyeurism."

"If that wasn't so damned close to the truth, I'd have a comeback," Fleet said.

Why had Carson left? The simple question that I had asked for years. Another woman? Traveling too much? It couldn't have been poker, because my mom loved the game and supported Ace teaching me how to play. There had to be something else, something no one would tell me.

An even larger question was why Carson had never once came home to see his family. To see me. Carson had given my mother good financial support and full custody of me. But nothing else. The son-of-a-bitch had given his duties as a father over to Ace and just walked out.

A hundred times I had thought about going up to my father in a casino and demanding an answer, but I could never bring myself to talk to the bastard.

Who really was Carson Hill? Maybe now that he was dead, I would get some answers, whether I wanted them or not.

CHAPTER ELEVEN

CENTRAL IDAHO MOUNTAINS. AUGUST 19

WE HAD GONE another five miles on the rough, gravel road when Fleet's cell phone beeped.

"Amazing the thing still works way up here," Fleet said.

"There are a lot of houses and money in this area," I said, pointing a big mansion up through the trees on the right. "The kind of people who won't put up with inconvenience."

"Oh, yeah, those types," Fleet said. "Club types. Nice of them to live up here."

"Second homes. Too far from good restaurants to be anything but roughing it."

"Figures," Fleet said.

He tucked the phone into its hands-free slot on the dash and clicked a button on the steering wheel to answer.

I stared at the nifty device. I owned an old Ford Taurus that mostly just stayed in the garage. But after riding with Fleet yesterday and today,

I was starting to think there might be some advantages to buying newer and more expensive cars. I had often wagered more than the value of Fleet's car on one hand of poker, but over the years, I just couldn't make myself spend the same amount of money on a car.

It seemed that some insanity just ran in my family.

Hell, I was so damned cheap, it had been everything I could do just to buy my little two-bedroom house on the north side of Boise when I got out of college, six blocks over from my mother's. Even though I was worth millions and had a couple million in fairly handy cash and bonds at that point, I didn't want to spend sixty-five thousand on a house. Heaven only knew what it was worth now.

Fleet had convinced me it was a good deal and had done the paper-work. All I did was sign my name a few dozen times and give Fleet the full amount in cash. It still bothered me a little, even though Fleet and I owned tons of business property in our different companies, more than I wanted to know, actually. And I liked riding in limousines and flying in our corporate jet between tournaments. But keeping track of it all was Fleet's job. And he just kept getting us richer and richer every year.

While on the road, I got suites in hotels, usually in the same hotel that a tournament was being held, and I had a permanent suite at the Bellagio in Las Vegas. I hadn't even bought enough stuff to furnish my house very well after I bought it. My mother and Fleet's wife had done a lot of the furnishing for me. Sort of sad for a man my age, actually.

Fleet got the speakerphone turned on, then said, "Go ahead. Your dime."

"Mr. Korte?" a soft, hesitant voice asked over the speaker-phone.

"Yes," Fleet said, sitting up, straightening his back, clearly dropping into his business mode.

Fleet had tossed his suit jacket and tie into the back seat, but still looked like an attorney fresh out of court, even though he wore a new pair of tennis shoes, bought at my insistence this morning on the way out of town.

"My name is Aaron Bearings."

I couldn't quite catch the accent. Maybe East Coast Washington area.

"Ahh, Mr. Bearings," Fleet said.

He quickly pulled over to the edge of the road and stopped. Too fast. A cloud of dust billowed around us, shutting out the sun. Luckily, Fleet had the air-conditioning system on and the windows rolled up.

"I have you on speaker phone in the car," Fleet said. "Jonathan Hill is with me."

"Mr. Hill, I'm so sorry for your loss."

"Thank you." As if the guy was actually sincere. Fleet had called Vegas and hired Bearings this morning to help with Carson's estate in Nevada. The guy was going to make a fortune off just the IRS problems caused by all the cash my dad had in the plane.

"And the name is Doc," I said, figuring that if I were going to have to be around the guy for all this, I might as well get that much straight up front.

"Doc it is."

"Have you started everything into motion?" Fleet asked.

"I have," Bearings said. "That's what I wanted to tell you. No complications that I can see so far. Mr. Hill—uh, Doc—you understand that I'm going to need you here in Las Vegas to sign some papers and deal with some other matters."

"We'll be down there in three days," Fleet said. "We'll inventory Carson's house and take care of bank accounts at that point. We're meeting with the NTSB on the crash scene in a few hours."

"Good," Bearings said. "I'll let you know if I run into any problems, but I don't expect any this soon."

"Thank you," Fleet said. "I'll speak to you tomorrow morning." With that, he clicked off the phone. Then, with a glance over his shoulder through the still-lingering cloud of dust, he pulled the car back onto the gravel road.

"How long is all this probate going to take?"

Fleet shrugged. "We might have it done in a year. More than likely longer. Depends on how much there really is, and if there are any surprises we don't know about yet."

"Hell, we don't know *anything* about the man. Who knows what could be waiting."

"By the time this is over, we're going to know more than we want to know."

"Wonderful," I said, with as much disgust in my voice as I could manage without spitting in Fleet's new car.

"Yeah, Fleet said, "I'm looking forward to it as well."

CHAPTER TWELVE

CENTRAL IDAHO MOUNTAINS. AUGUST 19

AS THE NARROW ROAD emerged from the heavy trees, I studied the meadow ahead. The Valley County sheriff's car was pulled off into the weeds, and another unmarked car was parked beside it. For the last ten miles, the road had been no wider than two tire tracks, winding its way along the stream-sized Middle Fork of the Payette River. I had no doubt that during spring runoff, the road was under water in a dozen places and this meadow was a swamp, if not a small lake.

The valley ended in sheer rock walls that towered over the meadow like buildings in central Manhattan. The river flowed between the walls and over a rock shelf in a waterfall that must be fantastic during high water.

"Looks like we're here," Fleet said, heading the Lexus across the meadow.

I glanced at the dial on the dashboard that said it was a comfortable seventy-one degrees outside the car. A person couldn't ask for a nicer day in the mountains. I just wished I was here for a different reason.

Any other reason.

No one was in sight, and no sign of wreckage. I felt a sense of relief at that. Relief like the kind you feel sitting in a dentist's waiting room when the nurse calls the person next to you.

"You ready for this?" Fleet asked, parking off the road beside the sheriff's car.

"Oh, sure, I love seeing where people were killed. Don't you?"

"I watch the Discovery Channel and programs about mass murderers. Wrong question."

"Does your wife know this about you?"

I opened the door and let in a blast of warm, dry air, then climbed out.

"She finds it disturbing," Fleet said, joining me at the front of the Lexus.

"I can understand why."

We started up the road toward the rock walls, Fleet's new tennis shoes squeaking in the dust.

I had been in a lot of places in the central Idaho mountains, but never here. And I was glad I hadn't. The place gave me the creeps.

Under the tall mountains and sheer rock walls, the meadow had a bottom-of-a-box claustrophobic feel. Downstream, behind us, the river valley turned so that the mountain walls closed off any open area in that direction. The valley made me feel as if I were standing in the bottom of a very deep well.

"Man, this place is weird," Fleet whispered, as if talking louder was going to make the mountains close in tighter. He pointed to an old fire ring beside the river. "Can you imagine camping in here?"

"Not a chance. I'm used to mountain valleys, and I can tell you that this one has giant rockmen who eat campers at night and lawyers during the day. I can show you spoor if you don't believe me."

"No, thanks," Fleet said, shaking his head at my stupidity.

"I guess my sense of humor sort of goes when I have to look at where my father was killed."

"No kidding," Fleet said.

The Valley County sheriff, Ray Hendricks, appeared from behind a boulder and came down a narrow trail at us. He was tall, heavy-set, and wore a tan uniform that looked to be about the color of most of the rocks around us. A wide-brimmed hat and sunglasses kept his face in shade.

I liked Ray a lot, and had known him for years. I figured him to be in his early fifties, but with Ray there just was never any telling. We had worked dozens of search and rescue operations together, and I wouldn't hesitate in trusting the man with my life.

"Sheriff Hendricks?" Fleet asked, stepping ahead of me and extending his hand.

"Mr. Korte, I presume," the sheriff said.

I could see the sheriff manage to contain a smile at Fleet's silk dress shirt, dress slacks, and new tennis shoes as he shook Fleet's hand.

"Doc, how you doing on this one?" Ray asked as he shook my hand. "I was stunned to hear it was your father."

"Doing fine, Ray. We weren't close."

Ray nodded, then changed the subject. "How was the river this summer? Didn't hear that anyone got into serious trouble over there."

"We didn't lose a one. The Henderson crew had a passenger break a leg. They had to chopper him out."

"One of these days I'm going to have to take a ride with you," the sheriff said.

"Make it late May or early June, and I can promise you a real thrill on the big water on the Middle Fork."

He laughed. "My heart might be too old for that."

Then Ray took off his sunglasses and looked me right in the eye, his expression serious. "Are you sure you want to see this?"

"Actually, I personally don't. I'd rather be sitting in a casino with pocket aces and a guy with pocket kings to call my raise. But I made a promise to my grandfather to stay on top of Carson's death. This is where he died, so here I am, right on top."

The sheriff shrugged. "Suit yourself. Let me show you what's left of the plane before Eric and the rest of the NTSB people get here and start blocking everything off. They can get kind of protective of a crash scene."

"Yeah, seen that."

Ray glanced at me, then smiled. "That's right, I forgot you were on the dive team for that kid in the pond. Ugly one, that one."

"Glad it wasn't me who found the kid."

"You should be. I had to pull the body out of the water, and I had nightmares for a month." Ray shuddered and then turned and headed up the trail toward the waterfall.

"You didn't tell me much about that search," Fleet said as we followed Ray.

"Nothing to tell. Two dead, a dad and his kid, the dad still in the plane upside down in the pond, the kid's body floated off."

"At first," Ray said over his shoulder, "the NTSB clamped a lid on that thing tighter than a virgin's ass. Then they discovered they needed our help. I love it when they come begging."

"I don't think they're going to need any help here," I said.

"Not likely," Ray said.

After about a hundred yards of climbing and walking through the boulders and brush, I caught my first glimpse of the plane. Seeing it made me go cold, as if I were studying a poker hand instead of a plane crash.

The wreckage was a part of the tail section. It lay twisted in some rocks along the left-hand side of the canyon, the shiny white paint looking very out of place.

No other part of the plane seemed to be close to it.

After another twenty steps, Ray stopped. We were a stone's throw below and to the left of the waterfall. The sound of the cascading water sounded almost playful, and very welcoming.

The sheriff pointed over the top of the waterfall.

"See that mark along the rocks there about two hundred yards beyond the falls?"

I glanced up, shading my eyes. It was clear what the sheriff was pointing at.

"Looks like someone dug into the cliff with a big knife," Fleet said.

"Tip of the wing, actually," Ray said. "From what I can tell, Doc, your father had engine troubles, more than likely engine failure, between the

Scott landing strip and Cascade. He didn't have the air speed to get over the last major ridge and into Cascade. He turned downstream and more than likely was trying to reach the meadow and the road."

The sheriff pointed back toward the cars.

I glanced back at the meadow below. The road would look possible for a landing strip. Ray's theory made sense from what little we knew.

I studied the rock walls that towered over us like thirty-story skyscrapers. You might be able to fit two lanes of traffic and a sidewalk between them, but nothing more. A damned tight squeeze for a dead-stick small plane.

"He got close," Fleet said, glancing back at the road.

"Hand grenades and horseshoes," the sheriff said. "Hand grenades and horseshoes."

CHAPTER THIRTEEN

CENTRAL IDAHO MOUNTAINS, AUGUST 19

I TRIED TO IMAGINE how it would feel to dead-stick a plane down this narrow canyon. More than likely just sheer panic and terror. While still in college, I had earned my private pilot's license, but hadn't much enjoyed flying. Too much work, too much risk, but mostly just too much money for so little return. After the flying lessons, I had never bothered to fly again, deciding to stay with airlines, bad food and all.

And Fleet had even ended that when one of our companies needed a big tax deduction and he bought us our own Gulfstream corporate jet, with beds and everything. That was one perk to being rich I tended to love and use a lot. I just didn't want Fleet to ever tell me what it cost to run the stupid thing.

The sheriff pointed to a spot that looked black and scarred on the cliff face downstream from the first mark. "The main body of the plane nosed in right there and just disintegrated. It's scattered in pieces along the base of the cliff for about a football field."

I couldn't imagine how fast Carson must have been going to have that sort of impact and destruction. A plane on takeoff or landing was usually going slow enough that most planes stayed pretty much intact when they crashed. Clearly Carson had a lot less control of his plane than he needed to make a landing in the meadow work.

"Was there a fire?" Fleet asked. "This area looks pretty dry."

"It is," Ray said. "Luckily, the only fire was small, burnt nothing but one tree and then went out."

"How did you find this?" Fleet asked.

"Mr. Hill activated a GPS emergency locator. Somehow, it survived the wreck. We had a plane buzz the canyon within twenty minutes and someone on-site within two hours, which is damned fast for this part of the country."

"Real fast," I said, impressed. "That has to be a record of some sort."

"I'm looking that up," Ray said, smiling.

"So only the body and the money were taken away from the scene?" Fleet asked.

"Yup. Everything else had to be left for the investigation."

The mention of the word *body* jolted me. No doubt I was going to have to identify my father's body at some point, or at least see it before any service.

Damn it all to hell. I suppose it was better me than my mother. Or Ace. Too bad Carson hadn't gotten remarried and had another family. Then someone else could have been taking care of this stupidity.

"And you've had someone on scene the entire time?" Fleet asked.

The sheriff pointed up at a rock ledge on the other side of the river from the crash site. For the first time, I noticed a man was sitting up there in a folding chair, his tan uniform perfect camouflage against the rocks.

"Wow, didn't even see him," Fleet said.

"He stayed on that ledge since right after we got on scene," Ray said. "He can see the entire wreck site from there. And he's not coming down until I hand over control to the government boys."

"Smart," Fleet said.

"Just experience," Ray said. "I've dealt with Eric and the NTSB people before. Too many damned forms to fill out if I do it any other way."

"How difficult is it to climb up there?" I asked, glancing at the rocks, trying to figure a way up.

The sheriff shrugged. "Wouldn't be hard for you, but I would suggest Mr. Korte here not try it."

"Not interested anyway," Fleet said, looking up at the rocks as if the idea of climbing them was grounds for an insanity plea. More than likely, it was, but when it came to the mountains or the river, simply craziness didn't seem to stop me.

"What's the best route up?" I asked.

"Head over the river there below the falls on those exposed stones, then take the best route you see on up. Watch for rattlers. They will be sunning themselves about now."

"*Rattlesnakes?*"

Fleet's voice echoed between the rock walls, a look of sheer terror filling his face. He looked around at the rocks and brush, jerking back and forth at any slight movement of a brush in the breeze.

We had been friends since grade school, business partners since our second year of college, and I hadn't known Fleet was afraid of snakes. His silk shirt would scare them away, if nothing else.

"Been around them most of the summer," I said, laughing at the panicked look on Fleet's face. "I know what to do."

"Just don't get bit on the balls," Ray said, winking at me before hitting the punch line of the old joke. "No one here to suck the poison."

Fleet now looked completely panicked, clearly ready to make a mad dash back down the trail.

"It's getting kind of warm out here," Fleet said, his voice higher than normal. "How about I just go back to the car to wait?" He turned and slowly started back down the trail, watching the ground carefully on both sides.

Ray smiled at me and then followed Fleet. "I'll go back with you."

"Thanks, Sheriff," I said.

The sheriff shook his head and somehow managed to not laugh.

I watched my best friend move away, almost tiptoeing in his business suit and new tennis shoes down the trail. Somehow, I resisted the urge to take a rock and throw it into the brush beside Fleet, just to watch him jump.

That would be a little too cruel.

CHAPTER FOURTEEN

CENTRAL IDAHO MOUNTAINS. AUGUST 19

I MADE IT easily across the water without even getting my feet wet. The waterfall sprayed up a fine mist that cooled the air. The river smelled of moss and wet dirt and looked just about as clear as it came. No doubt the river in the meadow below me was full of some nice trout.

I stopped and studied the rocks for the best route to take up past the waterfall. When the rain and snow started in the next few weeks, this river would swell up quickly. From the looks of the high-water marks on the cliff walls, the river often got twenty feet deep where I was standing.

It took me less than a minute to reach the top of the falls and another five minutes to reach the small camp of the sheriff's deputy on the wide ledge. The man had built a small fire ring, brought an air mattress for easier sleeping, and a lawn chair for comfort. He was in the process of tearing down his camp and erasing any sign that he had been there.

I stuck out my hand and introduced myself, not looking at the plane just yet.

"Ben Hendricks," the young deputy said, shaking my hand with a firm grip. "Sorry for your loss, sir."

"Thanks. You Ray's kid?"

"I am. My dad figured we should just keep things in the family up here." Ben hesitated for a moment, then went on. "I've sure heard a lot about you. The way you found that lost hunter two years ago up on Lick Creek Summit was something."

"Just played a hunch and got lucky," I said, smiling at the fact that someone had even noticed. "Thanks for watching over this mess. Had to have been a long night."

"Two nights, actually," Ben said. "This area gives me the creeps, and I'll be glad to be out of here, to be honest with you. Too many rockmen clattering around looking for lawyers."

I laughed. "You heard that, huh?"

"You can hear just about everything up here."

I nodded, then took a deep breath and slowly turned to look at the place where my father had died.

The sight of the wreckage scattered along the cliff wall looked more like someone had made an illegal trash dump. I had expected the sight to bother me, but for some reason it didn't. I had seen my share of small plane wrecks, and with this one I felt more curious than anything.

Maybe something would hit me later.

Maybe not.

I still wasn't caring that the bastard was dead.

The plane must have cartwheeled along the rocks and cliff face, coming apart as it went. Now the biggest section of the Piper six-seater was no more than four or five feet long. Off to one side, the engine compartment lay between two boulders, still amazingly intact.

The tail section had traveled the farthest toward the hoped-for landing site. Most of the plane rested in a rock field at the base of the cliff above the waterfall. Two parts of the plane, a wing tip and a chair, were in the small pool, and another chair lay tipped on its side near the water.

Flying a plane into a rock wall was a stupid way to go. Quick, but stupid.

I glanced back at the young deputy who had a worried expression on his face. "Do you know where his body ended up?"

The kid looked even more pained, but stepped up beside me and pointed. "We found your father still buckled in his chair in the rocks down by the tail section. He was pretty smashed up as well. You won't want to look at the body."

I stood there, taking slow, steady breaths, going over the details of the crash, the marks on the rocks, the positions of pieces of the plane, studying it like I studied the other players and their patterns at a poker table. I had promised Ace I would get it all, learn it all, so I would get him every damn detail.

After a few minutes, the faint sound of a vehicle coming up the valley echoed over the background noise of the gently flowing river. Whoever was coming was still a ways down the canyon.

"Looks like you get to be relieved soon. You need help getting this stuff down?"

"Thanks," Ben said, "but I can get it fine."

"I appreciate the tour. Don't step in any rockmen spoor on the way out."

"I'll try not to," Ben said, laughing.

On the climb down, I didn't allow myself to look again at the torn-up plane. I had seen what I needed to see to keep my promise to Ace.

That was enough.

I just hoped this wouldn't end up in my nightmares, right along with the bloated face of that child in the pond.

CHAPTER FIFTEEN

WHITE HOUSE, WASHINGTON, D.C. AUGUST 19

PRESIDENT DOLAN CHASE sat at his desk in the Oval Office, his jacket off and hung over the back of his leather chair, his tie loose, his sleeves rolled up. The frustration ate at him as he slammed the phone back into its cradle just a little too hard. He'd broken a phone already during his first year in office. He might break another by the time these calls were finished.

For the last two days, he had been trying to sway senators over to his side on a bill that would increase funding to schools. He wasn't sure of the exact count at the moment, but he had been promised a few things by a few senators, and had to give a few promises in return.

If this worked, all the compromising would be worth it. He would be known as the president who funded up the schools like they should have been funded decades ago. If he did nothing else during his presidency, this one bill might be enough.

He glanced up at the clock. Two hours left before the vote started, if it started on time, which was doubtful.

Outside, the threatened thunderstorms were starting to materialize as the afternoon sky turned dark. No doubt the award ceremony for the Red Cross would have to be moved from the Rose Garden. Probably better, anyhow. The humidity out there felt higher than a sauna at a fancy spa. He hated having the press see him sweat.

The next name on his list was Senator Conners, a Republican who hadn't voted for any of his bills. He hated the thought of even calling the egotistical little man, let alone asking him for his support.

He shook his head. Three years of law school and fourteen years in the Senate. You'd think he would have gotten used to this kind of pushing and shoving and trading by now. But he hadn't, never would. It grated on him.

A knock at his door came a respectable moment before Paul stepped into the room. Paul actually looked slightly harried, with his tie loosened just an inch and his jacket unbuttoned. That was about as casual as he ever got.

Dolan slid his notes toward Paul. "Having a little luck. How about everyone else?"

Paul smiled, and the smile actually reached his eyes. "Looks like we're up two votes at the moment, thanks to your calls. A couple of moderate Republicans have moved over."

"The two we hoped to get?"

Paul nodded. "But no one on the staff thinks we should completely count on that, and I agree."

"Then keep the calls going. And I'll call Senator Conners."

"Oh, yeah, good luck on that one," Paul said, shaking his head.

Then the smile left Paul's face like someone had pulled a plug on his chin. "Sir, I just got word that the NTSB is on its way to the site of the Carson Hill crash."

Dolan's heartburn flared. That Spanish pasta dish had been good at lunch, but he should have stopped at one helping. It didn't taste as good coming back up. He reached for the bottle of Tums in his top desk drawer, took one, and let the chalky taste coat his mouth. He was starting to get used to the damn things.

"We have a man with the NTSB team? And can we trust the son-of-a-bitch not to say anything about feeding us information?"

"It's a woman," Paul said. "FBI agent. I talked to Director Smith and got his help on this. I asked for Agent Heather Voight and got her assigned. You know her, that special friend of mine."

"The one you've been dating?"

"Yeah," Paul said. "And yes, we can trust her, sir."

"Good. I want to know what happened to Carson. Anything about the crash hitting the papers yet?"

This entire thing had him worried. Real worried.

"Nothing outside of Boise this morning. They haven't released Carson's name yet. I expect more tomorrow. Carson had a lot of friends."

"And a couple of enemies," he said.

"That too."

"Keep me posted."

"One more thing, sir," Paul said.

"Take your time. I am *so* looking forward to making this call."

Paul didn't even smile.

That wasn't a good sign. He must have more bad news.

Paul took a folded piece of paper from his inside coat pocket and slid it across the desk. "This just came across one of the wires. More than likely, a lot of places will pick it up tomorrow."

Dolan read the piece of paper, stunned. Someone had dug up and robbed the grave of Jeff Taylor. No reason for the robbery was given, no suspects had been found, and no mention of what had been taken from the grave.

Dolan took a second Tums and then put the bottle away, trying to think straight.

After a moment, he looked up at his chief of staff, who stood there shifting his weight nervously from side to side. Paul only did that when he was really worried. On this topic, they both had a right to be.

"Why would anyone do that?"

"I don't know."

71

He glanced at the news article again. Taylor had been dead for over a decade. Why the hell would someone pick now to dig up the jerk's grave?

"Weird, damned weird."

"That it is," Paul said. "But I thought you should see it."

He folded the article and flipped it toward Paul. "Forget it. We have enough to worry about getting this bill passed."

Paul looked for an instant as if he might disagree, then nodded. "Yes, sir."

"And Paul, make sure everyone stays on the phones right to the last minute. I want to get these schools funded the way they should be. We've been working way too long on this baby to let it slip now. No screw-ups."

"No screw-ups," Paul said, turning and heading back for his office.

After the door was closed, Dolan leaned back in his chair and closed his eyes, giving himself a moment before making the next call.

Why couldn't the past just stay buried?

CHAPTER SIXTEEN

LAS VEGAS, NEVADA. AUGUST 19

AFTER SPENDING the morning in the station, Detective Annie Lott decided that she needed to talk to Jeff Taylor's son, Brent. Maybe the kid could give her a clue, a detail that would be the lead she needed.

The day had grown typically August hot, and by the time the air-conditioning had completely cooled the big Buick Regal that her father had given her when her mother died, she was inside the parking garage of the Stardust.

Brent Taylor dealt poker in the Stardust poker room, one of the friendlier rooms in town. The Bellagio poker room might get a lot of the high rollers and host a couple of the World Poker Tour events, but the best poker promotions day-after-day for the grinders were often found at the Stardust.

She entered the cool air-conditioning of the busy casino. Around her the bright lights of the slot and video poker games flashed their welcomes, saying *Come play me, I'll make you rich in an instant.* She loved casinos, drew energy from them for some reason.

The place smelled faintly of smoke combined with a wonderful odor of baking bread coming from a café just off to the side of the main entrance. No doubt the smell was done on purpose, piped into the casino to relax people. Very few details in a modern casino were left to chance.

She headed through the rows and rows of slots, following what looked like a decent-sized aisle. Of course, no aisle in a casino ever went directly from one place to another. Too easy for people to escape that way. At every step, there was something to get your attention, to take your money, to make you look around.

That was another thing she loved about the places.

She walked into the medium-sized poker room and glanced around. About half the tables had games and a number of people sat around waiting. She hadn't played here that much. Too many what were called "rocks" for her taste.

The back wall of the poker room had signs indicating the current promotion, the amount of the bad-beat jackpots, and other listings. Nothing spectacular this week. Four televisions, sound off, were stuck up in the four corners of the room. All four were tuned to different sports events. Compared to the main floor of the casino, the poker room was morgue-silent.

The poker desk sat near the room's main entrance. Actually, it was a long, elevated counter with two people standing behind it, watching over the room like a guard station. The people behind the counter kept a list of those waiting to get a seat in each game on a big erasable white board.

She flashed her badge to the man behind the desk. "I'm looking for Brent Taylor."

"He's dealing on table ten in the back," the man said, pointing.

Within a minute, he had been relieved for a break and they were headed out of the room with him leading. In the years since his father had died, he had gone bald and gained a good hundred pounds. She would have never recognized him from his pictures in the files.

"I need to talk over my lunch," Brent said as he walked, "I only have a fifteen minute break since we're short-handed this afternoon."

"No problem."

"You got a badge?" Brent asked.

"Bright and shiny."

Brent only grunted.

She only had to show her badge once before they were in the big employee lunchroom. The place clearly got a lot of use. The room was huge, with low ceilings filled with recessed florescent lights. The floor was covered in a tile that looked faded, as if it had been mopped a few hundred times too many.

The sharp smell of lasagna filled the space, reminding her of a high school lunchroom.

"You want a drink?" Brent asked as he pointed to a table against a side wall, away from the other dozen employees in the room.

"No, thanks." She moved to sit down with her back to the wall. She couldn't imagine having to eat in places like this every day simply because the food was free and time on breaks was too short to go anyplace better.

Brent came back with a large dish of what looked like pasta in red sauce, two dinner rolls, and a glass of Coke.

"So, you trying to figure out who dug up my father?"

"I am."

"How about figuring out who killed him while you're at it."

"I read the file," Annie said. "Since someone has already dug up your father, I figured it wouldn't hurt to run a few modern tests on his body. Unless you mind, of course."

Brent stared at her, clearly stunned, a half-eaten dinner role in his mouth.

"I don't mind," Brent said, his attitude clearly a few degrees less hostile than a moment before. "What can I do to help?"

"Answer a few questions is all."

"Fire away," Brent said, digging into his pasta like a man who loved food, no matter how it tasted. From the looks of his weight, he had loved a few too many meals over the last dozen years.

"Some of these questions I have answers for in the file," Annie said, "some you answered before, but I want to see if an answer appears different in the light of the years going by."

"Makes sense to me."

"First off, do you have any idea who robbed your father's grave?"

"Not a damned clue," Brent said, "And I'll tell you, I'd like to get my hands on whoever it was that dug him up. The last thing I needed was to see the old man again. Especially after no one believed me about him and his murder. It's taken me this long to get past that, and now it's all back."

"They showed you a picture of his face, right? Identifying the body is procedure."

"I suppose," Brent said, chewing on the second roll. "Still sucked."

Annie could imagine. "You told the officer who contacted you that only a key was taken from the grave. Right?"

"It was the only thing in there with Dad besides his suit coat and shirt," Brent said. "I kept all his rings and his World Series bracelets. I have them in a safe-deposit box with my mom's jewelry."

"And you have no idea what the key was to?"

"Not a God-damned clue," Brent said. "But I'm convinced it got him killed. He told me before he died that he had a terrible secret that he needed to tell the world. He showed me the key and made me promise that if something happened to him, I'd keep the key safe. He told me that the key was to the secret."

"And he said nothing more?"

"He got killed before he could," Brent said. "I was so pissed off at the police and everyone back then for not believing me, I figured letting Dad keep the key was the safest. Guess I was wrong."

Brent went back to eating, and Annie looked at her notes. "You have any idea how long your father had that key before he died?"

Brent's dark eyes got a distant look in them. "I do remember that when Dad won his first World Series, he put his bracelet in my mother's big jewelry case in her closet, in a small drawer with his name on it. I sneaked into their bedroom and looked at the bracelet one day when he was gone. That same key was in there with his bracelet. I didn't want to get in trouble for looking at his stuff, so I never asked what the key was for."

"And how soon was this before he died?"

"Maybe five years or so."

"So that key goes back at least seventeen years. You sure it was the same key?"

"Perfectly sure," Brent said. "The thing was a bank key, long and thin, and had the number three etched large on it."

"Did you ever tell anyone about burying the key with your father?"

"I don't think so," Brent said, stopping to think for a moment. Then he shook his head. "Beyond family, I'm sure I didn't. Not the kind of thing that just comes up in a conversation, if you know what I mean."

"Good point."

"Who would have thought someone would go to all the trouble of digging up a grave to get a key? I've always wondered just what the hell that key went to. Clearly, my dad wasn't kidding when he said it was important."

Annie nodded. "I'm starting to believe that."

"It's about damn time someone does."

CHAPTER SEVENTEEN

CENTRAL IDAHO MOUNTAINS. AUGUST 19

THE SOUND of the government van echoed for over ten minutes through the canyon before popping out of the trees and starting across the meadow, a cloud of dust swirling behind it.

I always found it amazing how well sound traveled in the mountains, especially on clear, windless days like this one. Every summer, I warned the people on my rafts that a conversation about another person in another raft might be overheard as clearly as if the person were sitting beside them. No one ever really believed me until they got out on a calm area of water between the steep canyon walls and heard it for themselves.

As I reached the SUV, Fleet and the sheriff climbed out, Fleet staring around for any snakes.

Now I understood why yesterday and today were the first times I had seen Fleet any farther into the wilderness than the rough of Hillcrest Country Club. Fleet's Christmas joke gifts were going to get a lot more interesting this year.

The green van pulled slowly past us and off the narrow road into the grass and weeds. I caught a glimpse of two men in the front seats and a woman's face in the back.

"Three of them?" Fleet asked. "Seems like one too many."

"It is," Ray said. "Usually they only need two on small planes."

"Maybe a trainee," Fleet said.

I had a hunch it wasn't a trainee. My guess was that the crash was causing Eric and his NTSB crew some extra headaches. Three-point-six million in a duffel bag could do that.

We all moved toward the van with the sheriff leading, Fleet watching for snakes with every step.

The sheriff got to the van just as Eric climbed out.

"Sheriff," Eric said. "Good seeing you again."

I liked Eric, the head of the regional NTSB unit. I had from the moment I first met him on the dive into the lake for the kid. The guy seemed solid. He had on a Mariners baseball cap and a light, long-sleeved shirt over a tee shirt. He carried himself like he was in charge of every situation. He acted the same way, and people just naturally followed him.

"You, too, Eric," Ray said. "You get that little one born all right?"

"Two weeks ago. Healthy baby boy. Came in screaming." Eric beamed at just the mention of his new baby.

"Congratulations," Ray said. Then he turned. "Attorney Fleetwood Korte from Boise. This is Eric Berry. And you know Doc."

"Nice meeting you," Eric said to Fleet, shaking his hand.

"Congratulations on the new arrival," I said.

"Thanks. We love him." Then Eric hesitated, his eyes showing concern. "You sure you want to be here, Doc? I know this was your father and all, but I just can't let you up on the crash site."

"No need. I took a look from the other side of the canyon. That was enough for me."

Eric nodded and patted my shoulder as the other two members of the NTSB team came around the back of the truck. Eric introduced them.

Bud, Eric's normal second, had a pock-marked face and dark eyes that didn't meet another person's gaze. He had been at the lake search as well, and had seemed to be nothing more than manual labor.

I studied the third member of the team as she was being introduced. Heather Voight. She wore her hair blonde and stylishly mid-length, but it didn't look natural. She had on some makeup that accented her brown eyes, her skin was tanned and slightly freckled, and her build gave her the appearance of exercising a lot.

Nice package, but very out of place with Eric's NTSB team. Any western NTSB team for that matter. I figured her for an East Coast city type.

She took longer that she should have, staring into my eyes in our introduction. Not that I would have minded if there had been any hint of sexual tension about the stare, but there wasn't. She was studying me like a good poker player studied other players at a table, like I was a problem to be handled. Why, I had no idea, but I could hold anyone's gaze, and I held hers until she looked away.

Her hand was smooth, not work-worn like Eric's. A desk job was very recent in her past.

The three team members went to the back of their van and started getting equipment out. Heather bumped into Eric twice, and after a moment stood to one side and let the two men do the unloading.

"Sheriff," Eric asked as he kept unloading and checking equipment, "have you had the scene sealed off and guarded?"

"Since one hour after the crash," Ray said, a touch of pride in his voice. "My son has been on a ledge across from the crash site for the last two nights. He's not coming down until you reach the scene."

"Perfect," Eric said. "Thanks for the good work on that. And what about the money?"

"It's in the bank vault in Cascade, suitcase and all. You can look at it tomorrow, or whenever you get done here."

"Good," Eric said. "You did the right thing with that as well."

I motioned for Eric. "Got a second?"

Eric nodded and followed me a few steps away from the van, letting the other two finish unloading.

I kept my voice at a low whisper. "What's her story? She new to the area?"

"Totally," Eric whispered back. "Washington all the way. My guess is that someone stuck me with her because of the amount of money reported in the plane. Pain in the ass, if you ask me."

"But it makes sense."

"Only if you think like a government flunky," Eric whispered, shaking his head. "Paperwork on this is going to be a monster. Now she has to file a report as well. It never ends."

"I can imagine." I patted Eric on the shoulder.

"I'll keep you posted on what we find," Eric whispered, then louder he said to me, "Please stay here."

My plan had been to see the crash site, meet the NTSB team, and then head back to Boise, but now because of Eric's promise, I wanted to stay longer, see what they might come up with.

And I wanted to know why Heather Voight had been sent along. The money seemed like a logical explanation, but even the amount Carson had with him wouldn't get her sent from a desk job in Washington out here.

There was something more.

CHAPTER EIGHTEEN

CENTRAL IDAHO MOUNTAINS, AUGUST 19

AFTER THEY FINISHED getting all their equipment ready, Eric said, "Sheriff, would you give us a quick tour of what you know of the crash site?"

"Glad to," Ray said, starting up the road, followed by the other three. Both Eric and Heather had cameras slung over their backs, and both carried black suitcases. Bud hauled enough modern survey equipment to weigh down a large packhorse.

As they moved off, Fleet turned to me. "Why are we—"

I stopped him with a quick hand in the air and a headshake, fearing the question would be heard in the mountain air. I then pointed to the SUV.

After Fleet got the air-conditioning going, he asked. "So what was that all about?"

"The woman doesn't belong with the other two men."

"Hell, even I noticed that. Three-point-six million in cash can sure cause a lot of strange reactions."

"That's what Eric thinks. He said he'd keep me informed on what they find, so I figure we just wait around here long enough to see what comes up, and what their next move is."

"You worried about them, or the money?" Fleet asked.

"Actually, neither. I'm just doing what Ace asked me to do."

Fleet nodded. "Still, when we get closer to civilization, I'll get a judge on the phone, have him issue a court order stopping the NTSB from doing anything with the money besides checking it in the presence of you or me. I should have already done that. We might as well stay on top of that as well."

I nodded. "Good idea."

Fleet sighed and sat back in his chair. "This is going to take time, you know?"

"Yeah. You up for some fishing? There's a second pole in my gear from the river. Luckily, we didn't unload it last night."

Fleet looked at me as if I had suggested we both jump off a tall building. "In this snake-infested wilderness? *No thank you.*"

I laughed at my best friend. "Oh, come on, just on the river over there on the other side of the meadow. If we see a snake, I'll take care of it."

Fleet pointed to the briefcase in the back seat, his face as white as the frosting on the doughnuts he loved in the morning. "I brought some reading. I think I'll pass."

I gave him my best serious look, like I was actually trying to talk him into going across the meadow with me. "You know, a rattlesnake bite won't kill you. Maybe put you in the hospital for a day or so if we don't treat it right, but they're not deadly. Cute things if you don't bother them."

I didn't think it was possible, but Fleet's face got whiter, and even with the brisk air-conditioning, he started sweating and shaking his head.

I chuckled and sat back, enjoying the coolness, staring out the front windshield at the rock walls and towering mountains that locked in this valley.

Fleet took a deep breath and then sat back. "Sometimes, you just drive me crazy."

"One of my hobbies."

"I know that."

We sat there in the coolness for a minute, just watching in the general direction that everyone had gone.

"Why fishing?" Fleet asked finally. "Why now? Why here? That makes no sense to me, unless you just want to kill some time."

"There's that. But in case you didn't notice, sound carries out here. Especially in this kind of closed-in canyon."

"I caught that. I could hear you talking to the sheriff's kid up on the rocks when..." Fleet stopped, finally understanding what I was thinking. "You'll be able to hear every word the team says if you are sitting down by the river."

"On the money. Sometimes using what Mother Nature gives you is the best way to solve a problem."

Fleet stared around the outsides of the car like the snakes were circling and trying to get in. "I suppose that would be worth risking the snakes for."

I laughed and patted my friend on the shoulder. "I think I can handle it. You stay in the car."

I hadn't seen Fleet look that relieved since his future wife said yes to his stammering request for a first date.

CHAPTER NINETEEN

CENTRAL IDAHO MOUNTAINS, AUGUST 19

I SAT ON A HIGH ROCK above the small flow of water called the Middle Fork of the Payette River, doing my best to listen to the few words of conversation among the members of the NTSB team on the crash site above. They had spread out over the rock field, taking pictures and measuring and recording every detail of every piece of the wreckage.

I had crossed over the water to get to the exact right spot with the best sound, and also so I could face back up toward the crash site. Now my pole rested on the rock, tucked under my right leg, the line draping uselessly into the water. There was a hook on the line, but no bait. The last thing I wanted to do at this point was to actually catch a fish.

In the past three hours, the sun had left the valley floor, slowly working its way up the side of the mountain, but the heat seemed to have increased, with no wind to cool the valley floor down. I wished I had brought my DEET from my gear in the Lexus. The mosquitoes were starting to drive me nuts. Normally, they didn't bother me, but normally I was covered in

85

protection. If the biting got much worse, I'd have to go get some repellant and take a chance on missing something that was said.

So far, there hadn't been much talk at all from the investigators, but what there was I could hear as clear as a church bell on a summer night in a small town. Measurements had been called out, a rattler scared away from one piece of tail section, conversation about how much work it was going to be for the recovery team to get the plane out of the rocks.

But mostly there was nothing.

Mountain silence and the faint sound of running water.

I could go hours without playing a hand in a poker game if the situation called for it, waiting until just the right cards came along, the right position, the right opponent. Waiting for something that might not happen was a strength of mine. I suppose that wasn't a skill a person could put on a resume, but it had earned me a fortune over the years at poker tables.

A couple hours earlier, the sheriff, after showing the site to the investigators, had come back down the trail helping his son carry camping gear. Ray had packed his son into the unmarked car and sent him on his way, more than likely to a shower, a good meal, and a good night's sleep. Then, with a word to Fleet, Ray had headed toward the river, stopping on the other bank across from me and shading his eyes so he could see me.

"I'm planning on waiting around until they tell me it's clear," Ray said. "Normally, on small planes like this, it takes about three or four hours. I've had them take longer, not much shorter."

"Good."

I knew that every word the two of us said could be heard by the team, and I needed to be careful.

Ray went on. "After they get finished with this preliminary survey and photographs," he said, "the recovery team comes in tomorrow and moves the plane into a hanger in Boise. There just isn't much to do here."

I shrugged. "I think we'll wait as well. It was my father after all." That was what the NTSB team would have expected me to say, and I didn't want to disappoint since I was sure they could hear me.

Ray nodded.

"Besides, the fish are going to start biting at any moment." I moved my pole a little and smiled at Ray.

"I'll be in the car with your friend," Ray said, shaking his head and turning away. "It's too damned hot to fish out here."

Ray was right. It was too hot to fish, at least for trout.

I went back to waiting and listening and slapping at mosquitoes.

At just a little over three hours after the team started, Bud called out. "Eric, I think you should come and look at this."

"I'll be right there."

I watched as both Eric and Heather headed toward Bud, carefully working their way over the rocks. For a desk jockey, Heather looked to be holding her own pretty well. But I had no doubt she was going to have bruised and cut hands and banged up shins by the time this was over.

"What do you have?" Eric asked, kneeling like a golfer studying a break on a putt.

Heather got to a spot beside them and remained standing, watching the two men and occasionally glancing down at me as if she were afraid I might do something. I had no idea what that might be, but she kept a careful eye on me anyway.

I knew the crash site from my time on the ledge. They were looking at the engine and engine compartment.

"What do you see there?" Bud asked, pointing at something.

Silence.

It was as if the boxed canyon had just swallowed every sound, not letting anything escape.

"Take a picture of that," Eric finally said. "From all angles."

Both Heather and the other man started snapping pictures, the sound echoing down the canyon, their flashes lighting up the shadows around them.

It was all I could do to not drop my pole and run up there and see just what the hell they had found. But I stayed still, as if I actually were fishing and couldn't hear them.

"Could this have been caused by the crash?" Heather asked.

"Didn't happen that way," Eric said. He made a clear motion of glancing at me, then went on. I had no doubt Eric wanted me to hear what he was saying. He knew how sound traveled in the mountains, he knew exactly what I was doing, and he didn't seem to mind as long as I stayed off his crash site.

"See the staining in the wall of the compartment?" Eric said, pointing at something. "That shows it happened during flight."

I took a shallow breath, making sure I didn't miss a word.

"Are you saying this wasn't an accident?" Heather asked, her voice almost a whisper, yet still very clear to me down near the river.

Not an accident? For some reason, this being anything but an accident hadn't crossed my mind.

I took a deep breath and braced myself on the rock. Not an accident meant Carson's death was a murder.

What the hell had Ace known?

"It's starting to look like this plane was brought down intentionally," Eric said. He pointed at something else. "Get pictures of that as well."

"What is it?" Heather asked, snapping away beside Bud.

"Small remote detonator," Eric said. "Still intact. We might be able to trace it."

It took every poker skill I had at that point to not jump to my feet. I kept taking shallow breaths, working to keep my heart from racing and beating so loud it covered up what I needed to hear.

"A bomb?" Bud asked, his voice so powerful it echoed over the meadow. "You're saying this plane was brought down by a bomb?"

"Looks that way," Eric said, again glancing down at me to make sure I heard.

I didn't move.

Eric pointed at something again. "See right here? The detonation was set to shut down the engine and the hydraulic controls. A small, but perfectly placed charge, from the looks of it. But we won't know one hundred percent for sure until we get this all out of here."

"Sounds like a stupid way to try to kill someone," Heather said. "No real guarantee it will work. He might have landed safely."

"Have you looked around you?" Eric asked, his arm sweeping around at the canyon and rocks and trees. "No engine, no controls. He would have to have been amazingly lucky to survive."

"This guy's luck ran out," Bud said.

"Yeah, I'm afraid it did," Eric said, looking down at me. "Someone clearly wanted it to."

The three of them went back to work, taking pictures and studying the engine.

I sat on the rock, completely stunned, not even sure if I trusted my legs to get me back to the car.

My father had clearly been murdered.

My grandfather might have known about it. Or at least known the reason behind it.

And I had no idea what to do next.

CHAPTER TWENTY

BOISE, IDAHO. AUGUST 19

FBI AGENT HEATHER VOIGHT slipped into her jogging suit and took the towel to her wet hair one more time as she wandered out of the small bathroom and into her hotel room.

Back when she was doing field duty, she often woke up in these standard hotel rooms and couldn't remember what city or state she was in. All the hotel rooms these days looked and felt the same. A bed, a table, two nightstands, lamps, and bad art. She had come to hate the standard colors, the standard beds, the standard sheets, while at the same time getting used to living in them.

She missed her apartment, her two cats that she had allowed herself to get after the promotion to a Washington-based assignment, and her own furniture and things. She had no doubt that by the time she woke up tomorrow morning, she was also going to really miss her pillow-top bed.

She had CNN on the television and muted, a habit she had always had. It was company without being distracting, news without all the stupid, trivial announcer garbage. And every hotel, no matter how far out into the boondocks it was, had CNN on its cable listings.

She also had a traveling habit of wearing a jogging suit to bed. She had gotten called out quickly a couple of times on assignments and wasted valuable time dressing. You didn't get anywhere in the FBI by making people wait for you. At the moment, she was the only agent on this case, so she doubted she was going to get called out in the middle of the night. It wasn't the type of case that would have that happen. But the habit still died hard. She just didn't feel comfortable anymore sleeping in hotel rooms without the jogging suit.

Two years ago, she had been promoted to the Washington office and had thought she had graduated from field service once and for all. Now, here she was, back in the field, only this time she wasn't so sure how "official" her assignment was. She knew her being here was simply a favor for Director Smith and her boyfriend, Chief of Staff Paul Hanson. And they hadn't told her why, just where to go and what to do.

This Carson Hill had certainly been important to some very powerful people. Important enough to put her on the NTSB team to look at the crash site.

Important enough for someone else to kill.

She wished she knew exactly who Carson Hill had been. By tomorrow, she would know a lot more. She hated working blind, and the moment she saw the evidence that Carson Hill had been murdered, she knew she needed a lot more information about him.

She stared at her cell phone on the bed. She didn't want to make the call she knew she was going to have to make. After a very long day of climbing in the rocks and watching for snakes, all she really wanted was to watch a dull movie and sleep. She was going to be very sore in the morning, she could feel it. Working out in the gym in the city just wasn't a substitute for real field work, especially in the Idaho mountains.

"Better get this over with," she said out loud, then clicked off the television. She didn't need anything to distract her at this point.

Director Smith had told her to report directly to Paul in the White House, then send him an update. He knew of their relationship, figured it would just be easier.

It took a minute to get through to Paul and make sure her phone was secure and she was on a secure line. It always did take time, even with the private numbers she had. She knew he had been waiting for her to call, both to tell him what she had found and to say goodnight. Their ritual, if they weren't together, was for the first person to go to bed to call the other and say goodnight. Paul hadn't called, so she knew he was still up.

After she was connected, she started to tell him what had been discovered in the plane wreck.

"Hang on a second," Paul said. There was a click on the line. That happened at times. The White House was always a busy place, even late at night, especially for the Chief of Staff.

She sat on the bed, watching the blank television screen until Paul came back on the line and said, "Let me put the President on. He'll want to hear this."

That surprised her and made her stomach clamp down into a knot. While dating Paul, she had spent a number of occasions with the President. She liked the man and mostly believed in what he was trying to do in his policies. But she hadn't expected to talk to him about this. Clearly he cared about what had happened out here to Carson Hill. And more than likely, he was the reason she was here, not Paul. Her news was not going to make him happy, of that she had no doubt.

She glanced at the clock beside the bed. Almost midnight in Washington. What was the President still doing in the Oval? This was two hours past his normal time to retire to the residence.

Heather could hear another line pick up. Both of them were now on the line.

Then the President said, "Good evening, Agent Voight. What did you find on the crash site?"

Heather, as quickly and concisely as giving a report in a meeting, ran over the details of the crash site, and then the preliminary, on-location conclusion the NTSB team had come to.

"Explosive?" Paul asked, clearly shocked. "This was purposeful?"

"Yes," Heather said.

"The evidence is clear?" the President asked. "You're sure?"

"Ninety-nine percent. The plane didn't burn on impact, so the small explosion in the engine compartment is easy to see."

"Keep this quiet until you are one hundred percent sure," the President said, his voice carrying a harshness Heather had never heard before in him.

She took a deep breath, remembering Doc Hill and how he had sat on the rock below the crash site pretending to fish, listening to every word that the crash investigation team was saying.

"Sir, that might not be possible."

"And why the hell not?" the President demanded, his anger making her lean back on the bed.

She made herself pause to gather her wits before answering. "The victim's son, Jonathan 'Doc' Hill, was close by when the discovery of the explosion in the engine compartment was made. I'm sure he knows his father was murdered, and he looks to me to be the type to take action."

"Oh, no," Paul said, his voice sounding more worried than Heather had ever heard him sound in the year they had been dating.

"Damn!" President Dolan said, "If the kid is anything like his father was, I'm sure he *will* take action. Look, I'll make sure the head of the NTSB investigation team there keeps this under wraps. You keep an eye on the son, follow him, see what he knows and what he plans on doing. Hell, talk to him if you have to."

She was stunned that he had even suggested what he was suggesting.

"How should I approach him, sir?"

"Hell, tell him who you are, that I'm the one interested because I was a friend of his father's. I don't care how you handle it, just stay on this, stay on him, find out what this kid is thinking of doing about his father's murder, and report back to me or Paul regularly."

"Understood, sir."

"I'll talk to Director Smith, have him give you any help you need."

"Thank you, sir."

"And agent, do the best you can to keep the kid alive," President Dolan said, then broke the connection.

SECTION TWO

SURVIVAL

Patience is everything in a poker tournament. You are there to survive, build up your chips, be the only person left. You can't take stupid chances early on and expect that result.

CHAPTER TWENTY-ONE

Las Vegas, Nevada. August 22

"DOC, I THINK we have another problem."

"What, he had a second wife and she's home?"

"I wish," Fleet said.

Fleet had stepped past me into my father's house. I was in front of the alarm keypad tucked inside a stone column, one of a half dozen columns that ran along the front of this Las Vegas suburban mansion. I had just unlocked the place and turned off the alarms. The last thing I wanted to do was go in there, so instead I stood and stared at the neighborhood around the house.

Silent, hot, and sterile. The car radio had said it was one hundred and six degrees. A cool August afternoon, actually, for Vegas. But it was made hotter where I stood by all the rocks and concrete Carson had used to landscape his place.

I missed the coolness of the mornings on the river, even the biting cold of the water. I couldn't imagine why anyone lived in a subdivision like this, but the desert around Las Vegas was blooming with them, like weeds sprouting up everywhere no matter how much you tried to kill them. Every funny-named grouping had a fancy front entrance and lots of twisting streets lined with expensive homes spaced evenly. Right now, every window of every house I could see had the blinds or curtains pulled. Nothing was moving. No one had even looked out to see what we were doing.

I felt like I was in a bad science fiction movie and I was the only person left alive in the world. Where were the kids? Where were the people doing yard work, washing cars, living life? This was a street of homes, but it sure didn't feel like anyone lived here. I'd been in ghost towns with more life.

My mother had given me the code to turn off Carson's house alarm. Over the last two days, she had been so upset at Carson's death, I didn't want to press her just yet on how she knew the alarm code to his home after being divorced from him for decades. I just filed it away with the other hundred questions I was determined to finally get answers for. Including, of course, who killed the bastard.

"Doc, you need to see this," Fleet said from inside the open front door.

"Coming," I said.

Actually, I felt I didn't need to see anything in this house. Going into the home of a man I had hated since I was six was not a task I had been looking forward to. Sort of like crawling into a dentist's chair and saying, "Give me a half dozen root canals. And then pull a couple teeth just for kicks."

I'd rather stand in the heat and slowly just simmer in my own fat, but I doubted Fleet was going to let that happen, from the sound of his voice.

Actually, nothing in the past three days had been pleasant. Carson's body had been released to me two days ago, cremated yesterday. My mother had arranged to pick up the ashes, saying nothing to me.

We scheduled no ceremony. Ace had said he would remember Carson the way he wanted to and didn't need one. I certainly didn't care. I'm sure *Card Player Magazine* would run some article or two on him. I'd avoid those issues, just like I had been avoiding their phone calls to talk to me about his death.

Except for a very large trust set up for my mother, I was Carson's only heir, so even without my grandfather asking me to look into Carson's death, I would have been stuck with all the duties of the estate. Thank heavens Fleet was an attorney and knew what to do. He was taking the brunt of this for me. I was going to owe him big time for that.

After I had told Ace what I had learned at the crash site, he refused to say anything more. He wanted me to back off. He even released me from my promise to him. But when it was clear I wasn't going to just go back to my life without some answers, he made me promise to be very careful. I hadn't seen the old guy look so worried before. Clearly, he knew something he didn't want to tell me. I didn't push, but I would at some point down the road.

From behind me, Fleet said, "Doc, you really, *really* need to take a look at this before you touch anything else."

"Why?"

"Just come look, will you?"

I could tell he was starting to get annoyed at me. I sighed and moved away from the alarm control panel. There was just no escaping this, even by jumping into the hot oven of a dead subdivision. I took a deep breath of the warm air, and like walking into a torture chamber, I stepped into the darkened, cool house.

It took me a moment before my eyes adjusted to the dim light, then a moment longer to realize what I was looking at.

No damn wonder Fleet had been calling me.

What might have been a tastefully done living room looked like a hurricane had gone through it. Furniture was tipped up and the bottoms ripped open, art was off the walls, sitting on the floor, backs ripped open, and in a couple corners even the carpet had been pulled up.

Someone had clearly done a very careful search of Carson's home.

"Wonderful," I said. "Wasn't killing him enough?"

"Seems like it wasn't," Fleet said. "Don't touch anything and keep an eye on that door."

I doubted anyone was coming back at the moment, but I moved closer to the door and studied the big living room as Fleet dug his cell phone out of his jacket pocket and called the police.

So, this was the place Carson had lived. Even with all the destruction, it felt comfortable. I didn't want it to, but it did. All I wanted to do was go through the place, get the inventory for the estate, then sell it, furniture and all.

"Three minutes," Fleet said, hanging up after giving the police the address.

He looked around, studying the mess just as I had been doing while he was on the phone. "Got any idea what they were after?"

"Not a clue," I said. "Money, more than likely. They heard he'd been killed, decided to come raid his poker funds."

"I hope you're right," Fleet said, sounding as worried as I had heard him sound in a long time.

I didn't say anything, but I hoped I was right as well. I had a hunch I wasn't, and I was going to find out real soon why not.

CHAPTER TWENTY-TWO

LAS VEGAS, NEVADA. AUGUST 22

THE DETECTIVE who arrived with two uniformed officers was a middle-aged guy named Farmer. He had a bad comb-over covering a sunburned, balding head, and weighed sixty pounds too much for his five-foot-six frame, all carried like a bowling ball around his stomach. He was sweating almost constantly, even in the air-conditioning, and carried a bottle of water like it was a lifeline.

He had known of Carson and told me how sorry he was to hear about my father's death as I shook the detective's sweating, slick hand. I thanked him, because it was just easier than saying anything else.

I also managed to not wipe off my hand until his back was turned. Some of the politeness my mother had tried to teach me as a child clearly had stayed with me. Either that or I was just getting old.

Farmer and his men spent two full hours going slowly through the place, taking pictures, fingerprinting selective areas, and looking for who-knew-what. I had expected a quick stop-by from a patrolman, a nod that yes, we had been robbed, and a report filled out and filed, never to be looked at again. But that clearly wasn't the way it was happening. At one point, when I asked Farmer why they were doing such a careful job, he said that because of the nature of Carson's death, they were taking extra time and making sure everything was covered.

Made sense to me.

After they took our statements and did their fingerprinting and picture-taking in the dining room, Fleet and I sat at the big oak dining table and said nothing, just waiting and watching. If it had been up to me, I'd have gone out and sat in the car. But with a shake of the head, Fleet vetoed that idea for some reason. So we stayed, sitting, doing nothing but watching the police.

No matter how many ways I looked at this situation, Carson's death and this robbery, I didn't see money as the reason. And about an hour into the police nosing around, my hunch was confirmed. Farmer brought out a briefcase full of cash and sat it on the table. "Top of a bedroom dresser," he said. "It was searched and then left. There's cash everywhere, in bundles on the dresser, in one drawer, in a safe that was opened. Whoever did this wasn't looking for money, that's for sure."

"I figured as much," I said.

He looked at me like a beginning poker player, trying to pretend that by staring intently at me, he could get a clue as to what cards I held. "You know what they might have been after?"

I looked the detective right in the eye and told him the truth. "Not a clue. I wish I did."

Farmer nodded. "So, why so much money just lying around?"

"Carson was a typical professional poker player," I said. There looked to be about a half million in the case. "At least one who was winning. And you can bet we'll find even more in the cages at three or four casinos around town."

"Why?" Farmer asked, clearly puzzled at the idea of someone leaving more cash lying around than he made in salary in ten years. "He need this much?"

Fleet snorted, almost in disgust. "A professional poker player can't seem to go to the grocery store without ten thousand in his pocket. They feel naked without it."

"It's just part of the business," I said. "When you're playing well and things are working, you're flush with cash. Carson played in some high-stakes games where that much cash wouldn't get you a seat at the table."

"Oh," was all Farmer said. "You carry that much?"

I nodded. "I have at times." I didn't want to tell him I had less than a hundred in cash on me at the moment. I just didn't need money up on the river, and I hadn't bothered to get any out of my safe over the last few days. My mind wasn't on playing poker just yet.

With a shake of his head, Farmer left the cash with us and went back to looking the place over and taking pictures.

One thing had now been answered clearly. Money was not of interest to the person who did this. And was not a concern. We had a very rich robber here. And more than likely a murderer.

Two hours after they arrived, Farmer shook my hand once more with his slick grip and then Fleet shut the door behind them, trapping me in Carson's home.

I took a deep breath and pushed down the urge to dash for the door and the wonderful heat beyond. I needed to look through this place, at least once, then turn it over to Fleet and the people he would hire to help him inventory everything for the estate. Granted, I owned all this, but I sure didn't want any of it.

And I certainly didn't want to be standing in the middle of it all.

Fleet started turning chairs back upright, working to straighten out the place. I stood there for a moment, watching, then without a word, joined him. Cleaning the place up was as good as any way to do what I needed to do.

Chapter Twenty-Three

Las Vegas, Nevada. August 22

WE WORKED our way through the living room, picking up furniture, then the dining room, putting pictures back on walls, closing cabinet doors, putting any cash we found on the dining room table.

"Wow," Fleet said at one point as he picked up a painting that had the back paper ripped open. "Carson sure had great taste in art. There are some originals in here that are worth a fortune."

"More estate troubles?" I asked.

Fleet just laughed. "Yeah, but nothing I can't deal with."

"Have I said thanks yet?" I asked as I turned over an arm chair and slid it back into its old position near the wall, where the dents in the carpet showed that it used to be.

"A couple dozen times," Fleet said. "It's my job, remember. It's my half of this partnership."

"Yeah, but thanks anyway."

Fleet smiled. "You're welcome."

I stared at the ripped back of another picture as I picked it up. "At least we know two things about the person who did this."

"Not interested in money," Fleet said.

"That's one," I said. "And what he was looking for is small." I pointed to the back of the picture.

"Good point. I wonder what could be so important as to not be worth even taking the money out of here?"

"And killing Carson," I said.

"Yeah, that too," Fleet said.

We left the kitchen, with all the broken dishes and spilled food, for a professional cleaning service, and worked our way through a small office Carson had in one room, then down the hall and into the master bedroom.

I had been doing fine right up until the moment we stepped into that room. Then the urge to run for the hot afternoon sunshine grabbed hold of my stomach again. I didn't want to be in Carson's house, let alone his bedroom. That was just a little too close to a man I hated.

"Oh, my," Fleet said, stopping and staring.

It was a huge room, with a large king bed against one wall. There had to be a half dozen dressers, all with the contents opened and spilled on the floor. The center of the floor looked like the back room of a thrift store, the clothes were piled so high. Two large walk-in closets were also emptied and stacked onto the pile of clothes. It looked like each item had been carefully gone through. So, no doubt the object of desire was small. Small enough to fit into a pocket.

And a lot of the clothing was for a woman. In fact, it looked like one entire closet had been women's clothes. So Carson did have someone else in his life. That was something I was certain I wouldn't tell my mother any time soon.

"Shall we leave this for the cleaning service?" I asked.

Fleet shook his head. "Too much money in here. We need to go through this and stack the clothes back in the closets and drawers."

I nodded and dug in, trying not to think about the clothes being Carson's. Every few minutes, either Fleet or I would take a stash of bills to the dining room table. On my last trip out, I figured the table now held almost a million. And we hadn't even gotten to the floor safe in one closet yet.

I was standing beside the dining table, just finishing stacking about sixty thousand, when Fleet shouted.

"Doc, you had better come take a look at this."

I went back into the bedroom. Fleet was standing near one dresser, across from the bed. A half dozen or so framed pictures had been on the wall, and were now on the floor leaning against the edge of the dresser. And Fleet was holding another.

He turned it around as I came in. My college graduation photo, the one that my mother insisted that I have done. It was framed with some photos taken by someone in the crowd as I crossed the stage.

What the hell was it doing in Carson's bedroom?

Fleet placed it back on one of the hooks on the wall, then picked up another. It consisted of three matted pictures of my high school graduation. My official class picture, plus two others from the back of the auditorium.

I was so stunned, I didn't know what to say as Fleet hung the picture back up, then picked up another of my mother, my father, and me as a child. I have no memory of the picture being taken, but it looked like a happy time just before my father had left.

Fleet hung that up as well. The next framed picture was of me winning my first World Series of Poker bracelet. The last one was a picture I had given my mother of me standing beside a raft on the Middle Fork of the Salmon. How the hell had Carson gotten it?

My head was spinning as pictures of me filled more of the wall in Carson's bedroom.

Fleet hung the rafting picture with the others, then picked up the last one, a picture of my mother and Carson, smiling, sitting in some show on the strip, taken by one of the professional photographers that always go around at those events taking pictures of couples.

It was dated May 22 of the previous year. Their wedding anniversary.

Fleet put it in the middle slot on the wall and stepped back, not saying a word.

All I could do was stare.

Every belief I had held about my father, about my mother, about what had happened when I was six, had just been shattered.

It was clear that Carson had been at both my high school and my college graduation ceremonies.

I wanted to take the pictures off the wall and smash them into a hundred pieces, but just like in a tournament, when the cards didn't work, I somehow kept my balance.

Fleet backed up and sat down on the edge of the bed, staring at the wall. Then he said softly, and with great understatement. "Well, this is a stunner."

I glanced at the women's clothes, then back at the pictures. And suddenly some things fell into place. The clicks on the phone when I sometimes called my mother. More than likely the calls had been forwarded here. And her lame excuses at times about not being home when I would tell here I was going back to Boise for a few days without warning. More than likely, she had been here.

It was clear that Carson had really never left my mother.

Just me.

At the age of six.

Chapter Twenty-Four

Las Vegas, Nevada. August 22

DETECTIVE ANNIE LOTT pushed the Jeff Taylor pictures and evidence reports away on the oak kitchen table and sat back in frustration. She really wanted to just toss it all against a wall. Three days on this case and she wasn't one step closer to an answer than the moment she started. It felt like she was walking into dead end after dead end. Nothing made sense.

With its bay window looking out over her backyard, and her mother's big oak table, the kitchen was the most comfortable place in the house besides her big, pillow-top bed. She often sat at the table, staring out at the rock and desert flowers in her yard, thinking over cases or reading the most recent poker book or *Card Player Magazine*.

This kitchen was her favorite place. She had installed the best appliances and a top notch coffee maker. She had a state-of-the-art freezer and every dish and tool needed to cook any meal, all stashed in the beautiful oak and glass cabinets. She didn't use the dishes and pans that often, but just having everything here and ready was enough.

The window, the great recessed lighting, and the soft oak tones made the room her retreat from the real worlds of police work and professional poker. And she used it every day, at least to have her morning coffee.

Behind her, the timer dinged. The roast she had in the oven was fifteen minutes from being done. She had to get the potatoes going. She pushed herself to her feet and turned her back on the case papers.

It wasn't often these days that she cooked anything beyond a quick hot dish. She was just too busy, either with an investigation or playing poker. But she had wanted to tonight, since her dad was coming over. And right now, she had to admit, the roast smelled damned good. With the rich aroma of beef simmering in mushrooms and onions, her house actually felt like someone lived in it. Someday, it would be nice to get out of police work and just play cards for a living. Then maybe she'd have more time for cooking.

Of course, it would be nice to meet someone worth cooking for besides her retired-detective father. She and her last serious boyfriend had just drifted apart, mostly from her not having time for him. She couldn't really blame him for moving on. He had wanted someone to settle down with and have kids. That was never happening as far as she was concerned. She really didn't miss him, but she sure missed the sex.

She stacked the papers off to one side of the kitchen table, photos down, and set two places for dinner, using actual cloth napkins instead of her standard paper towels. She needed a favor from her father tonight, so she might as well treat him to a great dinner before she asked.

He had been one of the detectives on the Jeff Taylor murder before he retired. Maybe, if he was willing to talk about it, he could give her a few ideas, something she had missed in all the reports, or something that wasn't in the reports.

She spent the next fifteen minutes on the potatoes and salad before a knock sounded on her front door, and then the door opened.

"Decent?" her father shouted, just like he did every time he came over, his deep and powerful voice echoing through the house.

"In the kitchen," she shouted back.

A few moments later, her silver-haired father, retired Detective Bayard Lott, appeared beside where she was working and gave her a peck on the cheek. "Cloth napkins and a roast? This must be one damn big favor you need from me."

"What?" Annie said, trying not to laugh. "I can't just cook you a nice dinner without wanting something in return?"

"Oh, you could," her father said. "But it has never happened so far."

"Well, not a first tonight either," she said, laughing and turning to give him a big hug.

Her father, in his best years, stood no more than five-six. With no socks, she topped five-ten. Her mother had been shorter than her father, so she had no idea where she got the height. He had kept himself in top shape for his sixty-two years. Even while on the force, he had never let himself go as some detectives did. She admired that and a lot of other things about her father.

"So, this part of the favor?" he asked, pointing to the pile of papers as he moved toward the table to take his normal seat.

"Need some talking help on a case is all," she said, working over the salad one more time before putting it on the table between their two places.

"Jeff Taylor?" he asked, looking up at her. He hadn't touched the papers.

She smiled at him. "You reading my mind again, or did someone downtown tell you I had caught the case?"

"Just logical," he said. "I was lead on the Taylor murder case, and with your poker experience, I figured they'd toss you the grave robbery aspect of it."

"On the money," Annie said, turning back to drain the potatoes as the timer dinged once again to let her know the roast was finished.

"Mind if I look?" he asked.

"As long as it won't spoil your appetite, go ahead."

"I used to eat lunch through autopsies," he said.

As he flipped through the file, she took the roast out, letting the thick odor swirl hotly around her.

She slid the roast onto a serving platter, put the potatoes around it, spooned the cooked onions and mushrooms from the roast pan over the meat, then put the broth into a bowl.

As she put the roast on the table and sat down, her father, as she had seen him do so many times before, was studying the papers with an intensity that felt like he was trying to burn holes through the paper.

"As Mom used to say, *Food first, work second*."

He laughed and slid the papers to one side, admiring the roast with an impressed nod. "Five years, and I still miss her every day," he said.

"Yeah, me too," Annie said. The sudden death of her mother had taken them both by surprise. It had been everything they could do to keep each other going. It was then that Annie had decided that she wasn't going to wait to do things in life. She was going to chase her dream of playing professional poker sooner, rather than later.

Now, after five years, her father seemed to have settled into his new routines with his retirement. He had built a brand-new, state-of-the-art poker room in his basement, with an expensive table, a coffee bar, and wonderful, soft chairs. Once a week, he had four other retired detectives over for a game. Not only did they play cards, but each week they talked over some cold case, working to solve it between games.

The city loved what they were doing and supported their efforts in any way legally they could, since it allowed the paid detectives to stay on current cases.

Six months in, Annie had visited their game and called them "The Cold Poker Gang." The name had stuck. Now they were even called that downtown. In just under a year, they had closed five cold cases, a fantastic record. And Annie had a hunch, they were just getting started. Two more active detectives were retiring next year and joining the Cold Poker Gang.

"So, what do you want to know about Taylor?" he asked after a few bites of roast and the appropriate comments about its wonderful quality.

"I talked to Taylor's son, who still thinks his father was murdered because of something he knew, or was about to tell."

Her father shook his head. "It had all the signs of a robbery gone bad. Taylor had just taken down almost two hundred thousand that night."

"Wow, good night. And he had it on him, right?"

"Yeah, and he was on the way to his car on a side street. The money was missing and Taylor was dead from a blow to the back of the head."

She nodded. It was the kind of case that seldom got solved. No connections to the deceased, no witnesses, just a cold murder with no reason but money. It always took a lucky break or a murderer with a conscious or a bragging mouth to actually break cases like that. And with Taylor, in over a decade, nothing had surfaced. The case was about as cold as it got.

"So," her father said, "you think someone taking the key from his chest gives the son's theory some credence?"

"Don't you?" she asked. "Professional job all the way along, and clearly that key means something special to someone."

"The kid know what the key went to? Back when his father died, he didn't tell me he'd put the key there."

She shook her head. "He said he told almost no one. And that Taylor had had it for years before his death, tucked away for safe keeping with his World Series bracelet."

"That important, huh?"

Annie nodded and kept eating.

"Well, her father said, "the son had to have told someone, otherwise, who would know it was there?"

"I looked into that," Annie said. "Even the funeral director at the time didn't know. More than likely it's the ex-wife who told someone, but I'm planning on checking with the son again to see if he can remember exactly who he told."

"The kid was a drinker back then. He might have told a hundred people in a bar one night and not even remember."

"Wonderful," Annie said, shaking her head. There was nothing about this case that seemed simple. Nothing.

"You do some modern tests on Taylor's body, since someone did the favor of digging it up?"

"An entire battery of them," Annie said, "all showing nothing killed him but the blow to the back of the head. No drugs, nothing."

"Tough nut to crack, huh? So, what's the next step in the plan?"

"Poker," Annie said, smiling at her father.

"The big tournaments at the Bellagio?"

She nodded. "I figured a bunch of Taylor's old friends will be coming into town to play over the next two weeks. I might as well chase the idea that Taylor's son could be right about why his father was killed. Or at least see if I can find who knows what the key is all about. Maybe it was just some dumb bet. High-stakes poker players are known for making strange wagers outside the poker rooms."

"Tough wager for Taylor to pay off," her father said, shaking his head and laughing. "You need some stakes into a few of the tournaments?"

She patted his arm and smiled. "Thanks, Dad, but my poker fund is pretty healthy at the moment and growing."

"How healthy, if you don't mind my asking."

Annie felt embarrassed, but she told him the truth. "Over eighty thousand. Just in the poker fund, not counting my other savings. Not enough to buy me into that many of the big tournaments, but more than enough to keep me playing in the satellites to win my way into the bigger ones."

Her father actually whistled as he pushed his clean plate away. "That amount of money is downright living and breathing. Anyone ever tell you that you're in the wrong business?"

"Yeah, I've been thinking that."

Chapter Twenty-Five

Las Vegas, Nevada. August 23

SLEEP DIDN'T HAPPEN much that night in my normal three-room suite at the Bellagio. And when I did doze off, I kept dreaming about Carson standing in the back of my college graduation ceremony, watching me, yet not even bothering to walk up to me and shake my hand and say congratulations.

Not one damn word.

The dream kept morphing him into this ghost that wouldn't let me touch him, yet always floated around everything I was doing. That was enough to wake me up sweating every time. And I'm sure some shrink could have a blast with all the metaphors.

So most of the night I just lay there, thinking, staring at the ornate ceiling, the overdone Italian décor, and the television's blank screen.

Nothing made sense. By the time of my graduation from college, with my poker playing and Fleet's fantastic ability to invest my winnings soundly, he and I were fairly rich. I had moved up to playing in some of the bigger tournaments around the country. I knew what Carson looked like, had played cards in the same room with him. Why hadn't I seen him there at the ceremony?

Because I never once expected to see him there, that was why. I had always just assumed he didn't care.

That day, after the ceremony, my mother had encouraged me to go off and have fun with Fleet and my friends. "I've got more than enough to keep me busy," she had said.

Carson more than likely kept her busy. She had somehow kept the secret of their relationship for decades, and I hadn't noticed. So much for being an observant professional poker player. For twenty-seven years, they had kept me in the dark.

Now he was dead and I was so angry at my mother, I wasn't sure if I ever wanted to talk to her again.

Why had they done that? Did it have something to do with his murder?

Was my mother in danger now as well?

That thought sent me pacing through the suite for a while around three a.m. before I decided I needed to find out more before I did anything, including yelling at my mother in the middle of the night.

Not that she didn't deserve it.

I finally must have dozed off around four and somehow managed to crawl out of bed at ten with a plan. Not much of a plan, but considering how little information I had to go on, at least it was a plan.

I met Fleet at ten-thirty for breakfast in the Café Bellagio just off the main lobby, the twenty-four-hour restaurant that served just about anything at any time, with some pretty fine quality. Everything in the Bellagio was opulent Mediterranean style and richly textured. The Café was no exception, with large tables, comfortable cloth booths, and staff that actually smiled at any time of the day or night.

The thing you noticed most about the Bellagio was the openness, fantastically high ceilings, and light. Light seemed to flow in from everywhere, and the arch patterns helped that feeling. The second thing was the smell. There were always food odors wafting about from all the restaurants. The place didn't smell like a casino. And the Café always smelled like baking bread.

I couldn't even begin to remember how many meals I'd eaten in the Café Bellagio. I had even dated one of the waitresses, a wonderful woman named Traci, who worked there. We had gone out for a few months when I was in town. As with all my relationships, it had gone nowhere.

Fleet's plan for the day was to go back to Carson's house to start the inventory. He asked me if I wanted to go with him and I told him I had an appointment to put my head in a vise and twist it until the pain made me pass out, so I was sorry, but I just couldn't go enjoy any time in Carson's home.

He laughed. "So what are you really planning to do?"

"Didn't buy the vise excuse?" I asked.

He shook his head. "Not your style. You're more the crushing-your-self-between-large-rocks kind of guy. A vise would be just too pedestrian."

"True," I said, laughing. "Actually, I was thinking I'd play some poker, talk to some of my father's old friends, find out what I can about him. Later this afternoon, I might play in one of the satellites for the upcoming tournaments that start tomorrow, to get my feet back under me after the time on the river."

"And all the turmoil," Fleet said.

"Yeah, that too. It never hurts to spend a little money getting warmed up before paying the big money."

Like I said, it wasn't much of a plan, but at least it was a plan. And it kept me the hell out of Carson's house for most of the day.

CHAPTER TWENTY-SIX

LAS VEGAS, NEVADA. AUGUST 23

THIRTY MINUTES LATER, after a quick stop at the cage to get some cash from my deposit box, I walked into the poker room to friendly welcomes from friends and a bunch of sideways stares from other people. Everyone knew I was Carson's son, and that he had died in a plane crash. And everyone knew we didn't talk. So that made for some strange looks.

During normal times, the Bellagio poker room was a big, contained corner of the larger casino floor, with comfortable padded chairs, perfect lighting, and excellent dealers. It was divided off by arches that were open, but gave the room its own closed feeling of privacy. But during bigger tournaments, they removed a massive area of slot machines near the entrance to the poker room and expanded the poker area by five or six times, depending on the size of the tournament.

There were already a few tournament satellites going on in one corner of the sea of empty tables.

Even with the strange stares, it felt great being back in a poker room. I loved the river, but I loved poker rooms even more. And the Bellagio room was about as good as rooms came.

I checked in, asked the room manager a few questions about who was around, and decided to join the $100-200 limit hold'em game in the back corner that had an open chair and three of the old-timers who had known Carson.

This looked like a pretty good table for me, both to get information and win some money. Verne Adkins, a top live-game player, held the center five seat, with Hank Danning in the third chair and Loren Peoples beside him in four. All three of them had been close friends with Carson, and all three played a tight game.

They played the same time every day, like poker was their jobs, and went home for dinner with their wives no matter what was happening. I admired their skills and planned on staying out of their way while we played.

The others at the table looked like tourists, and at a glance I could tell the guy in the first chair was playing well over his bankroll, since he was sweating like it was a hundred degrees in the room. These three must be taking turns plucking him like a dead chicken.

I took the open chair beside Verne, stacked my chips, then reached into my pocket and pulled out a heavy rook-like piece and sat it beside my chips.

The little castle was made of some sort of silver alloy, stood about three inches tall, and was smooth and polished from so much handling. Carson, for years, had always used it as a card capper, and it had been on him when he died. The sheriff had given it to me with his possessions. I figured using it in this game would start a few conversations about Carson, if nothing else.

Verne stared at the castle, then glanced at me with a sad smile on his face.

"Figured I'd honor Carson a little in these tournaments," I said, picking up the castle.

All three of Carson's friends nodded, but said nothing. It was an uncomfortable silence, but just what I wanted at the moment, to get them relaxing a little around me and talking. For the first time in my life, I actually wanted information about Carson. It felt weird, damned weird.

For twenty minutes or so after I sat down, it was only basic chatter, like how was the river, how was my mother doing, that sort of thing. I was dealt one hand worth playing. A pair of jacks one off the button. Everyone folded to me and I raised, making it two hundred to go. The sweater in chair one, who was the big blind, called me, shaking his head as he did.

I put him on a bad ace, the kind of hand a weak player would chase with one hundred already in the pot.

Flop came ace, four, jack. I had a set of jacks. Sweater stared at the flop for a moment, like he couldn't believe what he saw, then fumbled one hundred out as a bet. I raised him to two, he reraised to three and I called.

His reraise told me that he had hit his bad kicker as well as his ace. He was sitting on two pair. Or maybe a set of fours. I was going to take most of his chips unless he hit another ace or a four.

Next card was a seven, he bet two hundred, I raised, he called. Next card was a nine and Sweater actually smiled. He clearly had fallen in love with his two pair and was going to go down swinging with them. He bet out two hundred, I raised, he reraised, and I capped it, forcing him to push in his last few chips. He flipped over his ace-four and I showed him my set of jacks.

As he stormed off and I raked in his chips, Verne shook his head and laughed. "It's going to be a lot tougher to get those from you than it would have been from him."

"I sure hope so," I said.

That was the first pot I pulled since leaving the river. It felt good, and helped shove back the lack of sleep.

After a time, I got the conversation going on Carson, as his three old friends relaxed and realized I really did want to hear what they had to say. And, more importantly, that I wasn't sitting there to take their chips.

Another tourist filled the empty seat and the game went on, with the four of us talking about Carson.

"You know," Hank said at one point, "Carson was one of the most generous players out here."

"I didn't know that," I said, not really believing Hank.

Verne laughed. "Can't tell you how many times your father paid a player's mortgage payment."

"You're kidding?" I asked, surprised. In all my hatred of the man, it would have never occurred to me he did things like that. I just always assumed he was a monster in all aspects of his life.

"They're not kidding at all," Loren said. "Hell, he paid for my kid's dental surgery and braces when I was tapped out. Took me a year to repay him."

I sat there, stunned, as story after story of Carson's generosity came from the three. I just couldn't understand how a man who could ignore his own child for more than two decades could be the same man these players were talking about. And the poker world was a small world.

Why hadn't I heard about any of this?

Oh, yeah, now I remember. I had made it clear that when I was around, Carson wasn't to be spoken of. Maybe that had something to do with it.

I sat there holding Carson's chess piece and listening to the stories. Then, as the dealer was shuffling, one of my fingers found a slight edge on the bottom of the castle and I pushed it.

The bottom moved aside and a key fell onto the table in front of me.

"Another surprise from Carson," I said, holding the key up and looking at it, then looking at the hole it had fallen out of in the castle.

The key looked like a regular bank deposit key, and the hole in the metal rook looked like it was made specially to fit the key.

"Put that away," Verne whispered to me, his voice firm and almost angry.

I glanced at him and could see the intensity in his eyes.

"You have no idea what you are holding." Verne's voice was a harsh whisper now, aimed only at me.

I slid the key back into the castle and then put the entire thing back into my front pants pocket. Only the other two friends of Carson noticed, but both looked puzzled. They clearly had no more idea than I did what that key was.

I started to ask Verne what he meant, but he shook his head and focused with unusual intensity on his new cards. It was clear he didn't want to talk about it. So I changed the subject, got them talking about Carson again, and the game went on.

About forty minutes later, Verne got up and headed in the direction of the men's room. I mucked my next hand and followed, finding him washing his hands and splashing some water on his face. He actually looked upset. And it clearly wasn't because of the poker game. He was a thousand or so up at the table.

"So," I said, coming in and standing beside him at the long, ornate marble counter with a dozen sinks under a massive gold-trimmed mirror. "You want to tell me what that key is for? You clearly know."

"For keeping secrets," he said.

He splashed more water on his face, then used a hand towel to dry off.

"What kind of secrets?"

"Deadly secrets."

"At least tell me something about it. Ace wants to know as well."

I figured using Ace's name might break Verne a little. Ace was a legend in poker circles, and he and Verne went back a long ways into the days when poker was a lot wilder and a lot more dangerous to play.

"Do they know why your father's plane went down yet?"

In all the papers they were still calling it an accident, and the sheriff had asked me, as a favor, to keep what I had overheard about the explosion quiet for the moment, to help them in the investigation. So I didn't know what to say.

But Verne read me like I read that sweater earlier. He nodded. "He was murdered, wasn't he?"

"Why would you think that?" I asked.

Verne waved the question away like I was a beginning player missing the most obvious piece of instruction. "He was murdered for that key.

Put it away and tell no one you have it, including Ace. You don't know what you have, or how dangerous it is."

Then, Verne turned his back on me and walked out of the restroom.

I stood there for a moment, trying to make any kind of sense out of any of what I had just heard, then shook my head and went back to the game. I apologized that I had to leave so soon, racked up my chips and headed for the cashier.

I had no idea what to make of Verne's comments about the hidden key, but one thing was for certain, I didn't want to hear any more stories about Carson right now.

CHAPTER TWENTY-SEVEN

LAS VEGAS, NEVADA. AUGUST 23

DETECTIVE ANNIE LOTT STOOD, leaning against the side of a row of slot machines, just over the rail from the tournament area, and watched a number of the satellite tables. She had to take the time to let herself calm down, chase out the mass of butterflies swirling around in her stomach. She loved the excitement of tournament poker, and in these big events, she loved how they made her feel as well. Excited, alive, and scared to death.

Everywhere she looked around the Bellagio poker room and tournament area, there were major professionals, some recognizable across the country from their tournament wins, others because she was starting to learn who the great cash game players were.

She felt at home here, but not as much as her favorite poker room at the MGM Grand. That room seemed to seldom attract the big names, and she could play and work on her game and build up her bankroll without worrying about being taken that often by a stronger player.

But here, in the Bellagio, today and the next two weeks, she would have to play at the top of her game to even have a chance of breaking into the money in one of these tournaments, let alone winning one.

After almost forty minutes of watching, she figured she had her nerves under enough control to actually play some cards. She moved over and sat down in a forming satellite at a table along the edge of the tournament area. She took the number six chair, facing away from most of the other tables. The rows of slot machines in front of her wouldn't distract her as much as watching the big names come and go.

She put the entry fee, two hundred and fifteen dollars in cash, in front of her. Two hundred of it went into the prize pool, the rest was the rake the casino took. Ten players at the table, winner take all. The first tournament tomorrow had a two-thousand-dollar buy-in, thus the reason for the structure of this satellite. Win this and you won your entry into the first big event.

She had just gotten comfortable when Doc Hill sat down beside her.

"Oh, my," she said under her breath. Every butterfly she had gotten rid of suddenly returned, bringing a few thousand more of their friends and family with them.

She couldn't believe he was sitting beside her. She smiled and nodded and he did the same.

He was even more handsome up close than his pictures in the poker magazines. He had an incredible tan, and his dark hair was lightly streaked by the sun. For heaven's sake, he even smelled wonderful, as if he had brought the freshness of the summer in the Idaho mountains along with him.

She had read a lot of articles about him, followed his wins and his life. She knew he guided rafters off and on all summer on the River of No Return in Idaho, even though he clearly didn't need the money. She had read another article about how he got his nickname from stopping just a few credits short of a doctorate in mathematics. She even knew who he had dated a few times.

He was the grandson of Ace Hill, one of the most famous old-timers, and the son of Carson Hill, who used to be a top high-stakes player before he died. She had no chance at all in this satellite if Doc Hill was in it. He was one of the best players playing currently, and was even leading the *Card Player* points list coming out of the World Series of Poker. He had won two bracelets this summer alone.

She tried to take a deep breath, but it sort of shuddered into her lungs instead. She felt frozen, feeling as if she were back in junior high and the cool kid had just sat down beside her. She should be past this sort of thing at her age.

"This is *stupid*," she said to herself.

"Excuse me?" Doc Hill asked, turning to smile at her.

She could feel herself blushing, her face growing hot. "I said that out loud, huh?"

He laughed, and she instantly loved his laugh, sort of low and real sounding.

"Yes, I'm afraid you did." He stuck out his hand. "Doc Hill," he said. "I watched you play a few times last spring, at the tournament here. And another time in a satellite at the World Series. It's good to finally meet you."

She couldn't believe he had actually watched *her* play. And remembered her. Somehow, that scared her even more. She liked the idea that no one knew who she was yet. It made her feel safe.

Somehow, she managed to shake his hand and say "Annie. Annie Lott."

His grip was firm and callused, and just his touch sent a jolt through her spine. His dark eyes held her gaze for a fraction of a second longer than any normal introduction.

Finally, he took his hand back.

"I don't remember you playing in satellites before," she said, hoping to somehow keep the conversation from going silent and uncomfortable.

"It's been a long few weeks," he said. "I figured I could use one or two of these to work a few of the kinks out."

"Makes sense," she said, nodding.

At that moment, the director picked up their money and nodded to the dealer. "Make sure you each have two thousand in chips. Dealer, put them in the air."

CHAPTER TWENTY-EIGHT

LAS VEGAS, NEVADA. AUGUST 23

ANNIE MANAGED to get enough of a look at her first two cards with her shaking hands to toss them into the muck. Doc tossed his hand as well, and then asked her where she had gone to school.

Between hands, they talked about her days at Princeton and his adventures on the river. The best hand she saw in the first fifteen-minute round was a pair of tens and there was already a raise ahead of her, so she had mucked them.

Doc hadn't gotten involved in a hand either, but by the end of the first round, two people were already gone. Eight left.

Somewhere in the middle of the first round, in the enjoyable conversation, she had relaxed and her hands had actually stopped shaking. She couldn't believe she was actually sitting there, playing cards with a very handsome, very famous poker player. She was going to have to pinch herself later.

Two more aggressive players were knocked out in the middle of the next round, leaving their chips with a man who she had a read on as a good player. He was clearly chip leader with about eight thousand. Six of them left, and next to her, Doc was still acting relaxed, talking to her, and tossing every hand away, sometimes without looking at them, depending on his position and what had happened ahead of him with the betting.

At one point near the end of the second round, he asked her what she did for a living.

"Detective in the Las Vegas PD," she said.

He looked into her eyes again with that. "I wouldn't have thought you were that old."

She laughed. "Thanks, I think."

She wasn't sure, but under the tan she thought that this time he blushed. She was just glad he didn't ask what case she was working on.

Halfway through the third round, she took down the blinds with a raise on a pair of jacks, and then won another pot on a race, her ace/king against a pair of fours with the ace hitting the turn. She had started with two thousand, now she had just over three thousand in chips. Not good, but not that bad either.

Doc was under two thousand, with the blinds at one hundred, two hundred, and didn't seem to care or even notice. She wasn't convinced he was even paying attention.

Another player got knocked out and stood, shaking his head at the loss. Five players left. Beside her, Doc sort of sat up, squared his shoulders, and looked like he was about to go to work.

Suddenly, she understood what he had been doing. He had been just staying out of the way of the dead money, the players who didn't have a chance to win, but might knock him out with a lucky draw. Now, with only five players left, he was going to start playing to win.

She had read about that type of strategy in a number of magazines and two books, but had never seen it so blatantly done before. She just hoped he didn't come after her first.

He didn't. The weak player in the second chair, under the gun, made a small raise of five hundred and suddenly Doc came alive, coming over the top of the man's bet with a reraise.

The guy clearly looked like he had swallowed something sour.

Annie folded, and so did the other two players in the blinds. The original raiser looked back at his two cards, then shook his head and mucked them.

The next hand Doc took the man's big blind with a decent-sized raise under the gun. Then, in the next hand, Doc took the guy's money again when the guy limped in on the small blind and Doc raised again from the big blind, again getting the guy to fold like tissue paper.

Annie was impressed. For three rounds, Doc hadn't played a hand, then in three hands, he had just simply robbed the weakest player at the table of almost two thousand in chips. It was a stunning run, set up perfectly. Doc might have been talking to her, but clearly he had been paying attention to the other players as well.

Doc folded his small blind to her big blind and then raised the next hand from the button. She folded her small blind; the big blind, who had the biggest stack, called, and so did the weak player Doc had been robbing.

After the flop, both checked to Doc, who bet, and they both seemed in a hurry to fold. Suddenly, Doc was gaining on the chip leader. What she was watching was play far beyond her level. Maybe someday she'd get there. At least she understood what she was watching.

Doc folded the next hand and she picked up a pair of tens on the button and raised. The chip leader beside her called her six hundred raise.

She caught a third ten on the flop, the big blind checked, and she bet over half of her remaining chips. The bet was too large to say anything to a good player except that her hand was weak. Usually weak players, when they have a strong hand, bet small to get people to call. She wanted the call, but she wanted the big stack to think she didn't.

Beside her, Doc nodded for some reason.

The chip leader thought it over and then called.

The board paired on the turn, giving her a full house. The chip leader bet out, enough to put her all in, and she called at once, rolling her cards over as she pushed her chips forward.

Doc again nodded as the big stack showed his smaller set. She couldn't be beat unless he hit quads, which he didn't.

As she stacked her chips, Doc whispered, "Nice bet."

"Thanks," she said.

Two hands later, Doc came in with a decent raise, she folded, and the big stack reraised, and Doc called all in. He had about three hundred less than the other guy. Doc rolled over a pair of kings, the big stack ace/jack. When the ace hit on the river, Doc stood.

Annie was impressed. He didn't seem upset or anything at the bad beat. She expected him to say goodbye to her, but instead just stepped back to watch the three of them finish the satellite.

Suddenly, she felt as nervous as she had when he sat down.

Three hands later, she reraised with all her money on ace/king, and was called by the big stack with pocket tens. Nothing hit and she stood up in third place. No winnings, but she felt good about how she had played.

Doc was nodding as he stepped toward her. "You played that right."

"Thanks," she said. She was almost glad she had gotten knocked out and was back talking to him. Satellites came and went, but how often did a player at her level get a chance to talk to Doc Hill?

Standing face-to-face with him, she was surprised how tall he was. She was tall, too tall she thought at times, but she still looked up into his eyes.

"You have time for some late lunch?" he asked, smiling.

She was going to have to be careful. That smile of his could melt just about anything, and it was having that effect on her legs.

"I'd love to," she said, trying to keep the stupid butterflies swarming around in her stomach from making her act like a schoolgirl. He was one of the best poker players on the planet, and extremely good-looking.

Was she in lust or just in awe? Or both?

Lunch with him to find out sure couldn't hurt.

CHAPTER TWENTY-NINE

LAS VEGAS, NEVADA. AUGUST 23

A STUNNINGLY GOOD-LOOKING COP, who could play poker. Who would have bet that was possible? And she had an education and was fun to talk to. There had to be something wrong with her. It was a good sign that I couldn't see what it was yet.

Besides, as a detective, she just might be able to help me with what I was dealing with on the death of Carson, maybe give me a perspective I couldn't yet see. But I wanted to get to know her better before telling her. Fact was, I didn't need an excuse. I wanted to get to know her better.

Period.

It had been a while since I had even had a date. I could just never tell if someone was going out with me for my money and fame, or because they were actually interested in me. And even real relationships, when I found them, didn't last long. Dating a professional poker player was not an easy thing to do. But that didn't stop me from continuing to try to find someone.

Just talking with Annie had been enough to keep my mind off Carson for most of the satellite and allow me to focus on playing. That help alone had been great. I had needed it after the conversation with Verne.

Deadly secrets. Carson was very dead, so Verne was right on that account.

I hoped to continue the distraction right through lunch as well. Anything to keep from going back to Carson's house. Those pictures in his bedroom haunted me, drifting around in my mind, appearing and vanishing without warning, a reality I didn't want to accept.

I had hated Carson for decades. Now I was so angry at my mother, I might end up hating her as well for what she had done.

"Where are we heading?" Annie asked as we left the tournament area, heading down one of the wide aisles between the thousands of slot machines, weaving in and out of the slow-walking tourists, going in the general direction of the main lobby.

"Café Bellagio," I said. "Why, is there another restaurant here?"

She laughed. "Not that I know of." Her expression changed. "Sorry about Carson. I heard you weren't close, but it still can't be easy. I wouldn't know what I would do if I lost my father like that."

I shrugged. "It's been interesting, that's for sure. So what does your father do?"

"Retired detective. Like father, like daughter. But he refuses to quit working. I'd quit in a blink if I was making enough money with my poker."

"Oh, you will make money with the poker when you focus on it, not an issue, as well as you play now."

She blushed, her skin turning pink right up under her beautiful hair. I was starting to enjoy that blush. Clearly the dream of playing full-time poker was very important to her. Before she could say anything, I went on.

"He's retired, but refuses to stop working? How does he manage that?"

"Cold cases," she said. "He and a bunch of his buddies work on cold cases with the blessing of the department. They call themselves the Cold Poker Gang because they talk about cold cases while playing poker in my dad's basement."

I laughed. "I think I'm really going to like your father."

She smiled. "He has his good points."

As we waited for the food, I asked her about some of the cold cases her father had settled and we talked about a few of them until lunch arrived. I liked Annie even more the longer we talked. There was a connection between us, an easiness that I often didn't feel around a woman.

"I'm sort of working on a cold case as well," Annie said as we started eating. "Half-cold, actually. The Jeff Taylor murder. You ever meet him?"

"Afraid not," I said. "He was just before my time. But I have heard that when he got on a roll, he couldn't be beat. So why the sudden interest in the Taylor murder case?"

She looked at me for a moment, puzzled, then nodded as if she suddenly understood. "Oh, you were still up in Idaho so you didn't hear. His grave was robbed. I caught the case since I play poker."

"Robbed?" I shook my head trying to figure that out, or even imagine it in a modern cemetery. "So why would someone rob his grave? Did he take his World Series bracelets with him or something?"

"No," Annie said, shaking her head. "That's what makes this so damn strange. The only thing taken was a key. His son Brent put it on Taylor's chest when he buried him. Brent said it looked like a bank key."

Annie shrugged and thankfully went back to eating, looking at her food instead of me.

For a moment I just flat couldn't breathe, then the years of poker training kicked in and I went behind what I called my shields. But not fast enough. Annie looked up and clearly saw that something about what she had said had surprised me.

Now she was staring at me with those wonderful eyes of hers, and I had no doubt she was seeing just how upset what she had said had made me.

Verne Adkin's words came back like they were being broadcast over a loudspeaker in my head. *He was murdered for that key. Put it away and tell no one you have it. Not even Ace.*

I focused on the hamburger I had ordered, trying to get my balance.

"Weird," I managed to say, looking up at Annie. She was still staring at me. "Anything about the key that gave you a lead?"

"Nothing," she said. "Taylor's son said it had the number three etched on the side of it. But otherwise it looked like the standard old bank deposit key."

Carson's key had a four scratched on the side of it.

They were connected.

"So why did his son bury it with Taylor?" I asked, hoping my voice sounded calmer than I felt.

"Brent said it was because his father clearly considered it important, but no one knew what it was for."

"Okay, that's strange," I said.

"Real strange. My father caught that case when it happened. Brent said his dad had been claiming he knew some horrible secret and was going to tell the world, and that was what got him killed."

My head was just swirling, and it was taking all my poker training and ability to think under pressure to keep myself balanced.

Annie went on. "It looked more like a robbery gone bad. The case went cold almost at once. My father never could get any traction on it. He said Taylor's kid seemed like a lunatic on drugs at the time."

"Didn't tell anyone about the key?" I asked.

"Not a word," Annie said. "But now with the grave robbery, dear old dad and his Cold Case Gang are going to give the entire thing another run, while I work this side of things."

Again, I was having trouble taking a regular breath. Verne's words again came back strong. When I had asked him what the key was for, he had said, *For keeping secrets. Deadly secrets.*

"Doc, are you all right?" Annie asked, a very deep look of concern on her face.

I must have been sitting, thinking, not moving at all, like I did when studying a situation at a poker table. She was staring at me and I didn't blame her.

I forced myself to sit up, focus back on my food, even though I wasn't that hungry suddenly. "Yeah, I'm fine. I was just thinking back, trying to remember anything anyone might have said to me about Taylor. Nothing's coming up, but if something does, I'll call you."

I could tell that she didn't completely buy my answer, but she didn't know me well enough to question it.

Annie nodded. "Or if you hear something over the next few weeks in the tournament. Any help on this is welcome."

I nodded. I couldn't decide if I should bring her in on what I was dealing with or not. I needed a night to think about that, maybe talk to Fleet and get his opinion.

"Look," I said, "I got a couple old-timers who are friends of mine. How about I talk to them tonight and we meet here for breakfast tomorrow?"

"I'd love to," Annie said, far faster than she should have. Then she realized what she had done and laughed, the blush coming up her neck. "Thank you."

"Anything to help out Las Vegas's finest." I said, smiling at her.

"I can use all the help I can get," she said. Then she blushed again.

I laughed. I had a hunch I knew what had just gone through her mind. It had gone through mine as well, but I was nice enough to not say anything. Although, I had to admit, it was tempting.

CHAPTER THIRTY

LAS VEGAS, NEVADA. AUGUST 23

STEVEN GLANCED UP as Doc Hill and his friend walked past, leaving the Café Bellagio. They had been sitting back near the windows, he was at a table closer to the lobby. He couldn't hear what they had been talking about, but it didn't matter anyhow. And he didn't care.

He pushed away his half-eaten Caesar salad and stood, tossing some cash on the table to cover his tab. Following every move he had planned, he picked up the morning *Las Vegas Sun* newspaper he had been reading, folded it, and stuck it under his arm. Without being in a hurry, he moved out of the confines of the restaurant.

Doc and his friend stood for a moment talking near the entrance to the restaurant, then parted. From the looks of it, the woman was going back toward the poker area. Doc turned and headed across the lobby toward the entrance to the south parking garage.

Steven stopped and stood beside a bench, making sure that was exactly where Doc was headed. The idiot actually had his father's key on him, and had been stupid enough to show it around at a poker table earlier this morning. He wasn't going to have it for much longer.

Steven watched as Doc entered the hallway leading toward the garage, then flipped open a cell phone and dialed a number. "He's on his way."

With that, he closed the cell phone, took a napkin and wiped any possible fingerprints off, then stuck the cell phone inside the newspaper under his arm. The phone would never be traced back to him even if something went wrong on the other side.

He strolled across the huge lobby, taking his time, acting like a tourist impressed with the overdone beauty of the Bellagio's front entrance.

Outside, he got in the line for a cab. He would go to the MGM Grand, drop the paper and phone in a garbage can there in an area of the walkway going to the tram that had few cameras, take the train up the Strip to where his car was parked in yet another Casino's parking lot.

Even in a city filled with cameras, there was no way anyone would trace him through all he was doing. And soon he would have his third key and Doc Hill would be dead.

Jeff Taylor's key had been his first. He had killed Benson James and his wife yesterday in Medford, Oregon, and taken Benson's key. That had been his second. Carson Hill's key would be the third.

And later tonight, he'd get a fourth.

After that, there would only be five to go.

This game was really becoming fun.

CHAPTER THIRTY-ONE

LAS VEGAS, NEVADA. AUGUST 23

I TRIED NOT TO THINK about what was facing me at Carson's house. What I hoped that I could do was go back, see how Fleet was faring, help out a little, then offer to buy Fleet dinner and escape. An hour in there, tops, if I was lucky.

Mostly, what I wanted to do was just go back to my suite at the Bellagio, rest, and think. There had to be something about what had happened when I found the key, and what Annie had told me about her case with Jeff Taylor that made sense.

But I couldn't figure out what it was, and that was driving me nuts.

I pulled my rented Lexus up in front of Carson's house and got out of the air-conditioned comfort into the blast of hot August heat. Fleet and I both had rented the same type car at the airport, and his was sitting in the driveway. Carson had a brand new Cadillac in the garage that I now owned, but I just couldn't make myself drive it.

Again, the neighborhood around me looked and felt like a ghost town. There was no desert breeze, or if there was, the houses blocked it. Silence and heat filled everything. What a horrible place to live.

As I was moving around the front of the car to head inside, a big, burly man stepped from behind a palm tree. He was wearing thin cotton pants, a white tee shirt, and no hat covering his tanned shaved head. He was well-muscled, like he lifted weights, and had a number of tattoos on his arms and neck.

In his hand was a pistol that looked frighteningly large. The big guy looked very used to handling the big gun.

He looked mean. Very mean. Not the kind of guy you want pointing a gun at you.

I stopped, keeping my arms away from my sides.

Around me the neighborhood continued its deathly silence, with blinds pulled over windows and no cars moving. Who would have thought that a suburban neighborhood in the middle of the afternoon would be the best place for a gun-point mugging?

"The key," the man said, his voice showing no nervousness.

Clearly, he had done things like this before.

Of all the things I expected a man with a gun to say, that wasn't it.

"What?"

"You heard me, asshole," the guy said, waving the gun at my face. "Give me the key or I'll shoot you and just take it."

I didn't have the key. After my conversation with Verne in the bathroom, I had gone to the Bellagio cashier's cage and gotten a second safe-deposit box. The key and Carson's card capper were in it. I always had such boxes at casinos, since poker tournament winnings were often paid out in cash. I had a regular one at the Bellagio, but I had decided to get a new box for Carson's key and card capper. I figured they deserved a resting place all their own. As far as I was concerned, they could just stay right there for the next twenty years.

I stared at the gun for a moment, then said, "Oh, keys."

I reached slowly into my pocket and pulled out my car keys, tossing them onto the pavement in front of me. "But I can tell you, it's a rental. They can track those things, you know."

The man glanced at the rental car keys, then shook the gun at me and smiled, showing me a nasty opening where a tooth had been. The ones that were still there didn't look that healthy.

I kept taking slow breaths, trying my best to stay calm, watching his every move. Clearly he was getting angry.

"Don't play dumb. Your *father's* key. The one you were showing around today at the Bellagio. The one that looks like a bank key with a number on the side."

Now I really was stunned. This big guy sure knew a lot about what I had been doing at that game in the Bellagio. There had been a number of men around that table that I didn't know, and a few others on the rail watching when I found the key. But this guy hadn't been there.

That meant he was hired, and more than likely, I was about to end up very dead right out here in front of Carson's house.

My only hope to get out of this was to just keep bluffing.

"I didn't know what it went to," I said, "so I tossed it in the garbage. Check the can by the poker desk."

I wouldn't have believed that bluff either, but it was the best I could think of.

"Yeah, right." The guy waved the gun slightly, clearly meaning that he would use it. "Hand over the key."

"Why would you want something I threw away?"

"Money. It's worth money you asshole. A lot of money. That's all I care about."

I kept bluffing. "If I had known *that*, I would have kept it. Actually, I might go back and dig it out. Who can I sell it to? You tell me and I'll give you a share."

"Quit screwing around," the man said, clearly getting angrier. He stepped toward me, the gun threatening. If I were a gambling man, I wouldn't have laid a bet on my odds of making it through the next minute.

I had nowhere to go. My only hope was to get closer to the guy, try to take the gun away before he could shoot me. I didn't give that plan much hope either.

"Search me if you want," I said. "I'm not lying to you. I tossed the thing away."

I raised my hands above my head and then took a half step toward the guy like an invitation. "Search my car as well. I just came straight from the casino and I honestly don't have that key. Trust me, I wish I did so I could give it to you. As I said, check the garbage in the poker room."

A good bluff always needed to have confidence behind it. Right now I didn't feel confident, just scared out of my wits, which was good in a way. Getting my fear across to the guy was the only way this bluff was going to work.

"Come on, search me if you don't believe me."

I stepped slightly closer again. I was now within arm's reach of the big gun.

And it looked even bigger the closer I got.

I put my hands on the top of my head and turned slightly, again getting just a little closer, pretending to give the guy access to the pockets on my right side. "Go ahead."

The guy laughed, and I was close enough to know he had garlic for lunch. "I'm supposed to get the key *before* I shoot you, but I think I'm going to just do it the other way around."

The guy glanced down the street, checking to see if anyone was watching.

I figured that moment was my only chance.

Like swinging an ax, I drove my right fist down on the guy's gun wrist, hoping like hell the gun didn't go off and shoot me anyway.

The gun clattered first on the sidewalk and then bounced into the street in front of the car.

The force of my blow spun the man a half step to the left.

Before he could get his balance, I hit him in the stomach with a full left hook, trying to drive my fist through his stomach and out his backbone.

I hated fighting, and as a rule just didn't do it, but when someone threatened to kill me, I tended to make an exception. And as Ace had once told me when I was a lot younger, if you're going to fight, do anything to win.

Anything.

My fist connected with solid muscle and I knew instantly that wasn't going to be enough to slow this monster down for more than a moment, so while the guy was still slightly bent over from my first two blows, I pretended I was trying to kick his nuts through a goal post about forty yards away.

My foot found something very soft and the force of my kick lifted the big guy almost off the ground.

He screamed, high and choking, a sound a man that big should never make.

Then he went down backwards.

His head hit the sidewalk hard with a sickening smack.

That was going to hurt. But I had a hunch a lot less than his nuts.

I stayed poised over him for a moment, breathing hard, but the guy was clearly out cold, his hands still clutched to his crotch. More than likely he was now burning his skin on the hot pavement.

Good. Let him burn. It might convince him to take up another profession.

I searched him quickly, finding nothing, not a wallet, not a piece of paper, nothing. Not a clue as to who had sent him.

I studied his face for a minute, making sure I would remember him if I ever saw him again.

From the way the guy's wrist looked, I more than likely had broken it. Too damn bad.

I stepped back and took a deep breath of the hot August air. What the hell were these keys, and why were they worth killing for?

I had a hunch I was going to have to find out the answer to that question before I got another good night's rest.

CHAPTER THIRTY-TWO

LAS VEGAS, NEVADA. AUGUST 23

KEEPING AN EYE on the big guy sprawled on the sidewalk, I picked up my car keys, then retrieved the gun. I quickly released the magazine from the pistol and made sure there was nothing in the chamber, which there wasn't. I put the ammunition in one pocket and the gun inside my belt against the small of my back, pulling my shirttail out and over it. I had no idea exactly what kind of gun it was, but it clearly looked like it had been used, and hadn't been cleaned in who knew how long.

As I finished, I realized my hands were shaking. Fighting was just not something I did. I would rather face a class IV rapid with the lives of passengers in my hands than fight a guy like this again.

Safer.

This was not the kind of adrenaline rush I liked. And I had no doubt that this time I had been lucky. The next time, I might not be.

I took a deep breath of the hot air and looked around the still-silent neighborhood, giving myself time to calm down and think. There was still no one in sight, nothing moving but the tops of the palm trees in the light afternoon breeze. The heat off the pavement made me feel like I was standing in an oven. I was going to have to get out of the heat, or at least into the shade pretty soon.

And I was going to need water.

I stared at the tattooed guy, wondering exactly what to do next. If the guy didn't move soon, I'd have to call an ambulance and get the police involved, but I really didn't want to do that just yet. I just hoped like hell I hadn't killed him. From what I could tell, he was still breathing, but I had no intention of going back over to him and trying to check.

As I was standing, half waiting, half trying to figure out what to do next, the guy moaned, long and deep, and his good hand held his crotch.

Then he quickly came to his senses.

He pushed himself to his feet, holding his wrist while holding his crotch. He couldn't stand all the way up and I could see the pain was bringing tears to his eyes.

He then looked at me like I was the devil. Broken wrist, burns on his legs and arms and back, a damaged groin, and more than likely a concussion. I had done a job on him, but it was far less than what he had intended to do to me.

"You want to tell me what this was all about?" I said, pulling out his gun and stepping toward him.

Panic replaced the anger in his eyes and he turned and staggered down the sidewalk, bent over, holding his wrist against his chest.

I had no doubt that he'd end up in a hospital with the wrist, crotch damage, and burns to his back. Even if I had wanted to chase him, I didn't need to. I could find him quick enough where he was going.

But I figured there was no reason to go after him. I would bet anything that he had no idea who was really behind this. More than likely, he was just the hired help, and after he had killed me and gotten the key, he would have been killed himself. He still might be, but at that moment, I didn't really care that much.

Criminals killing criminals. Just another way of Mother Nature thinning the herd.

I took a deep breath of the hot air and let my hands shake. Whoever had killed Carson was now after me, that much was certain. All for a key.

I headed for the house, the gun heavy in my hand. I owned a few rifles and a nice little pistol of my own. I would give this one to Annie when I had the chance. More than likely, it was attached to a few crimes beside my attempted murder. She might be able to do something with it.

I pushed the door open and was surprised to feel relief being in Carson's house instead of the horror and anger of yesterday. With the place straightened back out, it felt comfortable.

And more importantly, cool. My light shirt and pants stuck to me almost at once as the cool air allowed all the sweat I had been producing to stay on me.

"Fleet?" I shouted as I closed the door.

"Be right out," he shouted from down the hall.

I went into the kitchen, surprised that it had already been cleaned up. There was also no pile of money on the dining room table. Fleet had said he planned on getting it into a deposit box in a nearby bank. He must have already done that.

I opened the fridge to find bottles of cold water. I was making myself at home in my father's house. The world had really shifted on its axis.

I took two bottles of water back into the living room as Fleet came out of the back room. He was wearing dark slacks, a long-sleeved shirt, and tie. He had his tie loosened slightly, and his jacket was off, but that was all.

I laid the gun on the wood coffee table with a clattering sound, placing the magazine beside it. Then I dropped into one of the big chairs, surprised at how comfortable it was. Damn it all, I didn't want Carson's home to be comfortable. I wanted it to be as cold and aloof as he had been to me.

But after what had just happened, this felt like heaven.

Fleet stared at the gun like it was a snake, then took a step back. For a moment, I thought he might actually turn and run for the bedrooms.

"You want to tell me what *that's* all about?" he asked, a shaking finger pointing at the gun.

"Sit down," I said. "It's been a long day."

He sat on the chair farthest from the gun, on the edge, like he might spring to his feet at any moment and object to some important point in a trial. He glanced at me, then the gun every few seconds.

So I had another thing that I didn't know about my best friend, even after all the years we had been close and worked together. He was afraid of guns. Snakes and guns. No wonder he had gone into law and business.

While downing the first bottle of water and working on the second, I told him what had happened at the poker game before lunch, about finding Carson's key, about what Verne had said.

That information made Fleet forget the gun for a few moments.

Then I told him about meeting Annie, about Jeff Taylor's grave robbery, and his key. At that, I almost had to laugh since he was now sitting there with his mouth open.

"No wonder you got a gun," he said.

"I got that from some big guy with tattoos who tried to kill me outside the house here a few minutes ago. He was trying to get Carson's key, and I just didn't want to give it to him. Someone must have seen me with the key and sent him after it."

Fleet's mouth opened, closed, opened again, but no words came out. One of the best attorneys in the country and he couldn't think of something to say. That almost made getting almost killed worth it.

I laughed and he still couldn't think of anything to say, so I let him off the hook and told him what had happened outside, what I had done to the guy, the man's injuries, and everything he had said.

"We need the police on this," Fleet said after I had finished. With a glance at the gun, he gathered himself into the old "in charge" Fleet. Then he stood and turned for the phone.

"Not yet," I said.

"And why not?" he asked. "Someone is trying to kill you. Someone killed your father. Don't you think it's about time we get some police help?"

"Yeah, but then we'd have to tell them about the key, and maybe even give it to them, and tell them what happened to Carson and what we know about that investigation. I really don't want to do any of that just yet. I want to leave that key sitting right where it's at."

"So they can actually kill you the next time?" Fleet asked. "How about we cross that bridge of giving the key to the police or not after we get some help. Your life is more important."

"Tomorrow," I said, waving for him to sit down. "Right now we get out of here, head back to the Bellagio. In the hotel's security, I'll be safe, and tomorrow morning I've got a meeting set up with Annie. She is the Las Vegas Police. I'll get her and the police involved then."

"You promise?" Fleet asked, staring at me.

"I promise."

"Then let's get the hell out of here."

I stood and picked up the pistol and ammunition.

Fleet backed up two steps, his face whiter than normal, his gaze again frozen on the gun.

"Right after I lock this in Carson's floor safe."

"Real good idea," Fleet said, taking another step back. "Except for one problem. It's open, but we don't know the combination."

I shrugged. "I'll bet my mother does. We can get it if we need it."

I could feel my anger coming up at her again. I pushed it away. Now was not the time.

Fleet backed into the kitchen, staying away from the gun.

I didn't want to go past those pictures in the bedroom again just yet, but it was clear I couldn't get Fleet to take the gun to the safe.

He was afraid of snakes and guns.

I was afraid of some pictures on a bedroom wall and getting killed for some unknown reason.

We were a hell of a team.

CHAPTER THIRTY-THREE

VERNE ADKINS OPENED the front door to his Vegas home and stepped inside, letting the air-conditioning wash over him. The house felt empty, even more silent than usual.

He sighed and closed the door, locking it as he had done for years, even though it was still very light outside. He played poker every day from nine in the morning until six in the evening, five days a week. Just like working a real job.

And just like any job, he gave himself time to rest on the weekends. For almost forty years, the schedule had worked for him, making him a very rich man, with investments, stocks, and real estate all over Nevada.

His family and grandchildren would be very well taken care of when he died.

The schedule had not only allowed him to be a successful professional card player, but also raise a family in some sort of sense of normality. As far as his kids were concerned, Dad just went off to work in the morning and then came home for dinner. He stayed home weekends, went to games and school events just like any other parent. Normal in all respects, even though his job wasn't that normal.

Now his beloved Cannie was dead from breast cancer, his kids long gone into their own lives and families. The house was still the same, only these days it felt more and more empty and unused. Only his schedule kept him going. And sometimes he wondered if even that would be enough for long.

"Make no sudden moves," a voice said as he stepped into the dark, blind-shaded living room. His heart raced like it was about to explode from his chest.

In front of him a shadow moved, but Verne couldn't make out who it was since his eyes had not yet adjusted from the bright light outside.

"Turn on the lamp beside your chair slowly."

Verne did as he was told, then turned to find himself facing a white man with a gun standing about five feet from him. The middle-aged man was dressed casually in slacks, a light shirt, and a light jacket. He had dark, mean eyes and a slowly receding hairline. He was wearing white gloves and was holding a very nasty-looking gun.

Verne hated guns, almost more than anything else in the world. He hated them even more right now.

"What do you want?"

"I'm afraid I don't want much," the man said. "Just a special key."

Verne felt his legs go weak. Twice in one day, after all these years, the keys had come up. The robbery of Jeff's grave and Carson's death were part of something going on, someone working to get the keys at all costs.

He took a breath and faced the man. He had kept that key and its secrets for decades. He wasn't about to let it go now.

"Besides the gun, why should I give it to you? If you kill me, I can guarantee you will never find it."

The guy looked down at his gun as if just remembering he was holding it, then shrugged. "This was just to keep you calm at first."

The guy put the gun away in a holster under his jacket.

"I still would like to get the key. And I won't say please."

Verne stared at the man, now very surprised. "So tell me why I should give it to you?"

"You son drives a very nice Audi, light green, parks it in the same place in his corporate parking lot every day in Sacramento. Your daughter is clearly happily married and a mother of two wonderful boys. I bet you're really proud of those boys."

Verne said nothing, but he was fighting the desire throw up.

The man went on, his voice calm, as if he were just having a normal conversation. "Your two grandsons go to a wonderful preschool, well-thought-of in the Reno area. Your daughter picks them up at exactly four in the afternoon every day in her blue Plymouth van, and then they often go shopping for dinner. Your son-in-law gets home about six every night. The perfect family in all respects. You have to be very proud."

The man looked at Verne. "Would you like me to go on?"

"You wouldn't harm them?" Verne asked, his voice shaking, more afraid than he had ever been in his entire life.

"If I don't walk out that door with the key," the man said, "over the next week they will all meet with very sudden and tragic accidents. Even if you are dead before I leave. And if something goes wrong and I die here by some strange chance, they will die even more painful deaths."

"No." Verne couldn't hold himself up any more. He dropped into his favorite reading chair and just stared at the man who was threatening everything in his life that was important to him.

"I'm afraid the answer is yes. There is a very good reason to get these special keys all rounded up." The guy laughed. "At least I think it's a good one."

"Which one of those bastards do you work for?" Verne asked.

The man laughed and shook his head. "Who said I worked for anyone?"

Verne fought back the urge to just lunge at the man. If he did that, he had no doubt the man would kill his family. He could feel the coldness in the words. More than likely, this was the man who had killed Carson.

For twenty-seven years, Verne had worried about his family and the key he held. Now his worst fear was coming true.

He managed to point a shaking hand at the fireplace mantel. "The key is taped under the paper on the back of the picture of my wife."

"That-a-boy," the man said. He quickly stepped to the fireplace, picked up the picture, gently opened the back, pulled out the key, then respectfully replaced the back and the picture where it had been.

A smiled crossed the man's face, like no smile Verne had ever seen before. A cross between someone smiling while killing another person and a kid's smile seeing presents at Christmas.

The guy studied the key like it was a rare collectable, looking more and more excited by the moment.

"I have three of these now," he said, holding up the key. "Jeff Taylor's, Benson James', and now this one. I hoped to have four, but something didn't work out just yet."

He smiled and just stared at the key.

Finally, after a long moment, he seemed to regain a little control and put the key in his pants pocket.

Then he turned. "I just need a quick signature." He handed Verne a pen.

Verne felt like he had almost left his body, his mind was so detached from the horror that was going on in front of him. Maybe he was having the heart attack Cannie had always feared he would have. His mind felt like he was in a dark well looking upward at the light.

He took the pen and signed where the man wanted him to sign, not even caring what it was about. At this point, he would do anything to save his family.

Anything.

They were all that mattered.

"That is a very well-written note you just signed," the man said, "if I do say so myself."

Then the man moved around to Verne's right side.

Before Verne could even object, he took Verne's right hand, and put a small gun in it.

Then, like a parent directing a child, and before Verne could even realize what was happening, the man raised the gun to Verne's head and forced him to pull the trigger.

Darkness came instantly.

CHAPTER THIRTY-FOUR

LAS VEGAS, NEVADA. AUGUST 23

THE LAST PERSON I expected to ever be sitting across from me in my suite at the Bellagio was Heather Voight from the NTSB team in Idaho. Yet there she sat in all her blonde glory.

Wow, it had been one long day. I seemed to be having my share of them lately, that was for sure. And this day didn't look like it was ever going to end.

By a little after seven, Fleet and I had returned to the Bellagio and had finished a room-service dinner. When Heather called, Fleet was at the dining room table going through some papers he had found at Carson's house. I was sitting on the couch, some light jazz music on faint in the background, thinking about the day, trying to make sense of everything that had happened.

I spent many a night, after a tournament or playing in a live game, sitting on the big couch in my suite, just thinking.

My suite at the Bellagio felt more like home to me than the house I owned in Boise. And I had a hunch I spent a lot more days every year here than there.

The house in Boise was nice, sure, but this suite was actually my home, or at least that was how it felt. It had high ceilings, a large living room area with a big screen television that I seldom used, and wonderful large and very comfortable couches that I took naps on more than I wanted to admit.

Everything from the furniture to the rugs to the drapes was done in brown tones, with touches of stone in places around the room and covering the big fireplace. The decorating gave the place a very warm feeling, almost like I was back up in the mountains.

There was also a fully equipped kitchen and dining area, a fantastic bathroom with a whirlpool tub that I had never used and a large shower. The bedroom had a comfortable pillow-top bed so big I could lay sideways across it and not touch either side.

On top of that, they made the bed and cleaned every day. I had at least a dozen great restaurants inside the same building, and the Bellagio was easy to get to from the airport or anywhere else in Vegas.

It felt like the center of what I needed to do in Las Vegas. One hell of a lot better than my father's house, that was for sure. Just the drive from his place to the Bellagio took thirty minutes one way with good traffic. I could see no reason to waste an hour a day driving when I had the money to live like this.

Granted, I paid enough to the hotel in one year to buy another three or four houses in Boise. But it was my suite, I lived here. It was always available for when I needed it, and I kept a closet full of clothes and bathroom items here as well. No suitcases that way when I traveled back to Idaho. I had clothes at either end of that trip.

Over the years, Fleet had tried to get me to buy a house in Vegas, just because it made sense financially. But financially didn't concern me when I was here in town playing cards. Comfort did, and it didn't get any more comfortable than this.

Besides, I didn't spend my money on any other extravagant items. This suite was it. Worth every penny.

When the phone had rung, it had made both of us jump. I had already had uncomfortable conversations with Ace and my mother tonight while waiting for dinner to be brought up. I didn't want to tell either of them what was happening just yet, because I didn't really know. And my anger at both them had just made the conversations cold. And at the moment, I didn't really feel bad about that.

At least I hadn't yelled at my mother. I wanted to. Hell, I was an adult and had been for a dozen years. She could have told me about the relationship with Carson at any time, explained why he had left me, but not her all those years ago. But instead, I had to find it out this way. I was amazed I had stayed as calm as I had when I talked to her.

On the phone had been Heather Voight, the blonde from the NTSB team, who had clearly been added by someone in Washington. She had wanted to talk, she was in Vegas, and so I had invited her up.

"Oh, this can't be good," was all Fleet had said when I told him who it was.

Now she sat across from us in a sort of strained silence. I was a poker player. I could wait as long as she wanted to. She was the one who had wanted to talk, so I was just going to wait until she talked.

She was dressed in what I called Las Vegas business. Light tan slacks, a sandal-type shoe, and a light blouse with a light dress jacket over it. Considering that it had to be well over a hundred and ten outside, she was almost overdressed.

Finally, she shook her head and said, "I'm not sure where to start this, so let me just jump right in. I'm not normally a part of an NTSB team."

"I assumed as much," I said, giving her a break and helping the conversation along. "So who do you work for?"

"The FBI," she said. "Actually, on this assignment, I'm working for the President on a special assignment."

I glanced at Fleet whose eyes were getting larger by the second. Of all the answers she might have given, that was not one I expected.

She pulled out a badge and ID in a brown flip folder from her small purse and showed first me, then Fleet.

It looked to be FBI, very official and all, but to be honest, I wouldn't know what one of their badges even looked like. In playing poker, I had just never had a reason to get near the FBI.

Fleet studied the badge for a moment, then her ID beside the badge, then nodded. He seemed convinced.

"So, why would the President care about a plane crash in Idaho?" I asked. "Enough to send you along before anyone even knew it wasn't an accident?"

I knew that Carson and the President had been friends because the President had sent flowers to the funeral home. The friendship and the flowers had surprised me. Now I wanted to see what her reason was.

"President Chase and your father were good friends," Heather said. "He asked me to watch over the investigation for him."

Just as Ace had asked me to do for him.

I sat back. No surprise so far.

Fleet shook his head. "*The* President of the United States asked you to go to Idaho? Dolan Chase, *that* President?"

She nodded.

I tried not to smile. Clearly Fleet had not seen the flowers.

"Because my father was killed?" I asked

"Yes."

"And do you have any ideas who might have killed him?"

"Not yet," she said.

She didn't look happy about that answer, so I was betting it was the truth.

"And even if you did, you wouldn't tell us," Fleet said.

"Actually," she said. "I might."

She looked at me, holding my gaze. "Do you have any idea who killed him?"

"Not a clue. I didn't even know Carson. I'm finding out more about him yesterday and today than in the twenty-five years previous."

Heather sighed and sat back. "I assumed as much, but I had to ask. You didn't even talk to the man in over twenty-five years. How could you know him?"

That she knew that about me bothered me, but it didn't surprise me. She was FBI. I had a hunch she knew more about me than I wanted anyone to know.

"So, are you going to tell us exactly why you are here?" Fleet asked.

She glanced at Fleet, then back at me. "The President asked me to come here, talk to you, as a favor to him. He wants me to try to keep you alive."

"Alive?" I asked, sitting forward. Now she had stunned me.

"Alive?" Fleet said, his voice far too high.

An FBI agent had been asked by the President to keep me alive. That didn't bode well for my life expectancy.

Fleet leaned back in his chair and covered his face with both hands.

Heather nodded. "Alive."

I couldn't help myself. I laughed.

Come on, when does an average citizen get to hear the FBI say they are there to keep you alive? Never, so this had to be a joke. It sure seemed like a joke to my tired mind.

Heather stared at me, and Fleet just kept his face covered as he shook his head.

"I'm being very serious," Heather said after a moment.

"Well, that's all fine and good, as my Grandfather would say, that the Commander in Chief of this fine country sends someone to protect me from who knows what or who, but just where were you this afternoon when some big guy with too many tattoos tried to kill me right out in front of my father's house?"

I was laughing at the strangeness of it all because, to be honest, I didn't know how else to deal with what she was saying.

But Heather wasn't laughing. She turned rock hard and focused. I suddenly could see why a woman like her was a trusted person to the President. I wouldn't want to make her angry at me. In one look she went from harmless, overbuilt blonde to killer.

She asked two questions about the guy and what he was after and I told her what he looked like, what I had done to him, but left out the key part, saying I didn't know what he was after. I just didn't know who I could trust on any of this. And even though she had all the right papers and shiny badge, I didn't feel like I should trust her at this moment.

"I've got to get more help on this," she said, tossing her card on the coffee table and standing. "My number is there. Call me any time of the day or night if you need my help."

With that, she turned and left, pulling the door closed behind her.

"Oh, good," I said after she left. "Now she needs more help keeping me alive."

Then, all I could do was laugh again, even though my stomach felt like it wanted to reintroduce me to the dinner we had just finished.

"I stand with my original statement," Fleet said, his eyes closed, his head back.

"What's that?"

"This can't be good."

CHAPTER THIRTY-FIVE

Las Vegas, Nevada. August 24

SITTING IN A BOOTH, Detective Annie Lott watched Doc Hill come across the Bellagio Café toward her. Just seeing him again made her breath catch.

He moved through the tables like a skier cutting through a course, smooth and efficient, never missing a step. She had convinced herself last night that any interest he had in her was all in her imagination. She sure hoped she was wrong.

As he approached, he smiled and scooted into the booth across from her. Again, he smelled heavenly, like clear mountain air laced with pine trees on a warm summer's day. How anyone smelled that good in a casino, she didn't know.

By the time they had ordered and she had gotten a coffee refill, she had her nerves almost under control. Almost. And was starting to enjoy the breakfast a great deal.

Then Doc dropped a bomb.

"Someone tried to kill me yesterday. In front of my father's house."

"Are you all right?" she asked, looking into his face. He didn't seem to be injured or bruised in any way that she could see. "Did you report it?"

"I'm fine. And no, I didn't report it. The guy took nothing and ended up with a really bad headache, a very sore crotch, a broken wrist, and I'm sure some pretty good burns from taking a nap on the sidewalk in the middle of the afternoon."

Annie laughed, even though she didn't feel like she should. Someone trying to kill him wasn't a laughing matter. But Doc's attitude was so matter-of-fact, he made it seem that way.

"I got the guy's gun locked at my father's house. You can take it later. I have a hunch it might be interesting."

Annie nodded. "It might very well be. I'll stop out there later when you're there and pick it up."

Doc nodded, then dropped his second bomb. "Actually, it was clear the guy was working for someone, and he wanted my father's key. A key just like the one stolen from Jeff Taylor's grave. I didn't have it on me."

Annie stared at the handsome face of Doc yet again, stunned.

"Your father had a key like Jeff Taylor's?" she managed to ask.

"Yup," Doc said. "Let me tell you what I know."

"Please," Annie said.

"The NTSB is convinced my father's plane crash was not an accident. They are keeping that fact secret, so please do the same."

She nodded, but the news bothered her a lot. Something very big was happening, that was for sure, and the grave robbery was looking like just the tip of a very ugly iceberg.

"I found my father's key yesterday morning while I was playing cards with some old friends of my father's. It was locked inside his card capper. Verne Adkins was at the table and saw the key. He told me to put it away, that it was dangerous. Seeing it really upset him."

Annie's breath caught in her throat with the mention of Verne Adkins' name. Oh, God, he didn't know about Verne.

"I locked the key in a safe deposit box here in the cage," Doc said, going on, "then went to Carson's house where I met this big guy with a big gun who wanted the stupid thing. His plan was to take it and then kill me."

Annie nodded and said nothing. She could feel her stomach twisting tighter and tighter with every word. Clearly Doc had come down to breakfast from his room. He hadn't gone to the poker room and heard the news. She had to back him up a moment.

"Verne Adkins?" she asked.

Doc nodded. "Why? What happened?"

"Verne tried to commit suicide last night," Annie said as softly as she could. "A neighbor heard a gunshot and found him."

Doc sat back like someone had shoved him. His gaze stared off into the high ceilings of the restaurant. She let him sit like that for a moment, then she cleared her throat to get his attention. She needed more information.

"Did Verne say anything about what happened to your father?"

Doc nodded and came back into his eyes and sat back up, closer to her across the table. "He said that Carson might have been murdered for the key."

"Your father had a key, Taylor had a key," Annie said. "So maybe Verne has a key as well. Maybe there are even more keys than that, more people."

"Possible," Doc said, "but for what? Verne told me the key was to hide the truth, just as Jeff Taylor told his son. And that it was deadly. I have no idea what he meant and I couldn't get another word out of him."

"Something important?" she said. "Worth a lot of money maybe."

Doc shook his head. "I doubt it. Carson's home was searched for his key before I got into town. There was almost a million in the house at the time and none of it was touched."

"So, what number does your father's key have on it?" Annie asked, starting to get an idea.

"Four," Doc said.

"Taylor's was three," Annie said. "So there might be four keys, maybe more, which means more people are involved in whatever is going on."

Suddenly Doc leaned forward. "You said that Verne attempted suicide. Is he still alive?"

Annie nodded. "He tried to put a bullet in his head, but my old partner caught the case and told me he's going to live. He's actually awake and talking. The small caliber bullet just went in at a crazy angle, went around the top of his skull and came out his ear."

Doc suddenly went into motion. He pulled out a cell phone and flipped it open.

"Excuse me," he said to her as he dialed.

Annie watched as Doc asked someone named Fleet for a phone number, nodded, said thanks, hung up, and dialed another number.

The mention of Fleet's name made her realize just how little she actually knew about this famous poker player sitting across from her.

"Heather," Doc said, "A man by the name of Verne Adkins told me yesterday that my father might have been murdered. That man was shot last night. He's in the hospital, and I have a hunch he needs some protection. Can you do it?"

Annie was stunned at Doc's assumption that Verne hadn't attempted to kill himself, but had instead been assaulted.

"No," Doc said into his phone, as if answering her unspoken question. "Professional poker players don't kill themselves. Especially someone as solid as Verne Adkins. I've known him for years. Trust me, he didn't try to kill himself."

Silence for a moment.

"Good, thanks," Doc said, then flipped the cell phone closed and put it back in his pocket.

"Verne left a signed note," she said. "Gun was in his hand, gunpowder on his hands."

"What looks like a suicide is a suicide every time. Right?" Doc asked.

"Not always, but most times," she said.

"And what looks like a plane crash is always an accidental plane crash, right?"

"I get your point," she said. "So who's going to protect Verne if that actually was a murder attempt on his life? You know you have the Las Vegas Police sitting right here. I still am a detective and work half time."

Doc smiled. "I know, but I think it makes more sense for the person I called to do it. I'm sure she's going to work with your people as well. In fact, I'll bet on it."

"Do you mind if I tell my old partner what you are saying about the possible murder?"

"No problem," Doc said. "Just keep the keys out of it for now if you could."

"Understood," she said. Then she looked into Doc's eyes. "And that's all you're going to tell me, isn't it?"

"For the moment," Doc said, smiling.

God, she loved that smile, but the fact that he was holding something back from her made her angry. She needed to drop the in-lust schoolgirl attitude with him and start thinking like a cop, or someone was going to get hurt.

The waitress let him off the hook by bringing their food.

As they ate, Annie decided she wasn't going to push him just yet, but Doc went ahead and filled in a few of the smaller holes on what he had told her, like how he had overpowered the guy with the gun.

She smiled at that, since it sounded a lot like how she had taken down the guy down at the station. And her foot still hurt from it.

From what he had said, she had no doubt she could find the guy right now in a hospital somewhere. Spending that much time on a hot Vegas sidewalk meant the burns would be bad, not even counting the concussion, the damage to his crotch, and the broken wrist. She just might have a really large, imposing-looking detective do a stop-by to see if there was a little more information to be had from that guy.

Even though Doc wasn't talking with her about something he knew, she decided she would keep him up on what she was doing.

"I sent a few cops to put a scare into Brent Taylor's ex-wife last night."

"Jeff's son?" Doc asked.

She nodded. "Brent told me the ex knew about the key buried on Jeff. Brent said he thought his ex-wife might have come into a little extra money suddenly. It seems she had. Ten grand for telling someone she never saw about the key. She figured since it was buried, it wouldn't hurt."

"So, that part of the mystery is solved," Doc said, "which means your case is now connected completely with what happened to my father."

"I'm in this thing right up to my chin," she said. "So, knowing that, is there anything I can do to help *you*? You're the target it seems."

"Win that tournament today," Doc said.

She shook her head, not following. "What?"

"I'm going to go visit Verne in the hospital. I doubt I'll be back in time to play. You entered yet?"

"Hoping to win a satellite before it started," she said, feeling odd that she hadn't paid the two thousand entry fee. It was just too much for her stomach to handle. "But now, after this discussion, I think I have better things to do. You know, like trying to figure out who's trying to kill you."

"And you might get that kind of information playing in the tournament," Doc said. He reached into his wallet and pulled out a paid entry form. "Let's go to the desk and I'll transfer this over to you. I'll sponsor you."

"I can't let you do that," Annie said, stunned. "But just the offer made my day."

"I do it all the time for promising new players," Doc said. "I've seen you play a number of times now, and you're good. If you win, give me my two thousand back and twenty percent of everything you earn over that. Come on, you've been around long enough to know that's a standard sponsor offer."

She opened her mouth, but no words came out. She didn't really know what to say.

"Do we have a deal?" he asked, sticking out his hand over the dirty breakfast dishes for her to shake.

She hesitated for a moment, then took Doc's hand and shook it. "We have a deal. And thanks."

"Don't thank me. This is a business deal. Go make us both some money. I'll talk to Verne, maybe run a few errands, and come back, tell you what I've found out, and see how you're doing."

She nodded and smiled. One of the best poker players in the world had just shown faith in her ability in a big tournament.

No matter what else was going on, she was going to enjoy every minute of this. And with a little luck, prove that his trust had been warranted.

CHAPTER THIRTY-SIX

LAS VEGAS, NEVADA. AUGUST 24

I STOOD in the window of the ICU, stunned at the sight of the man I had been playing cards with yesterday. Verne had a bandage around his head and one side of his face was a nasty dark blue. He was attached to what looked like an entire wall of monitors and equipment, most of it on and blinking like a control panel of a large jet.

I had no idea if my finding Carson's key had led to this or not. I sure hoped it hadn't. But I had to find out if it did, and what was going on.

Verne knew. I just hoped that now he would tell me.

FBI Agent Heather Voight appeared at my elbow, staring in the window beside me. I glanced at her and nodded. She looked very official in her light blue jacket and dark slacks. She had her blonde hair pulled back tight behind her head giving her face a tight, take-no-prisoners look.

Every time I saw her, she looked harder and harder.

"His family has been here and are now down in the waiting room," she said without a hello. "The doctors say he's going to have very little brain damage. He was lucky."

"Thanks for keeping an eye on him."

"You were right," she said. "Even though he's not saying just yet, my people, working with the local police, are finding a number of very fishy things about all this."

"Such as?"

"Verne didn't own a gun and hated them, for starters. He wouldn't even touch one. He had a phobia about them. There is no record of him buying one lately, let alone one that can't be traced liked the one that was used."

"Looks like someone missed a little homework."

She nodded and said nothing more.

"Can I talk to him?"

"I assume it would be about why someone would want to kill him, you, and your father," Heather said.

"It is."

"I'd like to listen."

"How about I just tell you what he tells me?" I had no doubt that she was just going through the motions. If there wasn't a listening device already planted in that room, I would be surprised, and she wouldn't be doing her job.

"Deal. I've already cleared you with the doctors to talk to him for a few minutes. Go easy."

I nodded and stepped into the intensive care room. The sounds of the machines and the odor of ammonia come up and wrapped around me like an unwanted hug from a smelly stranger. I was used to the noise and smoke in a casino, and the roaring sounds of the river combined with the smells of pine trees and summer rains. These machine sounds and cleaning smells were alien to me. In all my life, I had never been in an intensive care room before.

I didn't like them.

But right now I was glad Verne was in this one and getting the care he needed.

I moved over and stood uneasily beside Verne on the side that wasn't bandaged. I had no idea what to do next. What looked like a heart monitor was beeping constantly, and an IV drip was attached to his arm. Up close, his face looked even worse, with the swelling closing his right eye completely.

"Verne, it's Doc Hill."

Verne opened his left eye and blinked, then looked around and focused.

"I really liked your father," he said, his voice rough and raspy. "Did I ever tell you that?"

"Yesterday."

"Good."

He sighed and closed his one good eye.

Clearly talking was very hard on him. I was going to have to keep this short today. But I had to know if what I had done caused this, or if he was a part of the group that had keys. So I decided to just ask directly.

"Did whoever did this to you get your key?"

Verne blinked for a second, then said with almost a sigh, "Yes."

"What was the number on your key?"

"Seven."

That rocked me. "Seven people, seven keys?"

"Nine keys," Verne said, his voice choking slightly.

"Nine keys, nine people?" I asked.

"Ten people, nine keys."

I had no idea why the difference, why one didn't get a key, but I decided I could ask that question later.

"What do the keys go to?"

"A box," Verne said softly.

"What's in the box?"

"Secrets. Ugly, stupid secrets."

With that, Verne seemed to just run out of energy and shrink down into his bed. I would have to wait to ask him more questions, even though his answers so far had only created more questions.

"Thanks, Verne," I said, leaning down and patting his arm. "Do what the doctors tell you to do. And tell the police exactly what happened. They can protect you."

"I'm not in danger anymore," Verne said softly, not even opening his good eye. "I gave him my key."

"You saw him?"

Without moving his head he said, "Yes."

"Then you're in danger. I've got some extra forces helping to watch over you."

Verne seemed to think about that for a moment, then he motioned me to come down close to him.

"Protect your family and friends as long as you have that key. Get Ace and your mother and your close friends safe *right now*. Don't wait one extra minute."

Then he pushed me away, a dismissal.

I sort of staggered out of the room in shock, trying to take in the warning that he had just given me.

Ace. My mother. Fleet.

Could they be in the same danger I had faced yesterday?

For some reason, I just hadn't thought of that possibility. But if these keys were valuable enough to kill Carson and attempt to kill me and Verne, then Verne was right, everyone around me was in danger as well.

I had to get them protected.

My heart felt like it was going to race right out of my chest.

I stopped beside Heather, trying to clear my head and catch my breath. I felt like I had just been sucker-punched. All I wanted to do was run from the hospital, get on the phone to Fleet, Ace, my mother.

"Anything?" Heather asked.

"Nine, possibly ten men are involved in something that is killing some of them. Verne didn't tell me why or who."

"Not even a clue?"

"I'm not sure he really knows. I've got to run. Thanks for protecting him."

With that, I turned and headed down the hallway toward the main entrance. The more I learned about Carson's death, the more confusing it got. But no matter how confused I was right now, I was going to take Verne's warning very, very seriously.

Nine keys, for some reason, were all valuable enough to kill for.

And I had one of them.

CHAPTER THIRTY-SEVEN

"THE LINE IS SECURE, SIR," Paul said to the president, pointing to the blinking light on the phone.

"Thank you," President Dolan Chase said. "Recording devices off in here?"

Around him, the Oval Office felt smaller than it normally did. He sometimes didn't much like this place, when the days got long and the decisions got ugly. And this was one of those times. It wasn't even dinner time yet and it had been a very long day.

Paul nodded. "They're off."

Dolan wasn't sure if he should trust that or not, but he wanted Paul to hear this conversation as well. He punched the speaker phone, then said, "What's going on out there?"

"I met with Carson Hill's son," FBI Agent Heather Voight said. "Both last night and again briefly this morning. He told me that an attempt was made on his life yesterday in front of his father's house."

"Did he say what the person was after, and did he get it?" Dolan asked, almost afraid of the answer.

"All he told me was that the guy was after something of value and got nothing but a number of serious injuries. We found the guy, clearly just hired by someone, at a local hospital. Bad concussion and burns. We will be talking with him later today. Doc Hill really did a job on him."

"Okay," Dolan said, shaking his head. "I assume you have people on Doc Hill now. I want you to keep us informed on everything he's doing. Understood?"

"Yes, sir," she said.

"Anything else?"

"I'm not sure how it ties into any of this," Agent Voight said, "but a man by the name of Verne Adkins was also attacked later last night. It was set up to look like a suicide, but through sheer luck, it failed. Mr. Adkins is now in the hospital."

"Not Verne," Dolan said. Verne was one of the nicest men he knew, with a wonderful family. The guy wouldn't hurt a fly, but he could sure take your money at a poker table.

"He was a friend of yours, sir?" Agent Voight asked.

Dolan glanced up at Paul, whose face had drained of all hint of color at the mention of Verne Adkin's name.

"He was. Keep him protected as well. If you need more help, FBI Director Smith will send it."

"I'm working with the Las Vegas bureau," she said. "I called the director and he called them. We already have Mr. Adkins protected, thanks to Doc Hill."

Dolan glanced up at Paul, very surprised.

"Doc Hill wanted you to protect Verne Adkins?" Paul asked.

"Yes. He called me this morning and alerted me. He was ahead of us with the connection of Verne Adkins to himself and Carson Hill. I don't know how he made the connection. Or even what the connection is exactly, to be honest. But I am now pretty sure it has something to do with some keys. Nine keys, to be exact, which means there are more people involved."

"All right," Dolan said, a little too fast. His stomach felt like he had just eaten the worst rotted meat available. He reached for the bottle of Tums in his drawer and quickly took three of them, letting the chalky taste fill his throat.

At the mention of the keys, Paul had dropped into a chair beside the desk and was sitting with his hands over his face.

After a moment, Agent Voight said, "Mr. President?"

"Yes," Dolan said. "Just thinking this over."

"I understand, sir," she said. Then hesitantly, she went on. "Is there anything you can tell me that might help in keeping Doc Hill and Verne Adkins safe?"

Paul looked up startled and shook his head.

"Nothing yet," Dolan said. "And thank you, agent, for the good work."

He clicked the phone off and stared at his long-time best friend and chief of staff.

Paul just shook his head and went back to staring at a spot on the floor between his legs.

There was nothing to say.

"Get some dinner," Dolan said. "We'll talk about this tomorrow morning. We might know more then."

As he stood and left the Oval Office, Paul was still sitting in the chair, his head still down.

Neither of them were hungry, of that he was sure.

And he doubted Paul would get much sleep tonight. He knew he wouldn't.

He was supposed to be the most powerful man on the planet, and yet he had no idea how to get this situation, and Doc Hill under control.

Chapter Thirty-Eight

Las Vegas, Nevada. August 24

I DIDN'T EVEN GET into the hot morning air of the parking area of the hospital before I had Fleet on the phone. He was at Carson's house, working on more of the inventory for the estate.

"Drop everything," I said without even a hello. "Get back to the Bellagio."

"Sure," Fleet said. "I've got a couple of errands to run, so it might take me—"

I didn't let him finish. "No, now. Just get to the Bellagio like you've seen a snake in the house. No side trips, nothing. I'll meet you in your suite and explain everything."

"There aren't any snakes here in the desert, are there?" he asked.

I could just imagine him looking around the floor in Carson's house for a snake. If this wasn't so damned serious, it almost might be funny.

"Believe there are for the moment and get out of there, get to the Bellagio. Trust me, there are no snakes in the Bellagio."

"On my way," Fleet said, hanging up before I could.

I climbed into my rental, got the air-conditioning going, then started to call Ace. I was halfway through dialing, then hung up. I decided that a few minutes one way or another wouldn't make that much difference. At least I hoped it wouldn't. I didn't trust myself to talk to him at the moment. Or my mother. I was just too angry.

It might be better to let Fleet do that when he got to the suite.

I wanted them safe.

And I wanted to know just what they knew as well. This secret stuff had gotten real old about the time that guy with the tattoos said he was going to kill me. Now, with Verne lying there injured, all the not knowing was just pissing me off.

I got across the strip to the hotel and had the rental parked in the Bellagio south parking lot in my reserved spot on the second level in almost record time. There was no doubt I was ahead of Fleet by a good ten or fifteen minutes.

As I climbed out into the heat, a long white stretch limo pulled up behind my car, blocking me in.

I couldn't see who was in the limo due to the dark windows.

I moved around my open driver's door, keeping it between me and the limo, waiting, ready to duck and move in any direction I needed to move, depending on what came at me. Behind me was a cement wall. I would have to move along that wall in front of twenty parked cars to get to the entrance. It wasn't much of an escape, but it was all I had.

A younger tourist couple was walking toward the entrance from another car, and three men were talking a hundred paces away.

Everything looked normal.

Except the white limo blocking me.

If some guy with a gun came out of that limo shooting, I was going to be in worse shape than I was in front of Carson's house.

The back door of the limo opened. "Doc, would you join me for a moment?"

I still couldn't see anything about the person behind the voice. It was just too dark inside to see anything but a shadow. And he wanted me to just climb in there.

The guy must have thought I was a total idiot.

"I don't think so," I said, staying right where I was. That guy yesterday had clearly been hired by someone with money. Enough money to have a white limo, more than likely.

I glanced around. Two Bellagio security cameras were pointed my way and not moving. Good. More than likely a security guard or two were already watching this very closely. Of course, if I ended up dead, it wouldn't do me a lot of good if they had my murder recorded.

An older man, heavy-set with thinning hair, climbed out of the limo and shut the door behind him, holding his hands away from his sides slightly to show me that he carried nothing. He was wearing a light dress shirt and light brown slacks with loafers. I knew him from somewhere, but at the moment I just couldn't place him.

"Doc," he said. "My name is Richard Scott. But everyone just calls me R.A."

Of course, now I knew who he was. I had seen his picture dozens of times. He was one of the five hundred richest men on the planet. He owned the ranch that hosted the Big Game, the private poker game Carson had been flying home from when he was killed. How the hell did he even know who I was?

And what was he doing here? He normally never left his ranch on the Salmon River before September.

"How about we get in out of the heat?" R.A. said. "I've got something to tell you about."

"I'm pretty comfortable right out here," I said, glancing at the security cameras in such a way that made it clear to R.A. that he was being watched.

R.A. shrugged. "Can't say as I blame you, after what happened to your father and then Verne yesterday."

I said nothing, figuring I'd just let him talk. He found me after all. And he clearly had something he wanted to say to me.

"Sorry to hear about your father," he said after a moment. "He was a friend and a great poker player. I understand you're almost as good."

"I play mostly tournaments," I said. "Carson was a good high-stakes specialist."

"That he was," R.A. said. "And he seemed to specialize in taking my money."

"I hear you can afford it," I said.

He laughed. "Yeah, I can. And I hear you can handle the white water on the Middle Fork below my ranch better than anyone."

I was not going to allow this man to get me off my guard. "I love that river. But I'm curious why you know so much about me."

"I like to keep track of my friend's families," he said.

Verne's words came screaming back at me. *Protect your family*. Was I already too late with Ace and my mother? The thought made my knees feel weak.

R.A. looked uncomfortable when I said nothing else, holding my composure as well as I did in any tournament when being stared down by someone who thought they could get a read on me. Around us, the morning just seemed to get hotter by the moment.

Finally, he wiped some sweat off his forehead. There was no wind blowing through the open garage at all, which made the heat even worse. At least we weren't out in the sun.

"Look, your father and I shared many events in our lives. Because of one of those events, someone now wants to kill me, and you as well."

I almost said, *Tough to kill yourself, isn't it?* Then decided against it and went another direction.

"You have one of the keys?" I asked.

He nodded and pulled a key out of his pocket that looked like Carson's, only this one was attached to a gold chain that was secured to a belt loop on his slacks.

"Which number?" I asked.

"Number two," he said. "Someone is trying to kill me for this key. I'm sure that's what happened with Verne and your father as well, and they dug up Jeff to get his. My sources tell me you now have your father's key."

I didn't ask him how he knew that, and there was no way in hell I was going to confirm that I even had the key. But his knowing that was just another piece of evidence that he was behind Mr. Tattoo yesterday. But as long as he was alone, and we were where we were at, I figured there was no harm in playing along.

"So, who do you think wants your key enough to kill you for it?"

"I think it's Nyland Harrison," R.A. said.

"I don't know him," I said.

"Nyland Harrison, up until about ten years ago, controlled the world's largest construction firm."

"I thought you owned that," I said.

"I do now," R.A. said. "Nyland drove his company into bankruptcy with a string of bad decisions after a dam he built in Northern California collapsed."

I remembered that. It happened back in 1995, in my first year of college. Ugly disaster. Killed over a hundred people in the valleys below the dam.

"So, why him?"

"Because he's gone crazy. He's so power hungry, he'll do anything to get his company back. And I'm betting he thinks these keys are the way to do it, if he can get enough of them."

"How many are there?" I asked.

"Nine," R.A. said, confirming what Verne had told me.

"And what is in the box that these keys will open?"

"Secrets," R.A. said.

I was getting disgusted at all the *secrets* people were keeping from me. "That's what Verne said. And trust me, if someone doesn't start telling me what these secrets are about, Carson's key is going to end up in the hands of the police very shortly."

R.A.'s hands came up like I had threatened to hit him. "Oh, God, no, don't do that. Never think of doing that."

"I've already had an attempt on my life because of that key. I think I'll be a lot safer the moment it is out of my hands, don't you? So why don't you just let me in on some of these dirty little secrets that are in that box, so I know what I'm protecting."

R.A. glanced around, the sweat pouring off his forehead. At the moment, there was no one around us, at least close enough to hear. Then he looked me right in the eye and said, "A murder. The secret is evidence of a murder."

I felt disappointed. After all the buildup, I figured it would be something more.

Then the pieces fell into place like a perfect poker hand coming together.

The FBI in Idaho.

Carson, Verne, R.A., and the President, all old-time poker players.

Nine keys. Ten men, Verne had said.

A murder at a ten-handed poker game. Nine survivors.

I just couldn't breathe.

Oh, God, could it be that the President of the United States was involved in a murder and a cover-up?

If it were true, that was certainly a secret worth killing me for. And a lot of other people besides.

CHAPTER THIRTY-NINE

LAS VEGAS, NEVADA. AUGUST 24

I STOOD, facing R.A. Scott in the hot late-morning, trying to decide how to ask my next question. He had no idea I knew that President Chase had sent the FBI to supposedly guard over me. Clearly, my father, R.A. Scott, Verne Adkins, Jeff Taylor, and the president had been involved in a murder and a cover-up a long time ago. And without that cover-up, Dolan Chase would have never gotten to be the president.

I suddenly had this very clear realization just how far over my head I was. We were talking about something here that could bring down a president. And a murder cover-up that had lasted for decades.

For all I knew, it was the President who was trying to round up the keys, having people killed. It didn't make much sense, but he clearly had the most to lose if he was involved.

After a long minute of us standing, facing each other, with R.A. sweating and looking lost in the memory, I finally asked him what happened.

"Third year of the Big Game," he said, sighing. "August, 1982."

"Twenty-seven years ago? That's a long time to keep this silent."

"It is, isn't it?" R.A. said. "I've never told anyone about it until just now."

"You still haven't told me."

He sighed again, looked around to make sure no one coming and going in the parking garage was close enough to hear. "A guy by the name of Kevin DeFoe was cheating us and we caught him."

"How *old west*," I said, my voice as sarcastic as I could make it. I was just trying to keep my balance and my mind working. "You catch a card cheat and kill him. Sounds like a bad movie."

"We didn't mean to kill him. He ran when I caught him palming."

"From your ranch?" I asked, surprised. "Where did the guy think he could go?"

R.A.'s ranch was inside the Idaho Primitive area, on the edge of the Middle Fork of the Salmon River. There was no road in or out of there, just his private air strip. No road at all for twenty miles, at least. Just a very long and dangerous trail along the river up to where we put the rafts in during the early spring. And there was nothing there most of the year when the water was low.

R.A. shrugged. "He just wanted away from us. I don't think he gave it much thought. We were all pretty angry, at least those of us who had been losing to him."

"So, let me guess, you chased him."

R.A. again nodded. "It was dark and he was starting to get away down the trail toward the river from my cabin, so I picked up a rock and hit him with it."

"You're kidding?"

He shook his head. "I wish I was. I used to be a good baseball player in my college days. I hit him square in the back with a perfect strike. Two others who were chasing him with me threw rocks as well. By the time we stopped hitting him, Kevin was dead. We didn't mean to kill him."

I had never heard a rich and powerful man sound so pathetic. But I was too stunned to care. They had killed a man for cheating at cards. And then covered it up for twenty-seven years. The president, Carson, Verne, and who knew who else.

"If it makes a difference," R.A. added, his voice soft. "Your father wasn't one of the ones chasing the cheater."

"It doesn't," I said.

R.A. nodded and waited for me to ask another question.

I wasn't sure which one to ask, so I backed up and came at everything from what was causing all the problems now.

"So, the keys are part of a cover-up in some fashion or another. How did that come about?"

"We all discovered that night how ruthless Nyland was," R.A. said. "Most of us just wanted to go to the police, your father included, to pay the price for what had happened."

"Why didn't you?" I asked.

"Because Nyland wouldn't let us. He wanted us all to sign a statement saying exactly what happened, who the rock-throwers were, include some pictures of the body and the location in the wilderness where the body was buried. It was his plan to put all that in a special safe-deposit box in a bank in Seattle that would take nine keys to open."

I just shook my head in disgust. An elaborate cover-up. A stupid one, actually. "What's to stop someone from bribing a bank manager to just use a pass key to open it?"

"It's a special box, made just for us. We paid for it for one hundred years and it will only open with all nine keys. No other way."

"So no one could go to the police with any real evidence of what happened unless everyone did. But I don't see why you all bothered. At the time, I'm sure it would have been ruled manslaughter and you all would have gotten off with probation."

"I know," R.A. said. "But Nyland would have none of it."

"And he could sway all the rest of you?" I asked.

"He was very persuasive," R.A. said. "Remember, he had all the real money at that time. And he had no morals about using it to get what he wanted, no matter what it took. And he didn't want this on his record. He was one of the stone throwers."

I just wasn't buying this. I shook my head. "I just can't imagine how one man could convince eight other men to cover up a murder."

"Family," R.A. said. "He used all of our families against us."

"How did he do that?"

"He threatened to kill them, anyone we cared about, if we didn't cover this up and forget it."

Verne's words came back once again, this time even louder in my mind. *Protect your family.*

"And he had the power and the money to do it," R.A. said. "Even if we exposed him and put him in prison, he threatened to still do it."

I glanced around, expecting Fleet to be pulling up. I had no sense of how much time had passed. I could understand a threat against family. Clearly understand. I was worried about Fleet right now.

R.A. looked directly at me, the first time since he started into the story about the murder. "Doc, Carson was against the cover up more than anyone. Nyland threatened you and your mother to sway him. You won't remember, but your mother ended up in the hospital, badly beaten before we could even get out of the wilderness. Your mother was used as an example of what Nyland would do to keep the silence. We all got his message."

I stared at the rich man sweating in the heat of the parking garage, trying to take in what he had said. My mother had been beaten? I had no memory of that at all. And she had never once spoken about it.

R.A. went on. "Doc, Nyland threatened you as well. If Carson didn't go along with the cover-up, you would be killed."

"I was only six in 1982."

"I know," R.A. said. "I know."

I let that drop for the moment, asked my next question. I was believing only parts of what he was saying, and I needed more. A lot more.

"So, what has changed now, after all these years, that would set Nyland off like this, if it is Nyland?"

I knew the answer to my own question. Dolan Chase had become President last year. That's what had changed. But I wanted to see what R.A. would tell me. Just how much of the truth he was willing to share.

R.A. looked pained. He glanced around, making sure no one was close, then took two steps closer to me. I held up my hand. The front door to my car was still between us.

He stopped, glanced around again, then nodded, seeming to make up his mind.

"Ten men in the game originally. Your father, Jeff Taylor, Verne Adkins, Kevin DeFoe, and Benson James were the professional card players. The businessmen were me, Nyland Harrison, Aaron Bell and—"

He stopped, clearly in pain, as if something was actually forcing him to not say what he wanted to say next. Finally he got out, "Are you sure you want to know this?"

"Let me guess," I said. "Dolan Chase and one other."

R.A. looked surprised, then nodded. "Paul Hanson, his now chief of staff. Neither of them were rock-throwers either."

"The cover-up is now all that matters," I said. "And the fact that people are being killed for those keys."

R.A. nodded.

"So the stakes of the cover-up changed when Dolan Chase became president. Talk about a skeleton in a closet. Chase has a real one buried in the mountains."

"He does," R.A. said. "And with the collapse of Nyland's company, and his son going to jail for the dam collapse, he has gotten desperate. Crazy desperate."

I nodded, staring at R.A. It was no wonder Carson had taken so much money from this guy. It was clear he was telling only partial truths, and had a real agenda. He was making what is known on a poker table as a semi-bluff, or a trap. He had no obvious reason to come and tell me all this information. There had to be another reason behind this move.

More than likely, it was an attempt on Carson's key in some fashion or another.

"So, we're both in danger from Nyland," I said.

R.A. nodded. "I have more resources to protect myself than you do."

"I can take care of myself just fine," I said.

He nodded, started to say something, stopped. I had no doubt he was about to ask for Carson's key, to keep it safe. But for some reason he didn't.

Was he continuing the semi-bluff?

Or was he just deciding to go ahead and kill me for the key anyway?

He reached into his shirt pocket and took out a business card, then laid it on the trunk of my rental car. "Call me if you need help."

Then he turned and stepped back to the limo, opening the door and ducking inside.

I didn't move, but was ready to if something came at me out of that car. Or from any other direction.

"Your father sacrificed a lot to keep you alive," R.A. said, his voice echoing from the shadows.

Then, before he had the door completely closed he added, "Don't make it all for nothing."

It wasn't until that white limo was long gone and I had turned to go into the Bellagio entrance that I actually let what he had said sink in.

Your father sacrificed a lot...

The images of those pictures of me in his bedroom came back into my mind like a fist to the side of the head and I just wanted to be sick right there between the cars.

August, 1982. The cover-up started.

The same month and year my father had left.

CHAPTER FORTY

LAS VEGAS, NEVADA. AUGUST 24

I MANAGED to get inside and to a couch tucked in between two marble pillars to the side of the wide hallway. Large green plants around the bases of the pillars gave the couch a private feel even though people were walking by within ten feet.

I sat, looking down at the white patterned tile floor, just thinking. At the moment, I didn't trust myself to walk any farther, or run into anyone I knew.

Your father sacrificed a lot.

Those words echoed like a bad movie effect in my head. I didn't believe everything R.A. had told me, but he was clearly telling some truths. I wasn't sure what was true and what wasn't.

What if part of his truth had been that this Nyland Harrison, or someone else, maybe even Dolan Chase, had threatened families? Mother had been beaten. Had Carson left to protect us? At six, I would have been easy to get to, and impossible to protect.

Is that why Carson pretended I didn't matter to him anymore, to keep me safe?

It felt like my entire world had just been turned upside down. I had hated Carson for so long, so passionately, I just couldn't make myself grasp the possibility that he might have left to save me.

Clearly, he had stayed married to my mother, and had Ace to look after me. And both had been overly protective at times, but I had just assumed it was normal stuff.

It had been twenty-seven years since 1982. After enough time of no threats from anyone, why hadn't Carson just gone home, and told me as well?

Or had there been more threats?

Jeff Taylor.

He had died in an unsolved murder in 1996. Was that one of the threats that had kept Carson silent? Or had my anger at him kept him that way? Now I would never get a chance to ask him.

But I sure as hell would ask my mother those questions. And it was far past time I got some straight answers.

When Taylor died, I was still in college, just thinking about going out and playing professional poker. Fleet was taking my local poker winnings and building a really nice fortune with it. I was an adult. I could handle myself. I could have been told, either by my mother, or Ace.

I was sure as hell going to find out why I wasn't.

And all that assumed I was jumping to the right conclusion with what R.A. had told me. There was a lot more going on than I knew right now. And I had no doubt he had been telling only half truths for some reason that was not yet clear.

"All right, think," I said out loud. "What comes first?"

The moment I asked the question, I had the answer.

Get Ace and my mother safe and Fleet's wife and kids safe.

That was the first and most important thing. They were the leverage that could be used against me, just as R.A. said they were used against Carson.

As Verne had warned me about.

I had no idea if it was R.A. Scott, or Nyland Harrison, or the president, or someone else entirely killing people. All I knew was that I had a key, and the keys held the secret of that supposed murder in Idaho, and someone was working to get them. I just had to make sure I couldn't be played like Carson was supposedly played.

"Doc?"

I glanced up to see Fleet. He must have walked past me, headed for the elevators to go up to the rooms before realizing it was me sitting there.

"You all right?"

"Fine," I said as I stood. "Just thinking while waiting for you."

"So, you want to tell me what's going on?"

"I'll explain it all shortly," I said. "Right now, I need you to get our plane to Boise for Ace and my mother and your family."

"My family? Why? When?"

"Right now, two hours ago. As soon as they can get to the airport in Boise, I want that plane waiting for them. And if our plane can't get there that fast, I want you to get another one and I don't care what it costs."

"You're scaring me," Fleet said, while at the same time pulling out his cell phone.

"I'm scared," I said. "If we have to call in favors from the police in Boise to get them all on that plane, we're going to do it. Understand?"

He nodded.

"And I want body guards waiting with a limousine at the airport to get them here. Make sure the guards are armed. Can you do that?"

Fleet stared at me, swallowed, then nodded.

"Get the plane on the way, then call your wife."

He took a deep breath and started to dial.

I pulled out my phone and called Ace.

When he answered, I said, "Doc here. Don't talk, just listen. I need you to pick up my mother and get to the airport as quickly as you can, no longer than thirty minutes, no extra stops. There will be a private plane waiting for you. I'll have a limo waiting on this end, and suites at the Bellagio."

Ordering him was something I had never done, or would have even thought to try to do with my grandfather. But at this moment, I didn't feel like having a conversation with him.

After he sputtered for a moment, he asked one question, very softly. "Is this about what happened to Carson?"

"It's about what happened to all of us a long damn time ago," I said, doing my best to just not yell at him. There would be time for my anger later, after he and my mother were safe.

"I understand," he said softly. "We will be at the airport within thirty minutes."

I didn't say another word, just hung up.

Fleet hung up at the same moment. "Another Gulfstream will be standing by in twenty minutes at the Boise airport. Ours is still down here waiting for us and would take too long to get there."

I nodded. "Ace and my mother are on the way to the airport. Get your wife and kids there without any delay. Not one extra minute. Make sure you get them all that protection and rides here on this end. I'll go get them suites. Your kids need an extra room?"

He nodded. "Yeah. Can I now ask what exactly is going on?"

"Put it this way," I said. "The guy who hired the thug to come after me yesterday will have no problem using our families to come after us and get Carson's key."

"Oh, shit," Fleet said, his face white.

"Get your family on the way. I'll tell you everything I know later tonight. It's a long story and there are parts of it I'm not sure of. But let me say this, the morning started with the news that Verne Adkins was shot last night. He survived, and I talked to him. He had a key and someone got it. And the President is involved in some way or another."

Fleet looked even whiter, like all his blood had vanished from his body.

"There's a lot more. But for now, just get everyone here, inside this hotel, safely. And don't you dare leave the hotel either, for any reason. Not one step outside, is that understood? There are some big nasty snakes just outside those doors."

"Not funny," Fleet said.

"I didn't intend it to be," I said, turning and heading toward the hotel front desk.

CHAPTER FORTY-ONE

LAS VEGAS, NEVADA. AUGUST 24

FBI AGENT HEATHER VOIGHT stood outside the window of the intensive care room and listened carefully to the phone conversation going on from Verne Adkin's hospital room. It was being relayed into her ear from the monitoring station they had set up in an empty room.

She pretended to be standing guard. She had three agents doing that in different areas of the hall. She had been here just waiting for something like this to happen.

It was her only hope at getting a real lead, since Adkins wasn't talking, and she doubted Doc Hill knew much more than she did at this point.

After Doc had left, Adkins had taken a short nap, which had allowed her to have a quick breakfast since Doc had woken her up with his call.

She had managed to eat a few bites, sitting on a couch in the hallway, when Adkins woke and asked for a phone. He was brought one, a phone that was bugged so Heather could listen in to both sides of the conversation.

She knew a moment after Adkins had finished dialing that he had called the Las Vegas number of a man named Aaron Bell.

"Verne, oh, man, I heard what happened. Are you all right?"

"A couple extra holes in my head, but nothing anyone would notice. They say I'm going to be fine."

"Oh, thank God," Bell said. Even through the tap, the relief in Bell's voice was clear.

"Aaron, protect your family," Adkins said.

Heather glanced around at the busy hospital wing. That was the exact same thing Adkins had told Doc Hill to do.

"Why?" Bell asked.

"Someone's making a move on the keys," Adkins said. "Got mine by threatening my grandkids."

"Son-of-a-bitch," Bell said. "I didn't think you'd ever touch a gun. Who's behind it?"

"I don't know," Adkins said. "I didn't recognize the bastard. More than likely hired help. Just get your family protected."

"Will do," Bell said. "Thanks. And take care of yourself."

After Adkins hung up, Heather desperately wanted to just go into the room and ask the wounded man what the keys were all about. He and Doc Hill had talked about keys as well.

"But keys to what?" she said out loud. She had a hunch that the moment she discovered the answer to that question, she would find out who was doing this. And why Paul and the President were so interested in all this.

And why she was here in the first place.

With one long look at the now resting man in the ICU, she turned and headed down the hall, leaving her unfinished breakfast behind on the couch. She was going to need even more help, which meant another call to Director Smith. And maybe Paul. She now had to put a round-the-clock watch on Aaron Bell.

If whoever was doing this made a move on Bell, she was going to make sure this would come to a very quick end.

CHAPTER FORTY-TWO

LAS VEGAS, NEVADA. AUGUST 24

I GOT THE SUITES for Ace and my mother, and the extra room for Fleet's kids, then headed through the midday crowds for the poker room. The tournament was scheduled to start in about fifteen minutes. I had no intention of playing. I just wanted to wish Annie good luck, and make a date to talk to her after she was finished. I didn't know how, but I had a hunch I was going to need her help.

And maybe all of the Las Vegas police department as well.

As I got closer to the tournament area in front of the poker room, I stopped and stepped off to one side of the wide aisle. My mind was swirling, and somehow I had to have time to put all of what I had learned today into perspective. And figure out what to do next.

I had no doubt I was just going to pace and worry until the plane from Boise got here and everyone was safely inside the Bellagio. Granted, someone could get to them here, even with all the security cameras. But on short notice, and at least for the night, it was the safest place I could think of. After they were here, I would have a talk with the manager and get his security people on higher alert. Maybe have Annie help me with that was well.

Right now, beyond taking care of that, I was having trouble thinking about anything.

I had to get calmed down and clear my head.

One of the final satellites broke, with a few handshakes around. In the early rounds of a poker tournament, my normal style was to do nothing but watch other players.

Maybe I should just go ahead and play, put myself in a place I was comfortable. No one would bother me, and I would have time to think. I always did some of my best thinking in the boring early rounds of tournaments.

Or on the lazy, calm water up on the river. God, right now what I wouldn't give to be back there.

Playing would be a waste of the two thousand entry fee, of that I had no doubt, but at the moment, it seemed like a small price to pay to help me get things into perspective.

I flipped open my cell phone and called Fleet.

"Everyone is on the way to the airport," he said. "I'm in my suite making sure nothing gets missed."

"Good. I got everyone suites, and later on I'll meet with Annie and get the police in on this as well. Anything I can do to help right now?"

"Got this part covered," he said.

"Okay," I said. "I think I'll sit in on the tournament for a while. But you can come and get me at any point."

"Trying to give yourself time to think, huh?"

"Yeah," I said, laughing. "You know me too well. You got guards and a limo lined up for this end?"

"I do," he said. "They will be at the airport in an hour and will wait. I'll get them all here safely," Fleet said.

"Good, thanks," I said. "You know where I'll be. Let me know when they arrive. Otherwise, I'll see you when someone takes my chips and kicks my ass out of the tournament."

He half-laughed. "Will you notice?"

"Probably not."

I hung up and moved forward toward the entry desk. Annie was standing off to one side, and when she saw me, her nervous smile faded. It dawned on me she must think I wanted my entry back, since I was here before the start.

Before I could say anything, she asked, "How was Verne Adkins?"

"Alive, talking, got a bad headache."

"Did you find anything out about what happened?"

"Not enough," I said. "I was right, he was attacked, and it was set up to look like a suicide attempt. The woman I called this morning is from the FBI. She's working with your department's people to keep him safe."

"FBI?" she asked, looking at me intently, "How are they mixed up in this?"

"Later," I said, avoiding her question. "After the tournament, I want to talk with you more about all this. I have a hunch I'm going to need your help in a very official way."

She nodded. "Good. Let's get your entry transferred back."

"Nope. We have a deal."

She looked puzzled. "You're sure?"

"Absolutely," I said. "I expect to make some money off of you."

"I'll do my best," she said. "But are you sure there's nothing we can do on the bigger problem right now?"

"Nothing," I said. "I'll explain everything later, I promise."

I bought into the tournament, then went back to her. "Two rules now that I'm playing. One, you take me out if you can. No laying down a hand."

"Wouldn't think of it," she said, nodding seriously.

"Two, I'll do the same to you if I can."

With that, she laughed. "Of that, I have no doubt."

For the next ten minutes, before the call to "Shuffle up and deal," I pointed out a few of the players already sitting at the table she drew, and what to be careful of with them. By the time she sat down, she seemed almost calm and cold and calculating. I had no doubt she was scared to death. I still remembered my early big tournaments.

But now these things didn't scare me. In fact, the early rounds bored me, and that was exactly what I needed at the moment.

Luckily, I had drawn a seat on another table clear across the tournament area from Annie. I doubted if I could have done much thinking with her close by. She had a wonderful way of distracting me. And right now, that was exactly what I didn't need.

I just needed to think.

Over the next three hours and the first four forty-five minute rounds, I played exactly five hands, tossing everything else away. I had actually managed to build a few extra chips over what I had started with as we went into the dinner break.

No one had talked to me. It had been heaven. I had had time to calm down, to go over what R.A. had said, what Verne had said, and what was happening with Heather from the FBI.

Now I at least had the basic outline of a plan. Granted, it was a plan that was going to need a lot of help, and a lot more knowledge about what had really happened in 1982.

But since Fleet had just come and told me that everyone had arrived safely and were headed to the hotel, I would be able to get some of that information very shortly.

A decade or so late, but at least I was going to get it.

CHAPTER FORTY-THREE

LAS VEGAS, NEVADA. AUGUST 24

ANNIE WAS ACTUALLY BUBBLING as we headed through the slots and evening tourist crowd toward the Café Bellagio for dinner. I had never expected to see a homicide detective actually act like a schoolgirl. It felt disquieting. And it made me smile. At this point, I needed a smile or two, and she was giving them to me as she talked excitedly about the first three hours.

"I've just about doubled up," she said. "I only played about twenty hands, but I took down all but one of them."

She looked over at me as we walked. "How are you doing?"

"Up slightly," I said. "David Phan was on my table, so I just stayed out of his way and let him play."

She nodded, understanding exactly what I had meant. David was one of the top professionals playing the game, and had an aggressive style where he often raised every other hand. He controlled a table from the first hand of any tournament, and I always just let him. I never saw any point in getting in his way early on. At this point, with about half of the entrants already knocked out, I bet he had one of the biggest stacks of chips in the tournament.

Annie kept talking about a few of the hands she had played as we neared the restaurant. I had a hunch it would just be the two of us for the first thirty minutes of our hour-and-a-half dinner break. Fleet was to meet everyone out front when the limo pulled up, get them into their suites, and then have my mother and Ace come down to the café.

But a tall guy with a light shirt on was standing near the entrance waiting for us. As we approached, he nodded to me, then asked Annie, "How are you doing?"

"Long way to go yet," Annie said. "But so far so good." Then, like flipping a switch, she reverted to detective mode. "Doc Hill, this is my former partner, Detective Dennis Boyne."

I shook his hand and he said, "Nice meeting you."

"Find out anything on who called Brent's widow?" Annie asked. "Get her phone records?"

"Got them," Detective Boyne said. "Someone made three calls to her, all from three different stolen cell phones, I'm sure long since tossed."

"Dead end," Annie said, the smile now long gone from her face. "Damn it all to hell."

I could have told her that the people we were up against wouldn't make stupid mistakes like talking on a phone that could be traced. My time thinking during the tournament had led me to that conclusion. We were facing a very organized and smart person who was after the keys and willing to kill to get them.

"Verne Adkins is recovering slowly," Detective Boyne said, "but there's enough FBI around him to stop an army. You want to tell me what that's all about?"

Annie didn't even glance at me. "Not a clue. Just work with them."

"We are," he said.

"You want to join us?" Annie asked.

"Got to get home. Dinner is waiting and long cold."

"Thanks, Dennis," Annie said, touching her old partner's arm. "I'll check in with you tomorrow."

"Good luck," he said, then turned and headed for the parking garage.

We got settled in the restaurant and the waitress took our drink orders. I looked seriously at Annie. "Would you mind doing me a favor?"

Annie smiled. "After getting me into this tournament, sure, anything."

"I'd like to have a short meeting with you on what's happening, after the tournament, after we win this thing."

"Good attitude," Annie said, laughing. "After I win it, don't you mean?"

"Even better attitude," I said. "But it could get late. On these first three tournaments, they're playing it all the way out in one day instead of going to a final table tomorrow."

"Not a problem. But any hints?"

"I have some new information," I said, "and I need help getting more. But right now, you need to focus on the tournament. One thing at a time."

Our drinks came just as my mother and Ace walked in. Fleet must have stayed with his family. I didn't blame him.

My mother looked almost out of place in the hotel. Her face, her walk, her posture looked extremely tired. Normally she was a solid woman with graying hair, who always dressed in pants suits and looked like nothing was every out of place in her makeup or her jewelry. Now, it was clear, she didn't have any makeup on and looked drained.

I understood why. Even though I was very angry at her for all the years of hiding so much from me, I was still very glad to see her here and safe for the moment.

I gave her a hug, shook Ace's hand as we always did as a greeting, then I did the introduction of Annie as Detective Annie Lott.

Annie was completely starstruck with meeting Ace. Sometimes I forgot just how much of a legend he was in the poker world.

My mother sat next to Annie, and by the time we were served dinner, they were talking like old friends. I was starting to like more and more things about Annie every minute. My mother had seldom taken an interest in anyone I had been with over the years. Yet, in ten minutes,

Annie had charmed and relaxed her, brought a little life back into my mother's face.

I just tried to stay silent, only contribute to small talk about how hot it was outside compared to the weather in Boise, and how this was the first time Ace had been in Las Vegas in August in twenty years.

Every so often, Ace would look up at me, and I would look away. Now, at dinner, wasn't the time to talk. And I certainly didn't want my anger coming out now. Not here. And I was so angry, I wasn't sure I could control it.

Tomorrow would be soon enough to get everything in the open, when they were refreshed and I had a night to calm down even more.

Then we would have a very long talk about a lot of years of secrets.

Very deadly secrets that just might end up getting us all killed.

CHAPTER FORTY-FOUR

LAS VEGAS, NEVADA. AUGUST 25

IT WAS ONE IN THE MORNING by the time I reached a turning-point hand in the tournament. Just twelve players left, six on each table.

I had been sitting back so much, sometimes watching the other players, sometimes just thinking about the plan that was forming in my head, that I was short-chipped. Fantastically short-chipped, actually. Or a better way of putting it would be *stupidly* short-chipped.

Under any of my normal tournament plans, I would have never allowed myself at this point to be this low. I would either be out of the tournament or have a decent amount of chips.

Now, because of not paying a lot of attention, I was going to have to make a move or just get blinded out very shortly. I couldn't remember the last time I had allowed myself to get blinded out in a tournament.

This clearly had not been one of my normal tournaments, but I hadn't expected it to be. But it had done what I wanted it to do, which was give me some time to just sit and think and plan. That I had accomplished.

Annie was on the other table of six, and doing fine, looking calm and collected behind a very large pile of chips. The woman could clearly play cards.

We were all in the decent money at this point, since they paid down to thirtieth place. I had never expected to make it this far as distracted as I was.

After dinner, my mother had gone to her room and Ace had gone to play in a ring game in the poker room. About two hours ago, he had waved goodnight, heading for his room.

They were under strict orders to not leave the hotel for any reason, and three guards that Fleet had hired were outside our doors, working directly with hotel security.

We had set up a time to talk in my suite at ten tomorrow, over a room-service breakfast. I had no doubt that was going to be an interesting conversation in all definitions of the word *interesting*.

I glanced down at my new hand to see ace-ten off-suit. I was one off the button and had two players fold to me at that point, with three players to follow. I only had one play as short-chipped as I was.

"All in," I said, pushing my chips slightly forward.

The button folded, the little blind folded, and I thought I might win the blinds when the big blind, a good player from Southern California, called.

I flipped over my ace-ten and he flipped over a pair of sixes. We had what was called a race, or a coin flip. Either hand had about the same odds of winning going into the flop.

Only problem was that if I didn't win, I stood up and sat in the bleachers. He still had a lot of chips left.

I hit the ten on the flop and no six came and I doubled up. I was still short-stacked, but not as bad.

The next hand I looked down at pocket tens, with a player with a big stack limping in under the gun. I was on the button now, so again I said, "All in."

Everyone at the table could cover me. But if someone called me and I won this one, I would become a factor again.

Both blinds folded. The limper, who was the big stack at the table, thought for a full minute, looked at me, then shrugged and called, flipping over ace-nine of diamonds. It was the right call for him to make since he had a lot of chips. My pocket tens had a decent advantage, which was better than a race like the last hand. If this tournament was being broadcast, which it wasn't, some broadcaster would have put up my exact odds of winning on the screen down to two decimal points.

I knew what my advantage was. Now if the pesky cards would just follow the odds.

They did. No ace or diamond flush hit the board and my pocket tens held. I had doubled through again.

Two of my friends at the table, top professionals in their own rights, just shook their heads. As someone once said about me in an article in *Card Player Magazine,* "Never give Doc Hill chips. He's dangerous when he has chips."

I now had chips.

I raised three of the next four hands with marginal starting hands and got no callers, building my stack with the blinds into the second biggest at the table. The big stack knocked out one player, and at Annie's table, one person took out two others in a huge hand that luckily Annie was only watching.

And then suddenly there were nine.

Final table.

We took a short break while the tournament folks moved everything to the main final table in front of the grandstands. If I thought Annie had been bubbling at dinner, she was on full artesian-well setting now as we moved away from the table to get a snack. It was great being around her. I had forgotten just how exciting and how much fun poker was.

With every sentence, she was reminding me.

She kept repeating, "Wow, only nine of us left."

And every time she said that, all I could think about was nine keys. Only in that real-life game, as far as I knew, there were still seven players left since I had stepped into Carson's spot when I inherited his key.

By the time we got back to the table, she had calmed down some, and I had decided I wouldn't think about what was going on with Carson's death and the keys until after the tournament. I had a pretty decent plan formed. I had stumbled along and somehow got into this position in the tournament, so it was time to take care of the business at hand.

Nine players, last man standing took the big prize.

I had a tournament to win.

As we started the final table in front of a half-filled set of bleachers, my mother came down from her suite and sat down in the bleachers. It was nice to see her there, no matter how angry I was at her.

Two hotel security and one of the hired guards had followed her in and taken up positions around her. That made me feel really good. I also could see at least two FBI types from Heather's people watching from other places around me. Right now, I was about as safe as I could be.

One hour later, there were only four of us left, and I was the big stack. I had turned on the attack mode and just gone after anyone who looked like they showed the slightest weakness in any hand. Pot after pot, I raised and just took down the blinds. I got called twice, once I folded after the flop, another time I took out two players with my pocket jacks against two smaller pairs.

Annie hadn't made many plays at all, seemingly content to just let her stacks of chips slowly dwindle while her position in the tournament went up with others going out. She was now the short stack.

What she had done was one strategy, and considering the level of players at the table and her inexperience, it had been a good choice. She had made a lot of money by doing nothing, but had put herself out of position to win the entire thing. Now, with only four left, she had to switch gears and she didn't seem to be doing that. If I survived all the craziness with the keys, I'd have to have a talk with her about that.

Finally, three hands later, with large blinds coming at her again, she pushed all in with only a glance at her cards. She had an ace, that much I could count on. She was good enough to know that at this point, in her short-stack position, with only four players, just about anything with an ace was a good enough hand to go with.

Heck, in her position, anything with a face card was good enough, but I bet she had been patient enough to wait for an ace.

The player between us folded and I looked down to see ace-jack off-suit. I called her and the other player folded to get out of the way.

She rolled over ace-six and no six hit the board and my jack played, so I took her out in fourth place.

She beamed, shook all of our hands, then almost skipping, headed for the tournament cashier to sign all the tax forms and get her cash.

Twenty-four thousand in cash.

I had a hunch that this success had just unleashed a monster, and would soon signal the retirement of a fine Las Vegas Police detective.

A couple hands later, when she joined my mother in the stands, she gave her a hug and then just sat there smiling, a lot of money in her hands. When she saw me looking at her, she raised the money and mouthed the words, "Thank you."

All I could do was smile. It always felt good helping a younger player.

I focused back on the task at hand. I had two top players to deal with, both experts from the live games in Southern California, both very aggressive.

Three handed no-limit poker. I was going to take advantage of their aggressiveness.

I was big stack by a long ways, so I had the luxury to be a little more patient.

I laid down the next two hands to raises, then raised the next two and got them to lay down their cards.

Five hands after Annie went out, the two of them got into an all-in fight and I folded my pocket threes and let them battle. One man crippled the other, and my king-ten in the next hand took him out.

Now it was just the two of us, and I had a decent chip lead, enough that if I got him all in and lost, I would still be in decent shape.

I was on the button and first to act on the next hand, and I looked down at ten-six off-suit. I just called, he checked, meaning his hand was bad or he was trying to trap me. He was good enough to make that play and I had no read on what he actually had. It could be anything.

The flop came ten, eight, seven, with two hearts to match my six of hearts. I had top pair with a gut-shot straight draw and a runner-runner flush draw.

He checked, I shoved all in, and he called, smiling.

So it had been a trap.

He rolled over pocket jacks.

It was going to take a little luck for me to pull this off, although, with two cards left, I wasn't that bad of an underdog. Any of the four nines or two tens would win it for me. Or two hearts, since he didn't have a heart in his hand.

A five of hearts hit the turn and suddenly my odds of winning went up a lot higher. I now had an open-ended straight draw and a flush draw, not counting the other ten that would give me a set. I had sixteen cards, or outs, to win this.

The four hit and completed the straight for me to end the tournament.

I was one-hundred and fifty-six thousand dollars richer.

Annie and my mother were standing and cheering in the bleachers.

I had to admit, it had been a really great planning session.

I might have to try that more often.

Chapter Forty-Five

Las Vegas, Nevada. August 25

STEVEN GLANCED at his watch. Four a.m.

Using his night-vision goggles, he stared down the faintly lit subur-ban street at Aaron Bell's home. This area was close to the university and was an older Vegas neighborhood, with lots of tall trees and green grass. Why anyone wasted the water to keep them green in the heat of August was beyond him.

There were lots of shadows and dark areas. Perfect for him to move around in.

The night had cooled a little, down to just under ninety. It felt almost chilly compared to the daytime temperatures.

Someone was watching Bell's home from a sedan just down the road. And the two were sloppy. Real sloppy. They had let Steven get close to them, within less than thirty feet, to take a look. They didn't seem like Las Vegas's best, more like government types. One was dozing, the other drinking coffee.

Even in the middle of the night, they still had their suit coats on and often had to run the air-conditioning. What idiots.

They were there because Steven had been careless and Verne had been lucky enough to survive. From now on out, there would be no attempt at covering the murders.

No point now. Besides, not covering them was a lot more fun.

Steven studied the sedan. Maybe they were FBI, he couldn't be sure, but it didn't matter, really. They wouldn't stop him or catch him.

The chances were they had bugged the home as well. They were sitting out here thinking that was enough, but that wouldn't matter either. It just made getting inside a slightly more challenging task.

Steven moved through a yard and into the back alley. He moved along the alley, making sure to not wake the big, friendly-but-noisy dog that lived on the other side of the alley.

He moved silently, like a shadow, staying to the blackest areas of deep shadow. He was dressed in all black, wore black gloves, and had black paint on his face. In the Army, he had been trained to move like this, with the night vision goggles. And to do so many other things. It was nice the training was finally coming in so handy.

He worked his way slowly into Aaron Bell's neighbor's backyard that bordered the Bell's suburban home on the right. The two families had been close over the years and had installed a joint barbecue pit that they shared between the houses. The area was fenced off from the street.

And the two idiots in the car.

Steven moved silently through the barbecue area.

The Bells had never bothered with a security alarm, but they did have a motion sensor light in the backyard that he didn't want to trigger. Staying low and against the wall, he moved under the light and to the back door, easily unlocking it and getting inside.

He moved slowly, staying where he had practiced moving a few times when the Bells were out late to a show. He knew the creaks in their floor and where to step to avoid them.

It took him less than five minutes to get silently through the house to the bedroom.

Aaron and his wife, Cindy, were sleeping right where they were supposed to be.

Steven moved to Aaron's side of the bed and then carefully put a gloved hand over the old man's mouth. He jerked awake.

Steven showed him the gun in the faint light.

Cindy was snoring lightly, her mouth open, facing away from her husband.

Steven leaned down and whispered in Aaron's ear, softly enough that the men outside wouldn't hear. "You want your wife and grandchildren to live, you'll tell me where your key is."

Aaron nodded under Steven's gloved hand.

Steven pulled his hand back just enough to allow the nose of his gun to take its place in front of Aaron's mouth.

"Softly," Steven whispered.

"Jewelry case in my wife's closet," Aaron whispered, glancing at his still-sleeping wife. "Top shelf, hidden pocket in the lid."

"Get it," Steven whispered. "Silently. You wake her up and you both die. And your grandchildren right behind you."

Aaron nodded, then climbed out of bed. He was wearing pajama bottoms and no top and had more hair than any man should ever have on his chest and back.

Aaron carefully opened the closet, took out the jewelry box, placed it on the floor, then opened it.

From a slit in the cloth lining, he took out the key and handed it to Steven.

Steven glanced at it, enjoying the thrill of yet another success, then tucked it safely in a pocket.

Four down. Five to go.

"Now, back in bed and just pretend this didn't happen," Steven whispered.

Aaron nodded and did as he was told.

"Thanks," Steven whispered. "And next time, don't cover up a murder."

He quickly shot Aaron in the head, then killed Aaron's still-sleeping wife. The sound must have made the agent with the earphones out in the car wet his pants.

Steven placed the gun on the nightstand. He wouldn't need that one anymore, and no one could trace it to him.

Then he quickly pulled out a device to disguise his voice as he headed for the door.

Trying to keep from laughing, he said into the device as loud as he could, "Hey, fellows, wake up. There be dead people."

Steven was in the alley before the men in the sedan even managed to get to the front of the house with their guns drawn.

CHAPTER FORTY-SIX

LAS VEGAS, NEVADA. AUGUST 25

THE NEXT MORNING, Annie was in the best mood she had been in since her mother's death, even with only a half night's sleep. She just couldn't stop whistling, and every time a song came on the radio that even had half a beat, she found herself dancing around the kitchen while she got breakfast ready.

This morning she was treating herself to something more than her standard breakfast bar and a go-cup of coffee. Scrambled eggs with ham and green peppers, toast, and fresh ground coffee. She figured she deserved it.

Having Doc Hill believe in her skill and talent, and then coming through for him, broke down the final doubts in her mind. She would still go at it slowly and carefully, but at least now she knew, deep down inside, that she could make a living playing professional poker given enough time.

When she finished eating, she went to work on what Doc had asked her to do. She had waited around after he won, watching him go through the paperwork and the photographs with his winning hand and all the money.

She very much wanted to be in that position shortly.

Then, after he put all the money in a safe-deposit box in the Bellagio cage, he had walked her toward her car, asking her to meet him in the morning, after he called, and in the meantime, look up some names for him.

Kevin DeFoe, Benson James, and Aaron Bell. He had said he thought they were involved with the keys. And he would tell her more in the morning, get the police, through her, involved.

"Everything?" she had asked him.

"As much as I know so far," he had said. "I promise."

She was going to hold him to that.

She desperately wanted to know why the FBI was guarding Verne Adkins, among many other questions.

She decided to first try to track down Kevin DeFoe.

She quickly discovered in one phone call to police records that DeFoe had been reported missing back in 1982 by a girlfriend. The report had never been cleared. With no leads, no body, no real relatives demanding work on the case, the report had been filed and not even noticed again. Luckily, it had been added into the computer files, or she never would have gotten the information.

Then she discovered, with a call to a friend in the State Police records, that Kevin DeFoe had lived in Laughlin and had been banned from two different casinos for vague reasons in the early eighties. He hadn't shown up on any police records or even renewed a driver's license since 1982.

There were no records at all of the other two names besides driver's licenses, Benson James in Medford, Oregon, and Aaron Bell in Las Vegas.

She got on the internet to look up any reference to the other two names. It didn't take her long to find Benson James.

He had been killed with his wife four days before in Medford, Oregon.

She sat back, stunned, staring at the computer screen.

"Oh, man," she said to herself, "the pile of bodies on this is getting deeper by the moment."

Her good mood about the tournament was now replaced with the focus of a very nasty case swirling around her.

She called the Medford police department.

A detective there named Ott told her that the double murder had been in cold blood, for no apparent reason. The murderer had left a gun that was untraceable and without any prints. There were no other clues, no suspects, nothing.

"Not even a motive," Ott said. "The Jameses were wonderful people. Retired, owned a small antique shop. Everyone loved them."

"No robbery?" Annie asked.

"Nothing that we can tell," Ott said. "No leads at all until you called asking about it. So, you want to tell me why you called, detective?"

"Just doing some basic research on a case," she said. "If I can tie this with your case, I'll call you."

"Please," Ott said. "We could use all the help we can get on this."

She promised she would, then hung up and called in downtown to tell her captain what was going on, but before she got a word out, he stopped her.

"We might need to call you back in to work, pull you off the Jeff Taylor case."

"Why?" Annie asked.

"Double homicide last night. Right under the nose of the FBI."

"Not Verne Adkins." The wonderful breakfast now felt like a hard ball in her stomach.

"No, he's doing fine, and still under heavy guard in the hospital. And I wish like hell someone would tell me why the FBI is there. No, this was a poker player named Aaron Bell and his wife, Cindy."

"Oh, no," she said.

"You know these people?" he demanded.

"No, but I'm already working on the case. And I'm on it full-time. All this somehow ties to Jeff Taylor's grave robbery."

"You've got to be kidding."

"I wish I was," Annie said. "And there are other possible murders, including two in Medford, Oregon a few days ago and a staged plane crash in Idaho."

"Oh, shit," the Captain said.

Annie went on. "And don't ask me how it's all tied together. I don't know yet, but I'm hoping to get more information this afternoon. I'll report in as soon as I have a little more."

She hung up before he could ask her any other questions, almost all of which she was sure she couldn't answer.

She grabbed her gun and badge and jacket and headed for the front door. No way was she waiting around now for Doc to call. She was going to him, and fast.

He had a lot of explaining to do, and he needed to do it quickly.

There were just too damn many people getting killed.

CHAPTER FORTY-SEVEN

LAS VEGAS, NEVADA. AUGUST 25

I WAS BACK UP and working with Fleet in his suite at eight.

It had been a while since I had gone with only a few hours' sleep, but at this point, sleep wasn't that easy to get anyway. And when I did manage to doze off, all I dreamed about was a combination of that tattooed goon with the big gun and Verne being forced to shoot himself in the head, all mixed in with images of Carson and the President.

Not great dreams.

I had told Fleet what Verne had said about protecting my family, but I had decided to not tell him what R.A. had said. I started to, then realized that there was a good chance that the walls had ears.

More than likely, with the FBI roaming around, very big ears.

I ended up just telling him there was more, but I'd tell him about that later, when we were in a little more secure place.

Fleet had set up two Internet-connected computers in his suite and I took one, sipping on an orange juice and munching on raspberry Danish.

It took some real work to keep the filling off the keyboard and I only half succeeded.

We were after as much information as we could get on R.A. Scott and Nyland Harrison. Fleet had asked why those two names, and all I had said was later. "Walls. Ears. Remember?"

He looked worried, but nodded.

The research didn't take that long. As R.A. had said, they were clearly bitter enemies, missing no chance in articles or speeches over the years to poke at the other. They both had owned large competing construction companies and the battle had been pretty level, from what I could tell, right up until the Clear Creek Dam broke in 1995.

The event ended up taking Nyland's company into bankruptcy from all the lawsuits, and put his son in federal prison in 2002, along with a few paid-off inspectors. R.A.'s company clearly gained from Harrison's loss, and he soon controlled a vast amount of the business, including a lot of overseas government contracts.

From all the records, after the bankruptcy and the trial, it looked like Nyland Harrison had dropped out of sight. Neither Fleet or I could even find an address or listed phone number for the man.

"I'll look up the documents on the son's case," Fleet said. "But I can tell you this as a friend, a partner, and as your attorney, if we're dealing with these two men, we're in way over our heads."

I laughed. "I knew that the moment that Heather and the FBI showed up."

"Yeah, that too," Fleet said, shaking his head. "Someday someone is going to have to explain that to me as well."

I smiled at my friend. "I know why, but until we get into a secure location where no one can listen in, I can't tell you."

"Secrets," Fleet said, clearly disgusted. "They are sure getting old."

"Couldn't agree more," I said.

"I'm going to make some calls," Fleet said. "See if I can find us a security company to help us out."

"If you do," I said, "I want it done on Carson's house."

Fleet turned to stare at me. "Why?"

I started to answer, but then he waved off the question.

"Control. I get it. Good security here in the hotel, but no control. We can control Carson's place. I'll get on it."

He turned and picked up the phone.

I finished the Danish, then went in search of Ace and my mother. For that same reason, the meeting with them this morning was going to have to wait.

I was still so angry at my mother that I wasn't sure I wanted to even see her right now. I just didn't trust myself to not explode.

I found Ace in his suite, alone, sitting at the table reading the morning paper.

"I'm postponing our little talk this morning." I made a motion at the room. "Walls more than likely have ears."

He nodded. "I was wondering about that. You need help? It just so happens I have a good friend here who specializes in different types of security. He owes me a few favors."

"Of course you do," I said, laughing. Sometimes I wondered why anything my grandfather did surprised me. I glanced at my watch. It was still over an hour before I was to call and then meet Annie in the restaurant. "Can he meet us in the restaurant for breakfast in about an hour, maybe sooner?"

Ace just smiled. "I'm sure he can."

I turned and headed for the door. "I'll stop Fleet from making any more phone calls. Tell my mother the meeting is off until later for security reasons. I'll meet you downstairs in an hour."

Ace nodded. "She'll understand."

"I'm sure she will," I said, not hiding the sarcasm and anger in my voice.

Ace said nothing, just picked up the phone.

CHAPTER FORTY-EIGHT

LAS VEGAS, NEVADA. AUGUST 25

I HAD FINISHED my third cup of coffee even though Annie was early arriving at the Café Bellagio. When I called her, she had said she was already on the way. I could tell from the call, and her face as she worked their way through the tables toward me, that what she had found from the information I had given her wasn't good. She wasn't smiling.

She looked very police official. Now I could see one of the reasons why she made detective at such a young age. She was a force coming at me.

The previous hour, Ace and I and Fleet had met with Mike Dans, a security specialist that Ace knew. For some reason, I liked Mike right off, and trusted him. He was a bear of a man with a large beard and moustache. He wore a large button-down shirt, Bermuda shorts, and sneakers, an outfit that said *I couldn't give a damn what anyone thought*. It also made him look a little like a tourist. A great disguise in Las Vegas.

After I shook his hand, I rounded up my original estimate of his age from mid-forties to early fifties, and I had no doubt he would take me in a fair fight.

After we were all introduced, and Mike and Ace spent a few minutes getting caught up like old friends did, Mike turned to me.

"Ace tells me you need help."

"We all do," I said. "Can you sweep a house to see if there are any listening devices, then set it up so that no one will be able to listen in to anything being said inside that house, including your own people?"

"If it's a standard house out in a subdivision, not a problem. It will take me about two hours."

"What kind of security can you provide for us after that?" I asked.

"What do you need?"

"An army," Fleet said.

Mike laughed, but then got serious when Ace and I nodded our agreement.

"I can get you a small army. What and who needs to be secured?"

"Ace, Fleet, his wife and kids, my mother, me, and the house. There might be others along the way. Everyone needs to be very secured from all sides against all levels of surveillance and attack twenty-four/seven."

Mike glanced at his old friend Ace.

"If what I think is happening really is happening," Ace said. "We may need more than that before this is over."

Mike nodded, now very serious. "Under normal circumstances, right here I'd say this was going to cost, and cost a lot, but I owe Ace so much that—"

I interrupted him. "Money is not an issue. Our lives are. We'll pay you above your normal going rate for all this, and if you can get us all through this alive, there will be a very, very large bonus."

"Very large," Ace repeated, smiling at his old friend.

Mike took a deep breath, then thought for a moment before he said, "Give me two hours and the house will be secure. I'll have at least two of my men shadowing each of you at all times starting within the hour, more as every hour goes by, no matter where you go, so don't worry about them if you don't spot them. Every man I have working for me is ex-Special Forces, and they all know how to move."

I liked the sound of that last little phrase. He had well-trained men if he thought we wouldn't see them.

"Can they all be trusted?" Fleet asked.

"Completely," Mike said. "They will die doing their job if they have to."

"Let's hope it doesn't come to that," I said.

Ace just nodded, but I could tell he wasn't sure it wasn't going to come to just that kind of battle.

Mike went on, clearly taking charge of security. "From now on, you're to only leave the hotel through the front entrance and into my cars. I will have secured, bullet-proof limos waiting for you at all times if any of you need to go anywhere."

He glanced at Ace, then back at me. "Do you know how long this is going to last?"

"Not a clue," I said. "But prepare for weeks."

"I will."

"Thanks," I said, shaking his hand after he gave each of us a card with his secure phone number.

Mike and Fleet and Ace then left to go up to Ace's suite to take care of the details.

I sat, thinking, sipping my coffee until Annie arrived.

"Not good, huh?" I said as she approached, the frown on her beautiful face not changing.

"Not good," Annie said, sliding in across from me.

It was great seeing her again. But after the conversation with Mike, I was starting to worry about her safety as well. Even though she was a detective, someone could still get to me through her if they realized how much I liked her. At the moment, I hoped whoever was behind this just thought she was the police and I was working with them.

"Well, spit it out," I said after the waitress came and took her order and cleared off some of the dirty dishes left behind.

"Kevin DeFoe disappeared in 1982. Nothing has been seen of him since."

"Okay," I said, nodding. "Another detail of R.A.'s story confirmed."

"You want to tell me why that got just an okay?" Annie asked. "And who Kevin DeFoe was?"

"I will, I promise," I said. "But not here. I have a security agency sweeping my father's house for listening devices and then putting up a secure area around the house where no one can listen in to anything going on inside. In three hours, there, in that house, I promise I'll tell everyone what I know. But I want to make sure it can't be overheard."

Annie stared at me for a moment, clearly deciding if that would be all right, then nodded. "That sounds reasonable. I'll be there. But I'm afraid there's a lot more that you don't know. Benson James was killed a few days ago in Medford, Oregon. No leads or suspects or motive."

All I could do was sit there and try to breathe normally. That meant whoever was doing this now had three keys at least.

"There's more," Annie said, her voice soft. "Last night, Aaron Bell and his wife were shot while still in bed. The FBI was guarding them as well and failed to stop it."

Or had a hand in it was what I thought, but I didn't say that out loud. I didn't dare.

Not here, not now.

I sat there silent, letting the waitress fill my coffee cup again and bring Annie her coffee. Four keys now in the maniac's hands, not counting if he had one of his own to start with. I had to assume he did.

And I had to stop thinking that there was only one person doing all this. More than likely, this was an organization.

Or the President himself was behind all this.

And whoever it was would soon be coming after me again, this time with all force necessary to take me out. The key I had of Carson's was possibly only one of four left.

Time was running down on this game and I was one of the next ones to be picked off. And the next attempt, they wouldn't send a stupid thug to do the job.

After the waitress left, I grabbed my cell phone and dialed Heather's number, motioning for Annie to excuse me for a moment.

When Heather answered with a "Yes," I started in on her.

"Aaron Bell. What happened?"

Heather took a deep breath. "I overheard Verne Adkins warning Bell to protect his family. I put two men on Bell's house and planted listening devices inside. The son-of-a-bitch actually taunted my men. We're going to find him and take him down, I can promise you that."

"I wouldn't underestimate whoever this was again," I said.

"Oh, trust me, we won't."

I didn't want to tell her that I didn't trust her one bit, or damn near anyone else for that matter. So instead I just said, "Good luck," and hung up.

"FBI?" Annie asked.

I nodded.

"And you're going to tell me why they are involved in this later?" she asked.

"I'm sure going to do my best," I said.

With that, I used my cell phone to call Mike upstairs in Ace's suite. I told him that whatever he was thinking about levels of security, triple it. And make sure that everyone he put on any of us could be trusted completely.

"It got worse?" he asked.

"A hundred times worse," I said.

Then I asked for my grandfather. I had the unpleasant task of telling Ace that his old friend, Aaron Bell, had been killed.

CHAPTER FORTY-NINE

LAS VEGAS, NEVADA. AUGUST 25

FBI AGENT HEATHER VOIGHT sat in her room at the MGM Grand and waited for a secure connection to the President. At least it was cool in here. She had spent most of the morning working the neighborhood around Aaron Bell's home, trying to get some sort of sense of how the killer got in there. It had gotten her nothing but overheated. She had been out there far too long in the morning desert heat. Even though she'd been drinking a lot of water, she still felt light-headed by the time she got back to her room.

She was going to have to force herself to spend a few hours cooling down in the air-conditioning and drinking sports drinks before venturing back outside again. No point in ending up in the hospital with heat stroke at this point. That wouldn't do Paul or the President or her job any good at all.

Two clicks on the phone and Paul said, "Yes, go ahead. The line is secure."

She was glad he was the one who answered. Maybe, without the President, she would get some answers to what was happening. Or at least maybe a hint or two. Paul owed her that much.

"Hi," she said. "We alone?"

"The President's in a meeting," Paul said. "Do you have a report?"

She could feel the coldness coming through the phone. He was angry at her. Very angry.

She dropped into official mode, her voice level.

"There are a couple problems. Doc Hill has hired a security team to guard his father's house."

"Good for him," Paul said. "Since you didn't have much luck protecting Aaron Bell."

Paul's words stung, but she deserved them. He was right. She had failed and two people were dead. She didn't want to even ask if Paul knew Bell, so instead she just ignored what he had said.

"Hill has also put in equipment that blocks our surveillance units on all levels. Very sophisticated stuff."

"Really?" Paul said, actually sounding surprised and a little worried.

She sure wished he would just come clean and just tell her what was so important to him and the President about this poker player. And the keys everyone seemed to mention.

The keys seemed the oddest part of all this. There clearly had to be something about those keys that threatened the President in some way.

Otherwise, none of this made sense.

When Paul didn't say anything else, she went on.

"Right now, Doc Hill and his family just moved in secured vehicles into his father's house. Right now, a Las Vegas homicide detective named Annie Lott is with them."

"Okay," Paul said.

"Hill has hired a very good security team who are standing guard around the house and patrolling the entire area. We've had to back off a short distance, but since he's blocked our electronic surveillance, it didn't matter."

"And no idea what they are doing in there?" Paul asked.

"Not a clue," she said. "What do you want me to do?"

"Stand off and watch, keep track of everything and everyone going in or coming out. Report to me regularly on all aspects of this."

"Including phone calls?" Heather asked, knowing she would be breaking a few laws if he wanted calls monitored.

"Including phone calls," Paul said without hesitation. "The President will talk to the Director and will cover you if he has to, but try to do it on your own."

"Understood," Heather said, but the phone was already dead.

Chapter Fifty

Las Vegas, Nevada. August 25

MOM MANAGED to not cry much as I moved her into Carson's master bedroom. I didn't say anything, or even make a move to comfort her, just because my anger was so close to the surface, I didn't trust myself. The pictures were still on the wall where Fleet had hung them back up, and the cleaning people had the place looking good and smelling fresh.

"I assume those are your clothes," I said, indicating the second closet. "I left Carson's clothes for you to deal with."

Then, before she could say anything, I turned and left, slamming the door so hard behind me, I heard something fall. I hoped it was one of those god-damned pictures.

Fleet took a second bedroom, Ace a third in the three-bedroom home. Fleet and Mike and Ace had decided it would be safer to get Fleet's family out of the area. They were now headed on our plane to a resort in central Idaho where a dozen of Mike's men could stand guard on them easily.

I planned on bunking on the couch, or if I really needed privacy, back in my suite at the Bellagio. But I wanted everyone else here, under full guard and protected.

Whoever was doing this would now have to come straight at me to get Carson's key. And that was exactly what I wanted, now that I knew most of what was going on.

I had to admit that the more I learned about Carson, the more I didn't mind being in his house. The brown tones, the comfortable couches and chairs in the living room, the workable kitchen felt very much like a home. I had no doubt my mother had had a lot to do with that. I wasn't about to forgive him or her for not trusting me just yet. Not by a long damn ways. I might never forgive them for that.

Mike showed me the protection for eavesdropping on our conversations, saying that he hadn't found a bug anywhere in the house. I had assumed he wouldn't. Anyone who knew me knew I wouldn't want to be in this house. And I was assuming whoever was after the keys had done their homework on me. So this house was the most unexpected and the safest place to come to.

And the easiest to defend.

At Ace's suggestion, Mike had also put a scrambler on one of the phones and had it routed in such a way that it couldn't be listened to in any fashion. I hadn't thought of that, but was glad it was done. The plan I had formed last night in the tournament would be well-served by a secure phone line.

I gave my mother a short time to get settled while Mike ran Ace and me, with Annie listening, through some of the security features he had installed in and around the house. After he left to go out to one of their big trucks parked on the street, Annie nodded. "He's good."

"The best in the country," Ace said.

Now, finally, it was time to get everyone on the same page, find out what had happened exactly all those years ago. I took a kitchen chair and pulled it into the living room.

Annie took the couch to my left, closest spot to me. I had to admit, I found I was calmer, more in control when she was around. We seemed to fit together, even think alike at times. After this was over, I hoped to spend a lot more time with her. But both of us had to survive this first.

My mother and Ace sat on the couch directly in front of me, and Fleet sat in the big chair on the right.

The tension in the air-conditioned room was thick enough to cut, so I decided to just outline what had happened that I knew of up to this point, starting with what I had discovered at Carson's crash site. I told them about finding a key in Carson's card capper, what Verne said about it, and the following attempt on my life out front of the house here.

Annie nodded. My mother and Ace looked shocked, but I didn't allow them any moment to ask questions. I wanted to ask them questions.

I told them about the visit of FBI Agent Heather Voight to my suite and what she had said her reasons to be there were.

With that, Ace nodded, but my mother just looked puzzled. Clearly, Ace knew that Carson knew the president. Chances are, Ace knew him as well, now that I thought about it. If Dolan Chase had been a high-stakes poker player back when I was young, of course Ace would have known him.

"I was given a few more pieces of the puzzle by a man named R.A. Scott. He stopped and talked to me right before the tournament yesterday."

"*The* R.A. Scott?" Annie asked, clearly shocked.

Ace didn't look happy with the news either, but said nothing.

"Yup, that one. It seems that in a high-stakes poker game at his ranch in Idaho back in 1982, there was a murder of a card cheat and the start of a cover-up."

I looked at my mother and Ace and then said, "Actually, a number of cover-ups."

Ace started to say something, but I waved him silent.

"Later," I said, not bothering to hide the anger. "We'll talk about that part of it *later*."

"The keys," Annie said, coming to their rescue. "That's why the keys and all the secrets. It's a murder cover-up."

I nodded. "Ten players in the game, nine keys for the players remaining alive. Proof of the murder is in the box that the keys open."

I stared at my mother and Ace. Both were looking down at their laps, saying nothing. So far it appeared I had everything right.

"Let me guess the players," Annie said. She held up her hand to check off the players in that poker game. "Kevin DeFoe was the cheater. He's been missing since that year."

I nodded, so she went on. "Your father, R.A. Scott, Verne Adkins, Benson James from Oregon, Aaron Bell, Jeff Taylor, and Dolan Chase."

She still held up two fingers. "Who am I missing?"

"Nyland Harrison," Ace said before I could. "A powerful and heartless businessman from Northern California. And Dolan Chase's partner, Paul Hanson."

"The President and his chief of staff?" Annie said, suddenly looking very worried. "Involved in a murder and cover-up? Oh, man, are we in over our heads."

"That's what I've been saying," Fleet said.

"That's why the FBI is involved," Annie said. "Now it makes sense. They're trying to protect their boss."

"Or actually just here to protect Doc," Ace said. "Dolan is a good man."

Annie snorted. "They were at Aaron Bell's house last night and couldn't protect him."

"Or they killed him themselves," I said.

Shocked silence around the room.

"He's the president," I said, going on. "He has the most to lose if this all comes out. I'm betting he's involved somewhere along the way."

I let that comment just float in the air like a bad nightmare.

Then I turned to my grandfather. "Who's this Nyland Harrison? I've heard nothing but bad things about him."

"And you haven't heard near enough," Ace said. "It was mostly his idea to do the cover-up. He threatened families of all the players if they didn't go along."

"Carson didn't want to go along, did he?" I asked.

Ace looked angry, but somehow contained it. "Carson was planning on going to the police when they all came out of the wilderness, and Nyland knew that. He had your mother beaten to stop him before they even got out."

I watched as my mother looked up at me. "The men who beat me said they would come for you next. Carson couldn't let that happen, so he went along."

"The bastard threatened you and your mother twice more over the next month," Ace said. "I got so angry, I contacted Mike."

"Same Mike?" I asked and Ace nodded.

"He's been around a long time, with a lot of contacts. He was going to take Nyland Harrison out for me, make it look like a nasty accident, but your father stopped me."

I stared at my grandfather. The man had constantly surprised me. I wasn't sure why this should have. He had made a living in the old days of poker, when often a gun was the only way to get your winnings out of a game, and the mob ruled Vegas. He knew his way in and around a lot of shady people.

"That was when Carson left," Ace said. "The three of us figured that if he pretended he didn't care about you or your mother, Harrison and his thugs would look for other ways to control him. He was right, it stopped at that point and never restarted until Carson died."

"We were going to tell you everything when you were in college," my mother said, tears filling her eyes. "We figured by then you would understand."

"I know," I said. "You didn't because Jeff Taylor was killed and you felt you couldn't."

Both my mother and Ace nodded.

Ace went on. "When you started winning tournaments and it became public knowledge that you and Carson hated each other, we let it go. It was the safest way to keep you out of this."

"And it worked right up until Dolan Chase became the president," I said. "Ten people started that poker game in 1982. There are only five still in the play left alive, since I have taken Carson's place in all this. I plan on winning this game."

"And how do you plan on doing that?" Ace asked.

"Assuming that Chase and Hanson are playing the same hand, that only leaves three suspects who have keys. R.A. Scott, Nyland Harrison, and the president. I have a plan to get two out of the three together for a showdown. And get the third party, the President, involved at the same time."

"You're losing me, kid," Ace said.

"Yeah, me too," Annie said.

"Aggression," I said. "With thought-through aggression. I'm going to assume, until we know different, that the killer is one of those three, and I'm going to go after the bastard and take him out of the game before he gets me."

"And just how the hell are you going to do that?" Fleet asked, looking very worried.

"Poker," I said, smiling at my partner. "A game of poker started all this, a game of poker will end it all."

CHAPTER FIFTY-ONE

LAS VEGAS, NEVADA. AUGUST 25

AROUND THE LIVING ROOM, they were all just staring at me as if I had lost what little sense I had to begin with.

"Okay," I said, "the plan is simply this. I'm going to use Carson's key as bait and lure whoever wants it into a trap."

"And just how are you going to do that without getting killed?" Annie asked. "Whoever wants those keys seems to have no fear of cold-blooded killing to get them. Very professional cold-blooded killings."

"As I said. Poker."

"I'm lost and getting very worried," Fleet said.

I laughed. "Look, we don't know which of these men is killing for the keys, or if it's someone else entirely. Right?"

Everyone nodded so I went on with the idea I had thought through in the poker tournament last night. "But we know that they each still have a key, and it's clear to me these keys mean a great deal to both R.A. and Nyland. Nyland because he started the cover-up, and R.A. because he visited me, more than likely on a chance I'd just give him my key to get rid of it."

"How does poker fit into this?" Annie asked. "I'm with Fleet. I'm still lost."

"I'm betting," I said, "that the two of them are willing to put the keys they own on the table and play me for them. I put up Carson's key, winner take all."

Ace nodded. "They'll play."

"I wouldn't," Fleet said.

"They will," I said. "Of that I have no doubt. I'm betting that one of them wants Carson's key enough to get it the way I'm willing to give it up. Both of them have hated each other for years, both are avid poker players. This all started over a poker game. I want to try to end it over one."

"Why will it end?" Annie asked. "Having only three keys is still no good if there are nine needed to get into that box."

"I agree," I said. "By my count, whoever is doing this has five keys right now, counting their own."

"Sure," Annie said. "And two are in the White House. I still don't see how this will end anything."

"It will end it for *us*," Ace said. "That's all that matters."

I nodded. "Ace is right. We're in danger because of my father's key. We get three of the available keys and destroy them in a public way, and we'll be safe."

"Or you lose the key," Fleet said, "and we win that way, as well, since whoever is behind the killings has no reason to hurt anyone here anymore."

"I'm going to win and put whoever is behind these murders away at the same time."

Fleet just looked disgusted. "Okay, I almost understood before you said that."

"By winning," I said, smiling. "It will drive the murderer to actions he will pay dearly for."

"That is *exactly* what I'm afraid of," Fleet said. "Why is that a good thing?"

"A sting?" Annie said. "Of course, a sting."

I smiled at her. She and I really did think alike at times. "A sting," I said, agreeing.

"What happens to this sting if you lose?" Fleet asked.

"I won't."

Ace laughed. "Oh, trust me, he won't lose."

Two hours later, I was ready to set the plan in action. We had talked it out, worked out details I hadn't thought of, then ran over the entire idea again, step-by-step. It was dangerous, but so was just sitting here waiting for someone to come and kill one of us for that stupid key.

"Ready?" I asked, glancing around. I was holding a phone in my hand and felt about as nervous as a beginning poker player going into a big tournament. I just hoped I wasn't dead money on this entire plan.

"Into the fire," Ace said.

"Make sure this call goes out on Mike's secured line," Annie said. "No telling who's listening out there."

"Yeah, Mike told me the house was being watched," I said.

"I noticed when we came in," Annie said. "More than likely your FBI friends. They looked Federal-level stupid."

"I hope they're the only ones watching," I said.

"Yeah, me too," Annie said.

I took a deep breath, then dialed the number R.A. had given me.

R.A. answered with a gruff, "Yes."

"Sir, it's Doc Hill. Would you be willing to meet me at my father's house for a meeting about the key?"

R.A. remained silent for a moment, then said, "Yes. That sounds like a good idea. Give me the address."

I gave him the address, then said, "My grandfather and my attorney will also be in on the meeting. Please come alone."

Again there was a pause. Then he said, "I'll be there within the hour," and hung up.

I made sure I had disconnected the phone, then nodded to everyone. "He's on his way."

My mother looked like she might just break down at any moment.

Ace was nodding and thinking.

"We better get a couple of Mike's people in here with us," Annie said, "just in case this goes sour right off."

"Well, that's confidence," Fleet said, looking very afraid and whiter than his normal pale skin.

I couldn't say that I blamed him.

CHAPTER FIFTY-TWO

LAS VEGAS, NEVADA. AUGUST 25

R.A. LOOKED a little nervous and sweaty as he came inside from the hot afternoon sun, leaving his limo outside running with the driver inside staying cool.

He had a good reason to be worried. I really had left him no choice. This was a logical continuation of the play for the key he had made yesterday when he approached me in the parking garage. For all he knew, I wanted to just give it to him now.

My mother was in her bedroom with one of Mike's guards. Mike and two of his men were stationed in the kitchen pantry and down the hall, out of sight. Annie was in Fleet's room, the closest to the living room. If something happened, there would be a lot of troops coming to the rescue.

Once we were settled in the living room, I got right to the point. "First let me be clear that neither of these men know what I'm about to suggest. This is my idea. I just wanted them here as witnesses to what we agree on."

R.A. nodded. "That sounds reasonable."

I went on. "I think we should set up a no limit hold'em poker game between you and me and Nyland Harrison with the keys as the stake to buy into the game. Winner take all three of the damn things."

R.A. sat back, staring at me, clearly surprised and thinking. So I went on, telling him the details.

"I suggest it would just be the three of us at your ranch in Idaho. I'll have a professional dealer come in with me so we make sure there's no cheating."

Annie had agreed to do the dealing in the game. Even though I didn't like the idea, she insisted that since this was basically a Las Vegas case, she had damn well better be on it. After ten minutes of arguing about it, I had caved in. The woman had a damn strong will.

"Why the ranch in Idaho? Why not here?" Fleet asked, following the script we had set up. I wanted Fleet to ask that question so that I could give an answer that would make sense to R.A.

"No one is there," I said. "I'll bet Nyland hasn't been back to the Big Game since that night in 1982, has he?"

"He hasn't," R.A. said, looking disgusted at the idea. "After what he did to your mother, he's never been invited."

"Good," I said. "I want Nyland to be as off balance as he can be. Returning to a place where he helped kill someone will put him in that state."

"So what exactly are the stakes?" Ace asked, just as he was supposed to.

"Nothing more than the keys," I said. "Nyland brings his key for the chance to play for my father's and R.A.'s keys."

"I'm not sure I want to give my key to Nyland," R.A. said. "In fact, I'm sure I don't."

"Trust me," I said. "You won't. I'll win the game and then I'll publicly destroy all three keys. No more reason for Nyland or whoever to kill anyone."

"And you're so sure you're going to win the game because?" R.A. asked.

"I do this for a living," I said.

R.A. was clearly *not* convinced. I didn't expect him to be at this point. He repeated what he told me the day before. "Nyland believes the keys are worth murdering for."

"So why take this kind of chance giving him your key?" Fleet asked me directly, right on script.

"A sting," I said. Just as R.A. had done with me, I was staying close to the truth. Just not giving it all. "During the game, we try to get Nyland to admit to at least one of the murders, or give us something we can track back to him."

"I'm an attorney," Fleet said, pretending to sit back and think. "And I have a few friends in Boise. I think I can make any recordings you get stand up in a court if I do a little preparation ahead of time and we watch the evidence chain of custody."

"I like *that* idea," R.A. said, smiling. "Get rid of that bastard once-and-for-all."

I never doubted that R.A. would like the idea. It played right into his desire to see his old enemy behind bars.

"If what you say is right about this man," Fleet said, "then he might try to kill you if you win the card game."

"I know," Doc said. "I'm planning that my winning will be what sets Nyland off so that he gives us the information we need to put him away. Don't worry, I can take care of myself."

R.A. nodded, buying into the trap. "And we destroy the keys when we have them all?"

"That is the idea."

"I'm in," R.A. said, standing and extending his hand to me.

I shook it, pretending I was happy to be doing so. Even for a professional poker player, that was a damn hard act to put on.

"When?"

"How about three days from today? Noon at your ranch."

"Sounds good. I'll set it up with Nyland," R.A. headed for the door. "I'll call you and let you know when he has agreed. But I have no doubt he will."

Neither did I.

Six hours later, I got the call.

"It's set," was all R.A. said.

SECTION THREE

A TURNING-POINT HAND

*At some point in every poker tournament,
a player must put everything at risk to advance.*

CHAPTER FIFTY-THREE

STEVEN JUST COULDN'T seem to stop laughing.

He walked outside his home into the warm evening air, trying to get himself back together by staring out over the rugged, pine-covered mountains and deep valleys that stretched into the distance. The sun was ducking behind a ridgeline of Mt. Shasta in the distance, filling the valleys around him with deep shadows while leaving the peaks bright with oranges and yellows. It was a beautiful time of the evening, a time he really enjoyed.

He took a deep breath and tried to calm down, but then the memory of the phone call with his father came back and he started laughing again.

He just couldn't believe it. Richard Scott had called his father to set up a poker game between Steven's father, Doc Hill, and himself.

And the stakes were their three keys.

Steven sat on a rock on the edge of a steep drop to an old construction site below and just laughed, the sound carrying out over the valley and the river below him. Finally, he managed to catch his breath.

The ironic thing was that Steven's father had called him and asked him to go along to the game, as a sort of second in the duel, as his stupid father had called it.

Somehow, Steven had managed to agree to go along without laughing, at least until he had hung up. Now, he just couldn't seem to stop.

His father had no idea who his own son had become.

While Steven was in jail for his father's mistakes, his pathetic father had told him about the keys and that night in 1982. He had spilled everything, including how he had forced the others to be part of the cover-up. It had been one of those far-too-regular soul-baring sessions his father had felt he needed and Steven had come to hate.

During that time, Dolan Chase was starting his run to the presidency, and his father had promised that when Chase got into office, he would pardon Steven because of the keys.

It hadn't happened. Steven had gotten himself out of the stupid minimum security prison on good behavior three months before Chase got elected.

Now Steven's father thought that by winning two of the keys at this game, he might get a start toward getting all the keys, and thus some business and respect back. His father had been a tyrant while running his own company. Now he was just plain delusional.

A lot of far more powerful people wanted control of those keys. And Steven was going to have that control.

Control over the President.

And just as important, or maybe even more, Steven would have control over the President's enemies.

His father didn't have the stomach for what it would take to get all the keys, or the knowledge of what to do with them when he got them.

But Steven did.

And, to his surprise, he was actually enjoying doing it. He seemed to have a special knack for killing, and the challenge of it was growing on him.

He thought about this special new session of the Big Game that Doc Hill had set up and that he was invited to and started laughing again.

It took him a good half hour until he stopped.

Chapter Fifty-Four

WHITE HOUSE, WASHINGTON, D.C. AUGUST 25

PRESIDENT DOLAN CHASE slammed down the phone, then stood and started pacing behind his desk in the oval office.

Paul stood in front of the desk looking pale and worried. "What happened?"

"Are the damn recorders off?"

Paul moved over to a control panel hidden under the bookcase and checked once more, then nodded. "They are."

"R.A. went into Carson's house and talked to Doc and Ace Hill. A couple Las Vegas detectives and other security people were in there as well, along with Doc's partner and lawyer."

"Oh, no," Paul said. "You think the kid gave him Carson's key? Does he even know what the keys go to?"

"He's not stupid," Dolan said, shaking his head at his best friend, then went back to pacing and talking. "Verne's injured, Doc is talking to R.A., and Ace is there now as well. I'm betting he knows everything."

"Oh, no," Paul said, moving over to a chair and slumping into it.

"I don't know what to think," Dolan said, frantically trying to work this through. "Any of them could do us some damage if we don't get them stopped."

"*Some* damage?" Paul said.

Dolan could hear the deep sarcasm in his voice.

"*Some* damage, like resigning from office, being tossed in jail?"

"Yeah, damage," Dolan said. "Blackmail at the least. God only knows what kind of damage could happen if someone on the other side got hold of this information and the proof. We've got to stop this, and stop this now!"

"And how do you suggest we do that?"

"Talk to that bastard Steven again. We need those keys here, in my hand, and I'm beginning to not care anymore what it takes to make that happen."

Paul started to say something when suddenly the phone line beeped.

"Get that, would you?" Dolan said.

He chewed on a few more Tums, then sat in his chair and leaned back, staring at the ceiling of the Oval Office. He had done that more than once so far in his short time as president. He had a hunch if he could stay in office, he would know every detail of that ceiling texture. No doubt many presidents over the years had stared at the exact same place.

Paul climbed slowly to his feet and picked up the phone . "Yes." Then a moment later, "Give me that name again and where exactly is he calling from?"

Dolan sat up and watched the puzzled and surprised look on his friend's face. Whatever this was, it had to be good.

Or very bad. In this office, you often couldn't tell which was which.

Finally, Paul nodded and said, "Put him through to this phone."

Paul leaned forward over the desk in the oval office and handed the phone to the President.

"It's Doc Hill, calling for you."

CHAPTER FIFTY-FIVE

LAS VEGAS, NEVADA. AUGUST 25

IT HAD ALREADY BEEN another long day, but there was still one more major detail to set in motion. There was one more player in this game that had to be invited to the table. And I was the only one who could do it.

I sat in the living room, across from Fleet, with the phone in my hand, thinking.

Actually, stalling.

Annie had left shortly after R.A. called back, and both Ace and my mother were taking a nap before dinner. The house had suddenly felt empty when Annie left. I wasn't sure what to make of that feeling. Clearly, I was growing to like having her at my side.

She hadn't much liked the idea that I wanted two of Mike's men shadowing her.

"Remember, I'm the god-damned police here?" she had said, getting angry at the suggestion.

I told her I didn't care what she was, and that had started a pretty good shouting match, with us standing face-to-face. I finally said that she had no choice if she intended on helping with all this. I wasn't going to take a chance on anyone getting her any more than getting anyone else around me. So it was either guards watching her, or she could just step out and not come back until this was over.

She had finally accepted the guards shadowing her. Mike promised they would stay out of her way as she left and all she had done was grunt.

We had all decided that going back to the Bellagio for a late dinner made as much sense as anything, since we hadn't stocked the house with food. Mike and his people said they could keep us safe and an eye on the house while we were gone. Annie said she would join us.

I looked at the phone in my hand again. I was really looking forward to getting all this over with, so I could just get back to playing poker.

I glanced at Fleet, who was sitting across from me in the living room, waiting for me to do what I needed to do.

"Butterflies?" he asked.

"Not really," I said, smiling. "Just worried that this call may end up getting one of us killed. More than likely me."

"And that doesn't give you butterflies?" Fleet asked.

"Butterflies are way too small for the worry I'm feeling. Bats. Large flying rodents swirling in my stomach."

"I'll match your bats and raise you a dozen more," Fleet said.

I looked at the secure phone in my hand, then dialed the number that Mike had found for me. It was a direct number into the White House, past the first levels of switchboards. I had no idea how he got it, and not in a million years would I have ever thought I would call the White House.

I got an operator, a woman with a nice voice and a charming way.

"I'm calling for Paul Hanson. Emergency business. My name is Doc Hill."

"I will connect you to his office." the operator said.

"Got through to the office," I whispered to Fleet.

246

"Step one," he whispered back.

A moment later another woman answered the phone. "Paul Hanson's office."

"My name is Doc Hill. I am calling for the President or Mr. Hanson."

"Would you please tell me what this matter is about and I will get you to the appropriate party?"

"Just give Mr. Hanson or the President my name," I said. "They will want to talk to me."

"I'm afraid both Mr. Hanson and the President are very busy men."

"I understand that," I said. "I am a very old friend of the family and this is an emergency. Just tell either one of them I am on the line and one of them will talk to me. I am calling from Las Vegas, Nevada. Please tell one of them. I'll hold."

Fleet had bet me that I wouldn't get through, especially at almost ten in the evening in Washington. I figured there was no way I wouldn't get through to at least Hanson. Not with what had been happening and how much those two men had to lose.

I sat, waiting as the phone clicked a few times.

"Doc," President Dolan Chase said, coming on the line. "I'm surprised and pleased at your call. I sure hope you don't mind being recorded. Most phone calls coming in here are, you know."

I liked how he had warned me about the taping system, to make sure I didn't say anything that could get him or me into trouble.

I gave Fleet the thumbs-up.

"Not at all, Mr. President. And thank you for taking my call."

Fleet's eyes got about twice their size and he started shaking his head back and forth like he couldn't believe any of this.

"Your father was a very good friend of mine," President Chase said. "I'm sure sorry about what happened to him."

"That's the reason for my call, sir," I said. "I am throwing a very special poker game in honor of Carson at R.A.'s ranch in Idaho."

"Really?" the President said. The tone of his voice had suddenly lost some of its phony political friendliness. "Who is playing?"

"Just R.A., Nyland Harrison, and myself. I know you can't join us because of your schedule, but I wanted to let you know, since you and my father had so much history between you."

There was a long silence on the line, then the President came back. "This sounds very interesting, and a fitting tribute to your father. What are your stakes?"

"Just some old keys," I said. "No money. You could say we're playing for a piece of history."

Again a longer-than-normal pause, then the president asked in a soft voice that had a lot of power behind it, "What would you do with a bunch of old keys?"

"Oh," I said, keeping my voice as light and as upbeat as I could do under the circumstances, "I'm not after the keys, just answers."

"What kind of answers?" he asked.

"Basic ones, sir," I said. "I hope this game helps me learn what happened to my father, and Verne Adkins and Benson James and Aaron Bell and Kevin DeFoe and Jeff Taylor."

Now the silence seemed so loud that my ears were ringing as I strained to hear anything from the other end of the line.

Finally, after a long ten seconds, the President said, "I hope it helps you find those answers as well."

He did not sound sincere.

"I'm sure you understand," the President said, "how much of a friend your father was to me."

With him repeating what he had said earlier, I knew I had accomplished what I had set out to do. I had made sure that even if he wasn't actually sitting in the game up in Idaho in three days, he would be there.

"Yeah, I do," I said, now not holding the sarcasm from my voice. "I got the flowers."

With that, I hung up on the President of the United States.

CHAPTER FIFTY-SIX

IDAHO PRIMITIVE AREA. AUGUST 26

ANNIE HAD NEVER HAD A TRIP like the one she had just finished.

At four in the morning, as the sun was just breaking over the hills, and the air still felt almost cool in comparison to the daytime temperatures, she and Mike had boarded a very swank Gulfstream private jet that was waiting for them at the Las Vegas airport.

The plane had an oak-trimmed interior, large, comfortable leather recliner chairs, a dining-room-sized table, and a flight attendant named Dan to serve her and Mike breakfast. And it was as good a breakfast as she had had in years.

She and Mike talked for a short time during breakfast about the Las Vegas police, then he laid out one of the chairs and went to sleep.

She managed to do the same twenty minutes later, giving herself time to enjoy her first flight on a private corporate jet.

This was Doc's plane, Fleet had told her, or actually it was owned by one of the many corporations Doc and Fleet owned. From what she had read, Doc and Fleet controlled a lot of companies and assets. Looking around this plane, she finally understood how great the rich had it.

And she liked it. What was there not to like?

The flight attendant woke them as the plane made its approach into the Boise airport.

Next, they had boarded a single-engine Cessna for the second leg of their flight, a fairly bumpy two-hour flight over some of the most rugged mountains she had ever imagined seeing up close. And sometimes the pilot got way too close for her taste.

She sat in the back seat behind Mike, trying to focus on the horizon so she wouldn't get airsick. Somehow, she held that ugliness off.

By nine in the morning, Las Vegas time, the small plane bounced to a landing on a small, rough excuse for a landing strip five miles below R.A.'s ranch.

Doc had given her a map with a trail marked on it, but basically all they had to do was follow the river upstream. She had asked Doc to let her look at a picture of R.A.'s ranch house to make sure they found the right one, even though Doc said it was the only house within twenty miles. She just found that hard to imagine.

Now, she and Mike stood to one side of the runway, their equipment and packs at their feet as the small plane took off, barely clearing tall pines at the end of the short runway.

As the sound of the plane died away, the intense silence closed in around her like a blanket.

She had been a Las Vegas native, born and raised. Las Vegas never slept, and the noise of the city went on all the time.

Here, there was nothing, no humans, no cars, no loud tourists. Nothing but crisp, cool morning air and silence.

A lot of silence.

And the air tasted and felt so fresh and clear and pure, it was almost like eating a wonderful dessert after a perfect meal.

She looked around slowly, taking it all in. The steep mountains, the forest, the intense blue sky. Now she understood why Doc came up here every summer. Maybe next summer she could join him for a trip.

She pushed that thought away at once. Until all this was settled, there would be no time for anything between her and Doc. And that also assumed he was interested.

"Never thought I'd see the day I missed the sounds of bumper-to-bumper traffic," Mike said, looking around at the tall peaks that closed the valley in. "This could get creepy."

"I kind of like it."

Mike just shook his head. "So, which way, Detective?"

The river was on the left of the airstrip as they landed, and the pilot had pointed out R.A.'s ranch as they flew in, so she knew exactly where to go.

"That way," she said, pointing to the opposite end of the runway that the plane had just left.

Three and a half very long hours later, they were in the trees at the end of R.A.'s private air strip, sweating, out of breath and hurting. It had been the longest and the toughest five miles she had ever walked. No wonder Doc always seemed to be in such top shape. She thought she had been as well, until she came into these mountains.

Mike was looking a little pale and she forced him to take some water, then down a large bottle of Gatorade and a salt tablet. Even though the temperature had to be thirty degrees cooler than Vegas, it still felt damned hot.

Doc had warned her at dinner last night that the hike would be tough, and that they needed to go slowly and take enough water. She had brushed his worries aside. After all, how tough could five miles be to someone as in shape as she was?

Stupid question. Five miles of a rough, uphill trail at eight thousand feet elevation. Now she knew. And she had a whole new respect for those hikers who could carry heavy packs and do ten miles a day. That should be an Olympic sport.

After resting, Mike looked better, so they worked their way up through the trees toward the house. Supposedly, R.A. had closed the place up for the winter when he left. But they were going to take no chances.

They scouted completely around the ranch, moving slowly and carefully. No plane, no sign of anyone at all.

At the single-story ranch house made of logs, they found a window into a dining area and she went to work on trying to open it without leaving any traces.

Beside her, Mike kept glancing around.

"You all right?" she asked.

"Sure, I just don't like going into a house without the proper paper-work is all, *Detective*."

She laughed and kept working on the window. "Don't worry, this isn't the first time I've gone into a place without the correct warrant."

"I'm not sure I wanted to know that," he said.

Once inside, they found the way into the house's attic space through a trap door in a bedroom closet ceiling. Mike barely fit through with his massive shoulders, but with her pushing, he made it.

In the attic, Mike set up the recording equipment.

Annie was impressed at the quality of the listening devices, and the fact that Mike was taking no chances in a machine not working. He set up three of them, in different hidden places in the attic, and used wires to run to the sensitive mikes he put down through the ceiling and into the light fixtures.

They had every room in the house wired within two hours, and within another hour, Mike had a satellite up-link working to send all conversation out of the house at the same time that it was being recorded.

Everything said in the house for the next three days would be recorded here, and listened to live in Boise. She had no idea how Fleet was going to be able to get any of this legally accepted in any court, but for the moment, she was going to leave that up to him.

By four in the afternoon, they were just finished policing the house to make sure they had left no traces. Suddenly, the sounds of a small plane broke through the stillness.

"We've got company," Annie said as they both stood listening to the plane circle and start its approach to the narrow runway cut out of the pine trees. "A day early."

As the plane landed and taxied to the other end of the runway, hidden from their view, they locked the window, went out the front door, locking it behind them, and headed for the river. They followed a nasty trail down from the house along a cliff face to the river's edge, then turned upstream toward where rafts put into the river in the spring. Someone would be waiting for them there.

"Too close," Mike said, glancing back.

The ranch couldn't be seen at all from where they were, and if anyone saw them, Annie was convinced they would just look like hikers with their backpacks working their way along the river.

But it had been far too close. With that, she had to agree.

CHAPTER FIFTY-SEVEN

IDAHO PRIMITIVE AREA. AUGUST 28

GAME DAY.

It was eleven in the morning, Mountain Time, when I climbed out of the small Cessna and helped Annie out. We moved over to the edge of R.A.'s runway to give the plane room to turn and taxi for a takeoff. The sun was hot, the air clear, the sky a deep blue you only see at high altitudes in the mountains.

It felt great being back in the wilderness area again, back in the fresh air and the peacefulness of everything here. It had only been a couple of weeks since I had left, but it felt like it had been a lifetime.

Now, instead of fighting the river and dangerous rapids, I was in a completely different fight for survival. And just like in the rapids, losing was not an option.

We watched the plane take off, then as the sound faded away, replaced by the faint rustling sound of the wind in the pine trees, I turned to Annie. She was dressed like a Las Vegas dealer in a white blouse and black slacks, and carried a rack of professional chips and a number of decks of cards, still factory sealed.

"This place is really something," she said, taking a deep breath and letting it out slowly.

"It doesn't come any more beautiful," I said. "You ready?"

"As I'll ever be," she said.

I was worried about her being in this dangerous a situation, and had said something about it to Ace. He had just laughed. "She's a Las Vegas Detective," he had said. "Trust me, you're the wimp of the pair."

I just hoped he was right. Last thing I wanted was her getting hurt, and no matter how much we had prepared for this, someone getting hurt or killed might just happen.

We walked over the rough ground past R.A.'s plane and his maintenance sheds toward the big house. There was no sign of anyone.

We had listened to everything that had gone on in R.A.'s house since the moment Mike and Annie had gotten back to Boise two days ago and Mike had set up the listening equipment base station for the satellite link in Ace's home. My mother, Ace, and Fleet were there now, well-protected by Mike's people and a number of Annie's father's Cold Poker Gang.

It seemed that when Ace offered Annie's father and a bunch of his retired detective friends the opportunity to come up to his house and play a little cards, none of them could turn him down. I just hoped Ace kept in mind those guys were retired detectives and living on pensions.

R.A. had remained clearly alone during the last two days, and had seemed to be in a good mood.

He met us at the door and shook both our hands, not really paying any attention to Annie at all, or even asking anything about her. We had prepared a very intricate story for her, but it seemed R.A. just didn't care.

Now it was my turn on stage.

I pulled out of a carrying case a small recorder, and while Annie set up the table, stacking the chips and getting ready, I showed R.A. how the recorder worked and asked him where we should put it.

He suggested an end table, and I hid it there in a drawer with the microphone tucked behind a lamp, then tested it.

R.A. seemed pleased that it worked. He, of course, knew nothing of the ones Mike had planted, and the entertainment we were offering everyone back at Ace's house.

As we were finishing, the sound of another small plane filled the area and a few minutes later Nyland Harrison's plane taxied up and let him and another man off near R.A.'s plane.

My first impression as Nyland came up on the porch was of a sick, old man, far too thin. His hair was gray and what little hair that was left was thin, showing age-mottled scalp. He had pasty-white skin and a toothy smile that he flashed far too often, with no real laughter behind it.

With him was his son, Steven.

Steven looked to be in his mid-forties and just flat scared hell out of me. I had been around some cold, mean animals before, and that was the impression Steven gave off. His dark eyes were dead-looking, and his powerfully built frame looked flat dangerous. Every internal alarm I had went off when I shook his hand.

And it took everything I could do to not wipe off my hand until he turned his back.

All Steven did was nod and smile at me, as if just shaking my hand amused him in some way.

Nyland and R.A. clearly hated each other, and didn't even bother to shake hands or speak in any way. It was clear that just getting either of these two men to talk wasn't going to be easy. I was going to have to push them.

Inside, I laid out the structure of the tournament, that each key was worth $500,000 in chips as a buy-in. The blinds were $1,000/$2,000 and would remain constant.

I took out Carson's card capper, clicked open the bottom, and took the key out. I placed it on the fireplace mantel and Annie slid $500,000 chips to a spot in front of my chair.

R.A. bought in as well, then so did Nyland, both without a word.

Now three of the keys were together on the fireplace mantel waiting for the winner to claim them.

It was time for me to go to work.

CHAPTER FIFTY-EIGHT

STEVEN WATCHED as the three men took their seats at the poker table. He had taken a bar stool and moved over against the wall across from the door, with his back to the wall.

Why men like R.A. and his father thought they had any chance in a poker game against a top professional player was beyond Steven. They were just throwing money after their egos and hoping that luck might help them.

Steven didn't believe in luck. He believed in careful planning and perfect execution. Luck should never play a part in anything.

This entire game just seemed funny, and a couple times as they were putting their keys on the mantel and getting chips, he had had a tough time just not laughing.

Doc Hill wasn't funny, though. The man looked hard and tough, and clearly didn't like or trust Steven. Doc was the only one who was a real challenge in the bigger game of getting the keys. Steven had underestimated Doc the first time by sending that idiot thug.

Steven would not do that again.

No doubt, this entire invitation to a poker game in the woods for the control of the keys had a dozen traps in it. Steven could think of at least a half dozen he could use here. More than likely, every word they were saying was being recorded, both by Doc and by R.A. It wasn't like that man to leave anything uncovered.

But his idiot father had been stupid enough to just walk into all this. The idiot didn't even realize he was the prime suspect in the murders of his old card-playing companions, and all this was more than likely being staged for his benefit.

There was an old saying in poker that is almost always true. If you look around a poker table and can't see the sucker, then more than likely you are it. Steven knew exactly who the sucker was in this game. His father.

Steven, on the other hand, was here to watch. At least for a while. He wanted to see the conclusion of what Doc Hill was planning before killing both R.A. and Doc and that pretty dealer as well, and then taking all the keys. It was nice of Doc to make Steven's task easier by getting these three keys together.

Wouldn't his idiot father be surprised when Steven killed everyone?

Surprised for a moment at least, right before he died as well.

The thought almost made Steven laugh.

Almost.

At the table, the first hand was being dealt. The game had begun.

CHAPTER FIFTY-NINE

IDAHO PRIMITIVE AREA, AUGUST 28

I WAS REALLY GLAD that neither R.A. nor Nyland had asked about Annie. She seemed invisible to them, and she was managing to stay that way as any good professional dealer did, dealing flawlessly, not saying anything, directing what action that needed to be directed by simply pointing.

Within the first ten hands, I got a sense of the two different styles of the two men. R.A. was reckless, and aggressive, and Nyland was careful and conservative.

I moved slowly, draining off a few chips here and there by making bad calls just to get information about the two of them. I watched how they moved, how they bet, taking in their patterns, hand motions, looks, and everything.

After about a half hour, I had a pretty good sense of both players. R.A. was up slightly, about fifty thousand, and I was down about the same amount, but no one had moved very far from our original stacks.

At the hour mark, when Nyland got up to go to the restroom, the chip situation was the same, but by then I knew how these two men played, and how to get to either of them.

I would have to work on R.A. first, let him give most of his chips to me, then go to work on Nyland. R.A. was too dangerous and wild of a player to leave in the game and try to control.

During the second hour, I stayed out of Nyland's way when he raised a hand, which wasn't that often, but I pushed R.A.

It was a simple professional's way of draining money from someone who thought they could play. I made him call small- to mid-sized bets with weak hands, and then fold when I pushed him with a larger bet on the next card.

Most players didn't notice this kind of grinding away of their chips, but when they suddenly did look down and realize their stacks were shrinking, they got in a hurry and made even worse decisions.

R.A. did exactly that. It was no wonder Carson had been able to take him for so much money.

Plus R.A. had a really nasty tell, one so basic it was in Caro's *Book of Tells*. When he had a strong hand, he sat back. Every time. When he had a weak hand and was in some action, he sat forward, as if paying more attention would help him figure out what to do with the hand.

So I stayed away from him when he had a strong hand, and ground at his chips when he was weak.

During the first two hours, neither man said much except to swear when they lost a hand.

Annie dealt flawlessly.

Steven just sat with his back against the wall, watching. He seemed to find the entire thing just flat-out funny. I wished I had a half-second of privacy to talk with Annie about her impressions of Steven as well. I had a hunch she was watching him the same way I was.

It was close to the end of the third hour and R.A. was getting panicked by his small stack of chips. I was in the big blind. Nyland had folded on the button, and the action was to R.A.

He glanced down and then, leaning forward in his chair, just called.

I looked at my hand. A pair of black tens.

The right play was to raise, but I knew R.A. had a weak hand and would fold if I did. I figured it was worth the shot at getting the right flop and trapping him, so I just checked.

Annie burned a card and turned the flop.

Ten, king, six, all rainbow suits.

I had flopped a set, but by the way R.A. sat back and stared at the board, I bet he had hit his king. And he might have had a six as a kicker, which gave him two pair.

Finally he bet out ten thousand.

I looked at the flop for a moment, then just called, still working the trap. From the looks of R.A.'s stack, he had about two hundred thousand left. If I did this right, I'd have that two hundred thousand in my pile very shortly.

Annie burned and put the turn card on the table.

Six of hearts. The exact perfect card for what I was doing. The heart matched the ten of hearts on the board, gave me a full house, and more than likely gave him a full house. Just a smaller one.

Every action R.A. was taking told me he had a really strong hand. If he could lean back any farther, he'd tip his chair over backwards.

The best hand he could have after his opening call was king-six which gave him sixes full of kings. He would have raised with a pair of sixes, or a pair of kings, so I didn't put him on either of those hands. My tens full of sixes beat him every day. He only had the two kings and the one six left in the deck that would save him.

He put about fifty thousand into the pot and then looked at me, smiling.

"Well," I said after a moment, "looks like you're going to get some of your chips back, but I have to call. I have too many outs."

I slid a matching stack into the pot.

I wanted him to think I was on a flush draw for the hearts.

The river was a five of hearts, putting a heart flush possible on the board. I sure hoped he thought I was on a flush draw and had hit it. That would make him greedy and reckless.

He bet out another fifty thousand, leaving himself with about a hundred thousand.

I raised all in, forcing him to put all his chips into the pot.

He just smiled and said, "Call. Hit that heart draw, huh, Doc?"

He flipped over king-six as I expected.

"Nope," I said, turning over my pocket tens.

He stared at the two cards for a moment, then exploded from the table. Without so much as a swear word, he turned and stormed off into the kitchen.

Annie pushed the pot toward me, as well as the rest of R.A.'s chips that were still in front of his chair.

Nyland only nodded.

Steven laughed.

R.A. came back with a drink in his hand while I was still gathering and stacking his chips. He pulled his chair four or five feet away from the table and dropped into it.

"Nice play," he said to me.

"Thanks."

I had about nine hundred thousand in chips, Nyland had the other six hundred thousand.

Now the real game was on.

CHAPTER SIXTY

IDAHO PRIMITIVE AREA. AUGUST 28

WITH R.A. OUT OF THE GAME, I switched gears and strategy completely. Where before I had been staying out of Nyland's way, I now pushed him by raising almost every hand.

And I went from being a silent player to chattering, playing with my chips, moving around in my chair. I had no doubt that would put him off guard. After three hours of playing cards with the man, he didn't look stable enough to handle quick actions and confusion around him.

So I had to throw confusion at him in every way I could.

Also, neither he nor R.A. had said a word that would be worth anything, so now it was my job to get Nyland upset, get him talking to the tape machines.

"So," I said, after I had raised five straight hands and he had folded every one of them. "You're just going to let me drain off your chips by taking all your blinds. At this rate, that will take until about seven in the morning."

He said nothing.

"I have the time. I'll get the keys either way."

He looked at his cards, then raised the bet to ten thousand.

I had nothing, so I reraised him another fifty thousand.

He stared at his cards and folded.

"Good, with bets like that it's only going to take until about midnight."

He glared at me. Out of the corner of my eye I could see his son Steven just shaking his head.

"So, beating up on my mother had to be some fun for you," I said as he looked at his next two cards.

He glanced up at me, clearly shocked that I would say such a thing.

"What?" I asked, pretending to look at the two garbage cards I had in my hand. "We're here to play for the keys. You don't think I know how you made it all happen? Wouldn't it have been more fun to just beat up on me? After all, I was six. Wouldn't that have made a better point to everyone?"

"I did what needed to be done," he said, pushing in a ten thousand raise.

I slapped my cards down hard on the table like I was angry.

Annie pushed him the pot.

I waited until we both had our cards again before saying anything more.

"We?" I asked. "Man, I've been told by everyone that it was just your idea."

"It was my idea," Nyland said. "But others agreed."

"My father didn't, so he had to be held in line by beating up on my mother," I said, pretending to be disgusted as I pushed in a ten thousand raise.

"There was a great deal at stake," Nyland said, his voice cold.

He called my raise, then put his hand on his cards. It was one of his tells that he had a very strong hand. More than likely a big pair.

"Yeah, I'm sure there was. Now people are dying because of your idea."

He said nothing, but I could tell I had him a little rattled.

I had a nine-jack off-suit. I was going to need some help very quickly on this hand, and even then it might not be enough if he had a big pair, which I was betting he did. More than likely I was going to have to make some big show of laying this hand down.

But thankfully, the flop was the help I needed.

Eight, ten, queen, all different suits.

I had flopped the nut straight. In heads-up play, this was a monster hand. I checked.

Nyland bet out fifty thousand, one of the biggest bets he had made so far.

I pretended to think about it for a minute, then I just called.

The river came a two of diamonds, with no flush possible at all on the board.

My hand was still the nuts. I was starting to feel like Johnny Chan must have felt against Eric Seidel in the World Series of Poker finals. He had a hidden straight and won the entire thing by trapping Seidel. A classic play. So classic, someone actually put it into a movie.

This was the same situation. It came up regularly in tournaments, especially in short-handed situations, and I loved being on the winning side of it.

I checked, shaking my head, pretending to be really angry at the conversation.

I glanced back at R.A. "Man, someday you're going to have to explain to me why beating a young mother and keeping this secret for all these years is worth the slap-on-the-wrist that would have happened if you had all just gone to the police at the time."

R.A. said nothing. He knew about the tape recorder I had brought with me.

I turned back to Nyland. "So, why was it worth it?"

He ignored me and bet out another $50,000. Now I had no doubt he had a big pair, maybe kings or aces.

I shoved a stack in hard as an angry call, letting him think he was just taking my money because I was upset.

I was trying to be careful to not say anything on the tape to give away what exactly the secret was. I wanted Nyland and R.A. to do it. But I had to keep pushing him.

"So, it's too hard to tell me, huh? Just easier to beat up on some woman. A real manly thing that was. Oh, that's right, you didn't even have the courage to do it. You ordered it done. I bet you were proud of that for years."

Annie burned a card and turned over the river card.

Ace.

Jack-king was now the only hand that could beat me, but I knew that he didn't have that. More than likely the ace had given him a set. At least I hoped it did. If he had pocket kings, that ace was going to slow him down. Either way, I still had him beat.

I was first to act.

"I'm tired of sitting across the table from a man who beat up my mother. Let's just get this over with."

I pushed all my chips toward the center, scattering some of them.

"All in," I said.

If he had the aces, he would call.

Nyland actually had the gall to look up and smile at me.

"I call," he said, turning over his pocket aces.

"Too bad," I said, smiling right back at him.

I rolled over my cards. "Straight to the queen," I said. "Looks like your sick dream of controlling the world has come to a very bad end yet again."

I had done my job. I had won the keys.

Now it was show time.

CHAPTER SIXTY-ONE

IDAHO PRIMITIVE AREA. AUGUST 28

NYLAND STARED at my two cards for a moment, then at the board, then back at my two cards, his pasty-white face getting red. Then he slid his chair back and stood.

I stood at the same time, moving back slightly so I could see everyone in the room.

Nyland strode over to the fireplace, picked up the keys and put all three in his jacket pocket, as if that was what was expected of him.

"Hey!" R.A. said, starting toward Nyland.

I reached out and stopped him.

Steven just stayed seated, shaking his head like he was amused at the entire scene. Nyland had brought his kid for a reason, and I had a hunch I was about to see what the reason was.

Annie stayed seated as well, the cards in her hand as she did her best to make no sounds and pretend she wasn't watching. I knew she was, and that she was ready to move the moment she needed to.

"Look," Nyland said, turning to face us all, a sickly smile on his face, "we all know that you two came here to give me your keys before something unfortunate happened to either one of you."

Out of the corner of my eye, I could see Steven shaking his head in disgust.

"Like what happened to my father?" I asked.

"That wasn't me," Nyland said. "I haven't killed anyone."

"Except the hundred-and-some people below a dam you and that incompetent son of yours built," R.A. said, glaring at Nyland, but ignoring the fact that Steven was right there in the room as well.

Steven sort of froze up, but still did not move off the bar stool.

Nyland glared back at R.A. and said nothing. Two old bulls in a stand-off.

"Why do you need the keys anyway?" I asked, trying to get one of them to say something for the tapes. "You still can't open the box."

"Oh, there are ways of getting the others," Nyland said. He continued to glare at R.A. "How about you? Why do you want them?"

R.A. took a step toward Nyland, and this time I didn't move to stop him.

Nyland shook his head at R.A. "I wouldn't."

Nyland looked just about as mean as they came.

Steven still had not moved.

R.A. hesitated, glanced at Steven, then back at Nyland.

"Nice playing with you, gentlemen," Nyland said, backing toward the door. "And kid. You're a better player than your old man ever was. Come on, Steven."

"You know we're not going to let you get away from here with those keys," I said.

"Oh, I think your grandfather will tell you right about now that you should let me go. Why don't you call him."

"You kidnapped Ace?"

"Let's just say I borrowed him until I get out of here."

I hoped that Nyland's voice was loud enough for the recording equipment. Even if we didn't get much on the murders from him, we now had him for kidnapping.

"But that's not going to stop me," R.A. said.

"Have you talked to your wife lately?" Nyland asked, glaring at R.A.

A second kidnapping charge. Nyland was burying himself and he didn't even know it.

Steven sighed and shook his head, as if his father was just a child who had gotten into some stupid problem.

R.A. moved to a satellite phone on a side desk and made a call.

"Put it on speaker phone," Nyland said, smiling.

I so wanted to just wipe that smile forever off his face with my fist, but I stayed where I was. He was soon going to a place that there would be more than enough people to make sure he never smiled like that again.

A woman answered.

"Dannie, are you all right?" R.A. asked, a real touch of concern in his voice.

"Fine, dear. But two men were arrested a short time ago trying to break into the house. It was kind of scary. Both are now talking to the police and everything's fine."

I let out a slow, silent sigh of relief. The police there had done their job. I had warned them what might happen and they promised to put men stationed around R.A.'s house and guard his wife.

"I'll be home shortly," R.A. said. "Don't go out."

"No plans to," she said.

He hung up.

The smile was gone from Nyland's face. He looked like he might just be sick.

I moved the few steps to the phone and dialed Ace's number, then put it on speaker phone as well.

"How's it going there?" I asked when he answered. I had no doubt everything was fine, but I had to play the hand out for Nyland.

"I've got a sum total of twelve bucks off that Cold Poker Gang of yours. They are the tightest damned players I've ever tried to pry a dime out of. And that Bayard Lott is a real player."

"Had any visitors?" I asked, keeping my eye on both Nyland and Steven, just in case they made a move during the call.

"Oh, yeah, that," Ace said. "Three idiots tried to break into my house while we were in the basement playing cards."

"What happened to them?" I asked.

"Last I heard, they were down at the police station singing some song-and-dance about some rich guy hiring them to kidnap me, if you can believe that. So, how's it going there?"

"I'll tell you all about it when I get back," I said, and hung up.

I turned back to Nyland. "My guess is that they are not going to let you keep those keys where you are going."

Chapter Sixty-Two

IDAHO PRIMITIVE AREA. AUGUST 28

"FATHER, YOU ARE as stupid as they come these days," Steven said.

I watched as Nyland stood like a child who was being forced to come inside when he wanted to play. The guy looked like he might just throw a tantrum at any moment. Or break down and start to cry.

I was betting on the tantrum.

"All I have to do is start talking," Nyland said, panic making his voice squeak. "Tell them what happened here in 1982."

"And not a soul is going to believe you," R.A. said. He stepped over to a small writing desk, opened a drawer, and pulled a silver-plated pistol from the desk.

He pointed it at Nyland. "Because you're not going to have those keys for long."

I had had no doubt that a gun or two were going to make an appearance. It had been my biggest fear, and now we were facing it. Annie and I neither one had brought a gun. Too many risks of being searched by one or the other of the players.

"Put the keys on the table," R.A. said to Nyland. "I've buried one man in these hills. I can bury another."

I had no doubt that statement was causing some comments from everyone who was listening. I was sure R.A. just figured he would destroy the tape on the recorder I brought for his scam.

Nyland stared at his old enemy for a moment, then with a glance at the gun, took the keys and put them on the table.

R.A. glanced at me, but kept the gun focused on Nyland as he picked up the keys. He pushed at something hidden in his shirt pocket. "Trust me, I was always going to leave with these keys."

Steven just sat, shaking his head, clearly trying to keep from laughing. I had no idea what he was finding so funny, but clearly he thought all this amusing.

I glanced at Annie. She was sitting, poised, ready to move in any direction she needed to.

I turned back to R.A. I still had a little work to do. "What do you mean by that?"

"You didn't really think I would just let you destroy the keys, did you?" R.A. asked. The he glanced at the front door.

The door was staying closed.

"You waiting for someone?" I asked. "Not too many people up on this part of the river this time of the year."

R.A. pulled out a small device from his shirt pocket, looked at it, and then pushed on it. Then he turned to the front door, expecting it to open.

Nothing.

The silence in the room was almost painful.

I had had no doubt that either R.A. or Nyland, or more than likely both would have people outside, people that got into this remote area in other ways. They weren't the types to leave things alone.

Now, clearly Nyland had expected to just walk away because of his kidnapping trick. So only R.A. had people out there.

"Actually," I said, after I let the silence drag on long enough to make R.A. squirm, "I don't think either of you is going anywhere but to jail."

I walked past the stunned R.A. and opened the door. It was black dark like it can only get in the trees in the mountains. Clearly the moon wasn't up above the ridgeline yet.

"Any problems out there?" I shouted into blackness.

"No, sir," a voice shouted back. I recognized it as Valley County Sheriff Ray Hendricks. "We managed to capture five wolves with big bites lurking in the trees and have them penned in the plane maintenance shed, if you'd care to see."

"Thanks," I said as he came up onto the porch out of the darkness.

I stepped back inside, making room for him to come in. "I think there are two more wolves inside here that need to join their friends in the pen, don't you?"

"From what I heard going on in here, I'd sure say so," the sheriff said, smiling at the two men and tapping an earplug showing them that he has been listening in.

"Father," Steven said from his bar stool, "you know you really *are* a complete idiot."

CHAPTER SIXTY-THREE

IDAHO PRIMITIVE AREA. AUGUST 28

"HANDS BEHIND YOUR BACKS, GENTLEMAN," the sheriff said, flashing two pair of handcuffs. "You're under arrest for attempted kidnapping, extortion, attempted murder, and as many other murders as we can pin on you both. And from the sounds of things, I guess I better start looking for that body you mentioned burying, Mr. Scott."

"I don't think so," R.A. said. He waved the gun at the sheriff. "I still have control here."

Before I had a chance to ask R.A. just where he thought he was going, and why compound the mess with even more charges, Nyland shouted, "No! I won't go to jail."

Moving very fast for an old guy, Nyland yanked a pistol out of his suit pocket and fired it at R.A., hitting him squarely in the chest.

The force of the shot slammed R.A. back against the wall.

The shot seemed as loud as a canon going off inside the contained space.

I moved instantly, since I was the closest to the crazy old man. Before he could get his gaze off of R.A.'s falling body and focus a shot on anyone else, I smashed the gun from his hand.

The weapon banged across the wooden floor toward the fireplace.

Annie dove for it, rolling once and coming up in a professional firing posture with the gun in her hands.

Steven hadn't moved from his bar stool, his back against the wall, his eyes cold and watching everything.

Nyland spun around. Then, holding his injured hand, he shoved the sheriff into me.

We staggered together toward the wall.

"Stop!" Annie shouted.

Nyland ignored her and bolted through the open front door, down the porch stairs, and along the trail headed for the river.

"Where the hell does he think he's going?" the sheriff asked as we untangled ourselves, then went for the door to follow Nyland.

By the time I reached the trail, Nyland had disappeared into the darkness.

The sheriff was right behind me as I started down the trail toward the river, doing my best to keep my feet. I had been on this trail a few times. I doubted Nyland knew the way well enough to make it very far in the dark.

The sheriff pounded along behind me, the bouncing beam of his flashlight giving me just enough light to see where I was going.

Suddenly, there was a scream from the dark trees ahead.

An ugly scream, like an animal trapped.

A few long moments later, crashing brush and a sickening thud echoed through the night.

That did not sound good.

I slowed, moving carefully to where the trail neared a sharp drop down to the river, then turned hard right. I was betting that Nyland hadn't made the turn.

"Slow down, Ray," I said to the huffing man behind me. The last thing I needed was him shoving me over the edge, and besides that, I didn't want him to have a heart attack right here in the middle of everything.

Carefully, we approached the turn in the trail.

In the beam of the sheriff's flashlight, it was clear what had happened. Or at least I thought it was for a moment.

Nyland's body lay crumpled against some rocks a good fifty feet down a steep bank. The dark swirling waters of the river lapped at the man's arm like a dog trying to wake up its master.

"I think he missed his turn," the sheriff said.

"Or he was trying for a new river high-dive record," I said.

"There is one?" the sheriff asked.

"There is now," I said.

We stared at the body for a few long seconds.

"My men tell me he's dead," a voice said from behind us. "Broken neck."

My heart felt like it was going to explode out of my chest. The last thing I expected was someone to come up silently behind us.

Completely silently.

The sheriff and I spun around to see a man dressed in all black, with a night scope pushed up on his forehead. His skin around the night-scope was painted black.

"Who the hell are you?" the sheriff asked between gasps for breath. "You damn near killed me there."

"Special Forces, sir," the soldier said. "We were sent to back you up, but your men did just fine without us. Good job."

The sheriff looked at me with a real puzzled look.

All I could do was shrug. This was one part of all this I hadn't set up. But I knew the President had to play a part somehow. I just didn't know where.

"Thanks, I guess," the sheriff said.

I turned and stared down at Nyland's body. "Broken neck?"

"Yes, sir," the soldier said, his voice colder than the night air.

I just nodded. I could see no point in asking anything more.

CHAPTER SIXTY-FOUR

BACK INSIDE the log house, R.A. Scott was also dead.

He had a good-sized puddle of blood forming under him, and his eyes were closed. The room smelled like gunpowder and blood and felt warm after the cold night air outside.

The door stood open and one of the sheriff's men was on station near the body as I came back in. No one else was in the room.

I had sent the sheriff's son down the trail to help his father with Nyland's body. Chances were they would just take a few pictures, then stand guard on the body until morning, when they could get more help in here. I didn't know many pilots who would try these high mountain grass runways in the pitch dark. There was just no reason.

Annie came out of the kitchen, wiping off her hands on a large dish towel. More than likely she had been washing off R.A.'s blood.

"Did you catch him?"

"He's dead at the bottom of a good-sized drop down to the river," I said.

"Where the trail turns hard right?" she asked.

I nodded. But I wasn't at all sure if the drop was what had killed him. I didn't say that for the tapes still working.

I looked around, then saw one of the keys a few feet from R.A.'s body. It was my father's key.

"Did you see the other two?" I asked, holding up the key before putting it in my pocket.

"They fell out of his pocket," Annie said. "I'm sure they were all right there where that one was."

They weren't.

"You think it would be all right if we searched his pockets?" I asked the deputy.

The young guy shrugged. "I can't see why not since you said the guy that killed him is dead as well."

"Very dead," I said.

Annie did a quick search, again getting her hands covered in blood.

After a moment, she rolled the body one way, then back the other, and looked under R.A.

Nothing.

"Where's Steven?" I asked, glancing around at the empty bar stool.

Annie shook her head. "I was taking care of R.A., trying to stop his bleeding. I didn't see him leave. My back was to the door. And the keys."

I looked over at the deputy. "You see another man leave here?"

"Not since I got here from the maintenance shed, sir," he said.

Annie went to wash off her hands again while I went back outside into the cold night air and toward the runway. Nyland's plane was still sitting there, and none of the sheriff's men guarding R.A.'s hired goons had seen anyone leave.

Somehow, Steven took his father's key, and R.A.'s key, and left me Carson's key right out in plain sight, where I would be sure to see it.

Steven was going to try to get out of the Idaho Primitive Area in the dark, and on foot. That wasn't a task I would attempt.

Maybe I should go find a Special Forces member to track him. Then I decided against that idea.

"Why would he leave your father's key and take the other two?" Annie asked, coming up beside me on the porch were I was standing, staring into the darkness.

"He wants to come after me personally to get it," I said. "It's a game to him, a challenge. We're playing heads-up now."

She nodded, then after a moment she said, "Well, at least we have figured out who our killer is."

All I could see was the image of Nyland's body at the bottom of that hill, his neck broken. And the Specials Forces soldier telling me that was the case.

"Yeah, I think we have," I said. "But I have a lot bigger question now. A very frightening question."

"What's that?"

"Is Steven working alone?"

SECTION FOUR

———

THE FINAL SHOWDOWN

In a poker tournament,
only one player remains alive at the end.

CHAPTER SIXTY-FIVE

PRESIDENT DOLAN CHASE sat at the dining table in the White House residence and just stared at his chief of staff. He couldn't believe what he had just heard. This was not the way things were supposed to have gone out there.

"You're telling me that Nyland is dead? R.A. Scott is dead? Doc Hill still has Carson's key, and Steven took the other two?"

Paul only nodded, looking almost sick, and clearly as unhappy as Dolan was feeling right at that moment. He should look unhappy. Their entire lives were just about to be flushed down the toilet, not counting what all this would do to the country if what had happened back in 1982 got out.

And what he and Paul had done to cover it up since.

"Have our names been attached to this in any way at all?" Dolan asked, "at least with anyone that matters?"

"Not that I know of," Paul said. "People are asking why the FBI is involved, but no one has a clue as to the reason behind it. A county sheriff heard about a body that R.A. buried out there, but doesn't know where to even start looking, or how old it is. And with R.A. dead, it's not a high priority."

"Good," Dolan said. "No one would connect us anyway, even with a body, without all the stuff in that damned box."

Paul went on. "Doc Hill knows we are involved, of course, but he has himself and his family surrounded by the Las Vegas police and his own private army. I have no idea who he's told, if anyone. More than likely no one."

Dolan could feel his stomach twisting up into a giant knot. This had to get settled in one way or another, and settled quickly. Having Carson's kid involved with this was throwing off all hopes of this ending easily.

"Where's Steven?"

"No reports yet. And I've tried to call him."

"Well," Dolan said to his best friend, "see if you can get your girlfriend to keep the lid on all of this from Doc Hill's side, make sure nothing goes south before it gets finished."

"How?" Paul asked, clearly not willing to face the last part of what was going to need to be done.

"How the hell would I know," Dolan said, managing to keep his voice level, even though he really wanted to shout. "Maybe make up some excuse to be out in Vegas yourself and have a little *talk* with her. Give her what help she needs. I'll talk to the FBI director and make sure he's on board."

Paul only nodded, then turned and left.

Dolan had no doubt Paul knew exactly what needed to be done, and over the years Paul had proven that when things got rough, he was the best person to have in the fight. He was quiet and unassuming at times, but he knew how to make things happen, sometimes legally, sometimes not, on all levels of business and politics.

And never once had he left a footprint leading back to either one of them. Dolan just hoped that this time wouldn't be the exception.

CHAPTER SIXTY-SIX

LAS VEGAS, NEVADA. AUGUST 30

I FELT RELIEVED to be back in Las Vegas. Yesterday, the sheriff had asked a lot of questions I just didn't have answers for, and a few I did, but didn't want to tell him. I hated withholding information from him like that. But if I told him everything, it would put his life and his family's lives at risk, and I didn't want to do that.

In the end, after officially interviewing both me and Annie, the sheriff was calling what happened up at R.A.'s ranch a murder and then accident. Since R.A. was dead, the sheriff ended up releasing the men he had captured around the cabin, but the men who Nyland had hired were going to do time on attempted kidnapping charges.

Everyone just sort of ignored all the tapes we had made, and Fleet was going to have Mike just destroy them.

Mike and his men had gotten us all back to Las Vegas safely on our company plane. Ace, Fleet, my mother, and I were now back in Carson's house and settling in.

After getting back to Vegas, Annie had gone back to her place to change clothes, then had come over, bringing a couple of giant pizzas for all of us. Mike's people were guarding her the entire way. I knew that as long as she was hanging around me, helping me, she was putting herself more and more in danger. She clearly knew it as well and hadn't complained about Mike's men tailing her once since we got back.

After dinner, my mother and Ace had both decided to call it an early night and were in their rooms. I was glad they were, actually. The longer I kept the anger bottled up inside me about not telling me the truth as an adult, the less I trusted myself to be around them. At some point, it was all going to come out. But Steven needed to be stopped first.

Annie and Fleet and I were settled into the living room, me on the big couch with my feet up on the coffee table, her with her feet tucked up underneath her in a big recliner, Fleet stretched out on the second couch.

If we didn't make this conversation real interesting very quickly, he would be snoring. He looked just about as tired as I had ever seen my partner look.

"So," she said, "what are we going to do now?"

"See if we can come up with a plan to get Steven before he figures out a way to get to me. He wants to play this game and I've just never been much good as a defensive player."

"That's a big *well-duh*," Fleet said.

"I like your style," Annie said, laughing. "Any ideas as to what to do first?"

I told them my hunch about Steven working for the President, something I couldn't tell her with all the recording devices getting every detail at R.A.'s cabin. I told her about the Special Forces man the sheriff and I had run into on the trail.

"You're kidding?" Fleet said, sitting up and staring at me. So much for his napping anytime soon. "The President wouldn't be able to order in men like that."

"Not kidding," I said. "And who knows exactly what a President can do and can't do these days. He said he was Special Forces. Night scope and the most silent person I have ever met. He was behind us and until he spoke, I didn't know it."

"Trained," Annie said, nodding.

"Really well," I said. "We didn't see him or any others after that, so neither the sheriff or I mentioned it to anyone."

"You think Nyland was dead before he left that trail?" Annie asked.

"Convinced of it," I said.

"Oh, great," Fleet said, sitting back and shaking his head.

"Steven would kill his own father?" Annie asked, seemingly stunned at the idea.

"I'm not sure Steven was a part of that decision," I said.

"The president?" Annie asked in almost a whisper.

"Maybe," I said. "But to be honest, I don't know for sure. There is so much we don't know about Steven. Those Special Forces may have just been some of his old army buddies up there helping him out for all we know. And he may be in on this alone."

"But you don't think so, do you?" Annie asked.

"No, I don't," I said. "The President and his chief of staff have everything to lose if this got out. Steven has everything to gain by working with them."

"Or with the President's loyal opposition," Fleet said.

"But if he gets Carson's key, he will only have seven keys without the two in the White House," Annie said. "That still doesn't seem to be enough."

"It is," Fleet said.

"How?" Annie asked.

I stared at Fleet. Somehow he must have already known that fact. "He's right, it is. I talked to Mike, showed him Carson's key, told him it was from the early eighties to a long-term bank box, and it was one in a series of nine. Then I asked him how many keys it would take to open the box. He said seven."

"How?" Annie asked.

"Keys back then were made in a sequence," Fleet said. "If the numbers of the sequence are clear, as they are in this case, it's easy to make two replacement keys that can fill the empty sequence spots to open the box."

I nodded. "I'm sure the President knows that as well."

"Oh," was all Annie said. "Then why didn't Steven take your key when he had the chance?"

"Because he didn't want the game to be over," I said. "So far, it's been frighteningly easy for him to get the six keys he has. He considers himself far superior to anyone he's dealing with. I know the kind. The winning isn't important to them."

"Okay, that lost me," Fleet said.

"Compulsive gamblers don't care about winning or losing," Annie said. "They just crave the action."

"Exactly," I said.

"And you're the only challenge he's had, right?" Fleet asked.

"Right again," I said.

"So what first?" Annie asked. "How do we bring this guy out to play?"

"Learn everything we can about the other player," I said. "Standard poker thinking. We need to know what he's going to do, how he's going to act before he does. Think you can help with that?"

Annie nodded. "I think I've got an entire city police force that would like to capture this scum. I'll get them started digging."

"And in the meantime," I said, smiling at her, "I'm wondering if we can get our dear FBI friend searching as well, without tipping our hand. I'm meeting with her to see if she really knows what's happening. I have a hunch she doesn't."

Annie suddenly looked worried. "You really shouldn't meet with her without me in the room, and a few of Mike's men around as well. More than likely she's reporting directly to the President and who knows, she could be working with Steven."

I smiled at her. "I'm meeting her in the restaurant at the Bellagio. Mike and three of his men will be there, keeping an eye on me. I already have it set up with Mike, and he's making sure the Bellagio security team is in on it as well."

DEAD MONEY

"Good," Annie said. Then she got a distant look. "I have a nasty idea."

"I like nasty," I said, smiling at her.

"Do I need to leave the room?" Fleet asked.

Her face turned slightly red, but besides that, she ignored both of us.

"How about you give your FBI friend a little piece of false information to give to the President? A little bait. See if it brings our friend Steven out of the wilderness. That way we'll know exactly who's working for whom."

"Oh, I like the way you think," I said.

Two hours later, we had a plan set to lure Steven out into the open, if he was attached to the President in any fashion.

A perfect trap.

As a poker player, I had set a lot of them over the years.

Chapter Sixty-Seven

Las Vegas, Nevada. August 31

FBI AGENT HEATHER VOIGHT sat in the back of the limousine on the tarmac of the Las Vegas airport, waiting for Paul to come out of the plane and cross the thirty paces of hot asphalt to the air-conditioned coolness of the car. At three in the afternoon, it was over a hundred and twenty degrees on that surface. It was amazing anyone could work out in those conditions.

Over the past two hours, since her lunch with Doc Hill, she had just twisted over and over in her mind what she knew and what he had told her. He had finally explained to her that the keys Verne Adkins had mentioned were to a safe-deposit box that held evidence to an old murder, part of a very old cover-up that was coming unraveled.

Someone who was after the keys was killing people to get them.

That all made sense to her, especially when he told her that the information in the box would expose a number of high-ranking people. He would not say who. But he did say his father had a key and that he now had it in safekeeping.

In Washington, the high-ranking people he mentioned could be anyone. She just hoped it wasn't the President. She liked him, thought he was doing the country a good job, at least in his first year. She didn't know what she would do if she found out it was him. She'd cross that bridge when she came to it.

Doc Hill had also told her that while up in Idaho, he had learned from R.A. that he had made copies of some of the stuff before it was put into the box back in 1982. Tonight, Doc and Detective Lott were going to get it from a secret wall safe in R.A.'s Las Vegas home.

"Why are you telling me this?" she had asked.

"Because I want your help in protecting us," Doc Hill had said. "I've got my people, but they are not at your level of expertise. And I'm telling a lot of people about R.A.'s wall safe in hopes that somehow the person behind all this will show his hand. If we have the items from R.A.'s wall safe, then the keys to the box are mostly redundant and depending on what's in that safe, could quickly become worthless."

"A trap?" she had said.

"Exactly," Doc had said.

She had no doubt she was part of the trap. She just wasn't sure how just yet. So she had agreed to be there as well with agents in conjunction with the Las Vegas police, protecting the outside of R.A.'s house while they were inside.

"It may take a while inside," Doc had told her. "I didn't get the safe combination, and his wife didn't even know the safe existed. So we have a professional safe person to help us get it open, all under an official warrant, of course."

Now, two hours later, some of the conversation still made no sense to her. But it had been given to her with the clear intention she would pass it on, and that was exactly what she intended to do.

She watched through the tinted windows as Paul came down the stairs of the plane and moved quickly across the hot pavement. He had on his normal suit and tie, and even in the heat looked good. She wasn't sure why she was attracted so much to an older man who didn't seem to exist outside of a coat and tie, but she was. There was just something about him that she had to admit she loved.

Paul climbed in beside her with a blast of hot air, closed the door, then gave her a quick kiss, far quicker than she would have expected considering how long it had been since they had seen each other. He was clearly all business at the moment. With luck, there would be more kissing and other exercises later.

"What's the status?" Paul asked. "Did you learn anything from Doc Hill?"

"Actually, a lot," she said. She told him about the keys and the reason for their existence.

"I knew about the keys and why they existed," Paul said. "Did Mr. Hill say who the people in power were that the information threatened?"

"No," she said. "So that's why I'm on this in the first place, isn't it? Not just the President's friendship with Carson Hill."

"Both," Paul said. "We needed you here, close to everything to keep us informed as to what was happening. We couldn't do it ourselves, and we couldn't do it through completely official channels. Just too many questions."

She understood that.

"Anything else?" he asked.

"Tonight, Doc Hill and the Las Vegas police department are opening a wall safe in R.A. Scott's home that has some copies of the items that are in the safe-deposit box. R.A. Scott supposedly made some copies of things before it was all put into the safe-deposit box. Doc Hill asked me to use my people to help guard the building while the Las Vegas police cracked the safe. I agreed."

Beside her on the seat, Paul had gone white and looked like he might throw up at any moment.

"Excuse me," he said, opening the door to the car. "I forgot something on the plane."

She watched him walk like a man being chased across the hot asphalt. He almost ran up the stairs onto the plane.

Now it was all clear.

Paul and the President were involved in the crime and the cover-up in some fashion. She now had no doubt. Doc Hill had used her like a paid messenger to get just exactly the information he wanted to get to the President.

But now she didn't know what to do.

Or for that matter, if she could, or should, do anything at all.

CHAPTER SIXTY-EIGHT

LAS VEGAS, NEVADA. AUGUST 31

STEVEN EASED his M21 sniper rifle over the edge of the back parapet wall of the Safeway building. From there he could see through some tall, thin trees and down the road toward R.A. Scott's Las Vegas home.

Steven was dressed in complete black, and had a night scope on the rifle.

It was just before eleven in the evening. The sun was long gone, and the only lights behind him were from the parking lot and the business signs and cars on the road. From the air, he would blend in perfectly with the black roof, but he didn't expect the police or FBI to have anyone in the air.

He studied the M21, the feel of it comforting in his hands. He knew the rifle better than anything in the world. He practiced with it almost every day when he was home. While in prison, he had missed it more than anything. It was nice he was getting a chance to use it in this game.

The rifle rested perfectly on the concrete edge of the roof. Through the scope, he looked for his target between the trees behind the store.

There was an older subdivision street back there, the entrance on a side street. It was a very private area of expensive homes, tucked in away from all the tourists.

Paul Hanson, Chief of Staff to the President of the United States, came clearly into Steven's view in the scope, sitting in the front seat of a rented sedan a block to the west of R.A. Scott's house. No doubt there was a Secret Service agent in the back seat, and FBI all over that neighborhood. Paul was sitting next to one FBI agent, more than likely his girlfriend. She was going to be in for a shock very shortly.

He laughed again to himself. They were so focused on someone coming into the area, trying to get into the house, that it hadn't occurred to them that the threat might come from outside.

Idiots.

Steven laughed again and had to pull back from the edge of the roof to get himself to settle down. Didn't these people know that he held all the chips, controlled the game like they were puppets?

The phone call from the President earlier had been so pathetic. "Rescue me, help me, save my poor do-nothing career. Get the documents from R.A. Scott's house before anyone else did."

The man was an idiot. How the hell he had ever become President was beyond reason. Steven hadn't even been at the original poker game where his father and others killed a cheater. But he knew, without a doubt, that the only real, hard evidence about what happened that night in 1982 was in that safe-deposit box in Seattle that could only be opened with nine keys.

His father had said that nothing else could have been outside the box, that he had been with the evidence the entire time after the murder. He had made certain of that.

But, of course, Steven's father had been controlling that night, just like he had tried to control everything in Steven's life. And Steven had believed his father when he told him because he'd had no reason at all to lie.

On the other hand, Dolan Chase and Paul Hanson were being shoved around that fateful night, having a very bad experience, their families threatened by Steven's father. It wasn't a surprise that twenty-seven years later, they bought in to this stupid trap.

And more than likely, this had all been set up by Doc Hill. It was his style of play, just as he had trapped Steven's father in that last hand of poker.

Doc Hill was the only opponent worth going up against in this game. He had let Doc keep his father's key for that very reason, to keep Doc clearly in the game. And as soon as tonight was over, Doc would be Steven's next challenge.

He was so looking forward to it.

But first Doc needed a lesson. Right now, Steven was going to do what poker players called "advertising."

He was going to show that he should never be underestimated again with a stupid trick like this.

Doc needed to come to this contest with his full game, or not at all.

Steven calmed himself as he had been trained to do in the service, then rested his rifle on the edge of the wall. He set the sights on the back of Paul Hanson's head. It was nice of the poor idiot to come so far to die. It saved Steven a planned trip to the East Coast to kill him.

The wind was calm, the night air thin. And he knew the exact distance within a few feet.

He adjusted for the fall over the distance.

He then took a breath and let it out slowly.

Then he pulled the trigger, keeping his focus completely on his target.

The side window of the sedan shattered inward.

The White House Chief of Staff smashed forward into the dash. A large part of the side of his head splattered on the inside of the FBI's rented car.

Steven laughed, sighted, took another breath, and fired again.

Paul's body jumped under the second impact.

Steven fired quickly a third time.

Again the body jerked.

Then, working steadily, Steven picked up his brass, shouldered his rifle, and went over the edge of the roof, disappearing into the darkness of the trees and the neighborhood before anyone really had time to move.

That should wake Doc Hill up.

And just about everyone else in the country as well.

He was going to be the most wanted man alive.

God, this was fun.

CHAPTER SIXTY-NINE

LAS VEGAS, NEVADA. AUGUST 31

I HEARD THE SHOTS, faint pops, from where I was sitting on one of R.A. Scott's beautiful leather couches.

The sounds seemed to be far off in the distance. They could be from blocks and blocks away.

Annie, Mike, and I were in the living room. About six of Las Vegas's finest were stationed around the house at the different entrances. Mike was sticking to me and Annie like glue since Annie hadn't allowed any of his other men to be on the scene.

He had not been happy with that, but Annie had stood him down, glaring eye-to-eye with him and stating flatly that this was a Las Vegas police sting and she was in charge on scene. Her people would cover the house. Period.

Mike had finally agreed, and stormed off to set up what he could.

I watched that confrontation with renewed awareness of how little I really knew about Detective Annie Lott. And how much more I wanted to know. But I knew one thing for certain, she was one tough cop.

Now, White House Chief of Staff Paul Hanson and FBI agent Heather Voight were outside, along with a few dozen FBI agents and a dozen Las Vegas police.

I wasn't sure with this much fire power if Steven would get anywhere near this house, but both Annie and Heather wanted to make sure everything was covered in case he did. The idea was to bring him down. Verne had identified a picture of Steven as the shooter, so at least he was wanted on one charge of attempted murder.

Annie glanced up at the sounds, waiting, clearly alert, her hand on her gun.

"Those were shots," Mike whispered.

Annie nodded.

We had had a couple false alarms already in the last two hours. Chances are this was just another.

Annie, Fleet, and I had spent all afternoon, after my meeting with Heather, doing research on Steven. The more I learned about him, the more I was convinced he wasn't someone to take lightly.

When Heather had called back with some basic information I had requested from her, she had told me that she and Paul Hanson would be outside the house, in charge of the FBI detail there. I was stunned that Hanson was here in Las Vegas, but not surprised. Hanson and the President had a real stake in all this. Very real. It was the reason they had sent Heather in the first place.

"Shots fired," Annie whispered, motioning me to get down as she dropped to a crouch on the carpet, gun out.

Mike moved between me and the front door, his gun out as well.

I slid off the couch and also crouched, ready to move quickly if I needed to. I was carrying a pistol as well, but I kept it holstered for the moment.

Annie had a communications link with the FBI tucked in her ear and her gun had appeared in her hand faster than a card in a magic trick. I sure wouldn't want to get into a fast draw contest with her.

We waited.

We had the living room lights on, so it felt damn odd hiding in the middle of the floor behind a leather couch in a fully lit room.

"Oh, shit, no," Annie said, listening to something coming over the communication link.

She slowly stood and put her gun away.

Mike and I both stood and faced her. She looked white, like all the blood had drained from her body.

"What happened?" Mike asked.

She shook her head, clearly having trouble saying what had caused her shock.

I touched her shoulder gently.

She looked up at me and I knew something really horrible had happened. Her eyes looked almost haunted.

"Paul Hanson has been killed in a car down the block. Sniper."

"Oh, no," Mike said, turning away.

All I could do was drop onto the couch and just sit there, thinking about one of the details about Steven we had discovered this afternoon.

He had been in the Army.

He was an expert shot and had been trained as a sniper.

We had been trying to play him, and he had played us like we were beginners.

CHAPTER SEVENTY

PRESIDENT DOLAN CHASE ripped the phone from the wall and smashed it against the big window in the living room of the residence. The phone bounced, shattering and scattering plastic parts all over the carpet and window ledge.

Chase couldn't believe that the bastard Steven had double-crossed him.

And killed Paul.

Paul couldn't be dead. Paul had been at his side for thirty-five years.

"Oh, God, what have I done?"

He dropped into a chair and just sat, staring at the floor, not seeing anything but all the good years with his best friend.

What had he done?

He wanted to be sick.

He wanted to cry.

But instead all he did was sit and stare at the floor and think of Paul.

Everything was over. All the dreams and goals he and Paul had were now done.

Paul was dead.

He couldn't do this alone. He wouldn't even survive the questions about this alone.

Penny came out of the bedroom, pulling her bathrobe tight around her.

He looked up as she glanced at the shattered phone, then moved over to him. She sat on the edge of the chair and put her arm gently around his shoulders.

"What's wrong? What happened?"

All he could think to tell her was, "I killed Paul."

CHAPTER SEVENTY-ONE

LAS VEGAS, NEVADA. SEPTEMBER 3

THE LAST TWO DAYS were two of the longest I had ever remembered living through. Most of the press ignored me, thankfully, as they focused on the cover story of a serial killer named Steven Harrison murdering old friends of the President.

The fact that Carson's plane crash wasn't an accident came out, and the fact that the President had known about the threat had also come out as part of the cover story. It explained nicely why the FBI was working on the trap to catch Steven Harrison the night Paul was killed.

There were a ton of questions as to why such a high-ranking government official was there, why he wasn't in a bullet proof car, things like that. Then it came out that Paul had been dating Heather for the past year, and his presence there that night with her suddenly made sense to everyone.

So now, after two days, the press and public's reaction was anger at this insane Steven Harrison.

And anger at the police and FBI for not catching him.

Verne Adkins had refused interviews and been put in protective custody by the Las Vegas police. And after a couple times with the press about my father, I refused any more as well.

The focus of everyone, including me, was on finding Steven Harrison. But Steven Harrison had vanished.

Outside of Carson's home, the FBI had disappeared as well, but I had Mike and his hired people double the security. I had no doubt Steven was coming for Carson's key. It was only a matter of time now.

I just wanted to beat him to the play, because if he came at me, he would have the control. I hated that, both at the poker table and in real life. I wanted to be the one in control of the situation, and I wasn't going to get that control back by sitting around.

Today, the news was focusing on Paul's funeral and the grieving President. I was tired of it. The President had told Steven where we would be, what we were doing, and was totally responsible for his best friend's death. I had no sympathy for the man.

None.

So, instead of watching any more news, I turned off the television and turned on a light jazz station on the radio. I called and invited Annie over to help Fleet and me search for Steven.

My mother, who was doing a great job of staying away from me in Carson's house, had curled up with a book in the master bedroom, and Ace headed in a protected limousine to the Bellagio to play in some ring games. Fleet's family were still well protected up in Idaho at a retreat and Mike had layers of protection around the house.

Fleet had amassed boxes and boxes of old records about Steven Harrison and his father through varied sources before Paul was killed. Most of what he had gotten was financial records, records from the bankruptcy of Nyland's construction company, court records from Steven's trial, parole records.

Tons of paperwork with mind-numbing details in it. But somewhere in those piles of boxes stacked against one wall of the dining room, Steven had to have left a trace as to where he was hiding.

I knew he had money. I knew he had to have shelter somewhere. And no one, no matter how smart, could manage to not leave at least a slight footprint in this information-filled society. The key was finding it.

Annie looked tired and a little haunted when she arrived, although I had to admit, I had missed her and her wonderful smile. Mike had been keeping me up on what she was doing, since he had a half dozen security people on her and around her house. Except for a little sleep, she seemed to have spent most of her time answering questions and in front of a police review board.

"Paul's death wasn't your fault," I said to her as she stood in the kitchen watching me as I got ice-filled glasses of water for both of us.

"I know," she said. "But it was my idea to try to lure Steven out that way."

"I have no doubt that Steven was going to kill Paul one way or another," I said. "And given enough time, he will kill the President as well if not stopped."

Annie looked at me, clearly shocked that I would suggest such a thing.

"The game," I said. "Think of a poker tournament with only one person left standing at the end. He took Taylor's spot at the table, when he killed Carson and didn't get the key, I took Carson's spot."

"So the keys don't matter to him?" Annie asked.

"I doubt they do beyond being the bait that lures the President out into the open, causes him to make mistakes. They are important, sure, like chips, but only for the power they hold."

"So you think he was actually working for the President?"

"I do," I said. "But I doubt the President expected Steven to kill everyone. I figure that at first Steven contacted the President and offered to round up all the keys, including Taylor's."

"For a price, of course," Annie said.

"A price that the President and Paul would expect to have to pay, yes. Then, once Steven started killing people, the President sent out Paul's girlfriend to have the FBI try to stop him."

"But you think the intent for Steven was to kill everyone in that game right from the start?"

I nodded. "I'm sure of it. And he underestimated me originally, and we underestimated him the other day."

"That we did," Annie said.

"Trust me," I said. "That won't happen again. On either side."

CHAPTER SEVENTY-TWO

LAS VEGAS, NEVADA. SEPTEMBER 3

SIX HOURS AND A DINNER BREAK LATER, Fleet glanced up from a pile of legal paperwork from Nyland's bankruptcy hearings. "I might have something here."

"What?" Annie asked, rubbing her eyes, both of which had turned slightly red a few hours before. She needed a good night's rest, but I doubted any of us were going to get one until this was all over.

I was at the point where I had paperwork blur, and everything was looking the same. I had slowed my reading down so much, I was staring at each line on each piece of paper, making sure I understood it before moving on.

This entire idea had seemed stupid about three hours ago. Now it felt just foolhardy and a complete waste of time. We only had one more box of paper to go. We'd get through that, but I wasn't sure how.

"What did you find?" Annie asked.

"I think I might know where he lives," Fleet said.

Now that was enough to get me excited. Both Annie and I sprang to our feet to join Fleet where he sat on one couch.

I had started to assume that Steven lived like I did, with no real base. But unlike me, Steven owned no property or companies, rented no suites that could be traced, had no bank accounts under anything close to his real name, and used no credit cards, at least under any name any of us could find.

The guy acted like a complete ghost. He had disappeared completely from all records the moment his parole ended last year.

Annie sat on one side of Fleet, I took the other.

Fleet pointed to a section of a document he had been reading. It was one of the final judgments on the bankruptcy.

"Nyland reserved a small parcel of land near the dam site, you know, the dam that collapsed in 1995."

"Why?" Annie asked.

Fleet shrugged. "He claimed it was for long-term study of the dam failure. The court allowed it. It might only be that, but it's the first odd thing I've found in all this."

"It's worth a shot," I said.

"Let's see what happened next with that property," Annie said, standing and moving toward the secured computer Mike had set up in the living room.

"Wait!" I shouted.

I had promised myself I would start treating Steven with the respect of someone with a mind. He had completely out thought all of us so far. And more than likely, if Steven was half as smart as he seemed, he was going to know when someone went snooping at that property's records, especially if he actually was living on it.

"Why?" Annie asked, glancing back at me, but not sitting down.

"I'm going to call Mike and get him to make the search without footprints or tripping alarms along the way."

Annie nodded, then smiled. "Good thinking. We don't want to alert Steven."

"Exactly," I said.

"Sometimes, I love the computer age, sometimes I hate it," Fleet said.

"Which is it today?" I asked as I picked up the phone.

"I'm not sure."

It took Mike a half hour to join us.

We kept working on the rest of the paperwork while we waited, and when he arrived, Fleet showed him the document and what we wanted him to do.

After twenty minutes of intense work on the computer, his big frame hunched over like a kid playing a video game, Mike finally glanced up at the rest of us, smiling.

"What?" I asked as we gathered behind him to look at the screen over his shoulder.

"You were right to call me," Mike said. "There's an alert on the information that would have sent out an automatic signal, called a ping, to the person who set it up."

"Did you get around it?" Fleet asked.

Mike looked almost insulted. "Sure did. No one knows we are looking at this."

Mike pushed his chair back and stood to stretch, letting me at the computer to take his place.

"Don't touch anything," Mike said. "Just read."

I put my hands on my lap and read. And I really liked what I was reading.

Mike had pulled up a simple building permit, permission to put up a three bedroom manufactured home on the property reserved out of the bankruptcy.

Property that overlooked the remains of the old dam Steven had built and gone to prison for after it collapsed.

The owner's name on the permit was Steven Harrison.

CHAPTER SEVENTY-THREE

LAS VEGAS, NEVADA. SEPTEMBER 3

"THE BEST WAY is for me to go in alone first," I said.

Annie and I were standing in Carson's living room, face-to-face, arguing about how to approach and take down Steven Harrison in his remote home. So far I had stopped her from alerting anyone to what we had found, but not by much. Twice she had had her phone in her hands. Twice I had talked her down like a cop talked a man off a high ledge.

And so far we had only shouted at each other once.

Mike was still sitting at the computer, watching the argument with a smile on his face. Fleet was back on the couch pretending to study more of the paperwork.

"Not going to happen," Annie said, shaking her head. "Sorry."

Without a doubt, Annie was the smartest and strongest woman I had ever met. And the most stubborn, a great trait to have playing poker, but annoying as hell at the moment.

"Annie, think," I said, looking directly into her eyes. "Think about who our opponent is and what he's managed to accomplish so far."

"I'm well aware of that," she said. "That's why this isn't up for debate. You are not going in there alone. You are a poker player, *remember*?"

I cut her off before she could call me a complete idiot. "Steven had an alarm on anyone just looking up his building permit. You alert anyone in your department that we've found him, mount any kind of raid on that remote place, even as quietly as you can, and he'll be gone long before you can get there."

"You think he's tapped into *all* the police agencies?" Annie asked.

"I know he is," I said.

"How could you know that?" she demanded.

"Because it would be what I would do in his situation," I said.

She opened her mouth to answer that, then stopped.

"We underestimated him once," I said, "and Paul Hanson is dead. Let's not do it again."

I turned to Mike. "How easy would it be for someone with your skill to know when the police in an area were alerted to a problem, the FBI, even the Secret Service?"

"Not easy, but very possible," Mike said. "Very possible, and with this guy, likely. I have to agree with Doc on that part."

Annie shook her head and Fleet, who had been sitting on the couch during the entire discussion, did the same.

"So, even if I give you that much, why the hell do you think you should go in there alone?"

"To slow him down, surprise him, interrupt his escape plan. Whatever I need to do."

"And two or three or a dozen of us can't do that?"

I pointed to a map of the area Mike had found and printed out. "The area is as rugged as the mountains in Idaho. I'm used to it. I spend a large part of every summer in country like that. And I only need to get in there before you sound the alarm to slow him down, or if nothing else, see which way he flees."

"In poker it's called a showdown," Fleet said, still pretending to read. "Head-to-head. The two survivors face off. It's the only way any tournament ends, and you're talking to one of the best at this sort of thing."

"So you agree with me?" I asked Fleet.

"Oh, hell no," he said, looking up at me. "But I do understand it."

"So I go along?" Annie asked.

"And me?" Mike said.

"Not me," Fleet said. "Too many snakes, I'm sure."

I laughed. "I need you both to get everything ready, so that when the call is turned in, you'll be on scene very quickly."

"You need Mike only for that," Annie said. "You're not going in alone and that's final. Remember who is the detective here."

"How quickly do you need someone in there?" Mike asked before I could start the argument again.

I took a deep breath and made myself calm down. "From the maps and the looks of the roads in that area, I figure he thinks he has ten minutes to get away. Maybe fifteen. He has to really know that area and I'm sure he's prepared."

"He's not going to push that time limit," Annie said.

"How fast can the local police have all the roads blocked, and men on the way?" I asked.

Annie shrugged.

"Fifteen to twenty minutes at best," Mike said. "There are a number of roads in and out of there. But we can have me and maybe a half dozen of my men in a helicopter waiting within eight minutes. I can guarantee he's not tapped into my communication network, and if he is, I just won't tell any of my men where we are going."

"Why eight minutes?" Fleet asked.

"That's far enough away it won't spook him, or trigger any alarm, but close enough to get there fast."

"See?" I said to Annie. "Only eight minutes alone."

"No," she said, staring at me. "Not alone. We're going in together to slow him down and that's the end of the discussion. Otherwise,

I pick up the phone right now and do what I should be doing and report this."

"All right," I said. "We go in together, *Detective*."

She just stared at me, not at all happy with my tone. I could feel the coldness of her eyes. Ace was right, I was the wimp in this pair, and I'd be damned smart to remember it in situations like this.

"Sorry," I said.

She nodded and said nothing.

"You know," Mike said, "you better start working together on this right now. Both of you can get awful dead awful fast in eight minutes."

"Oh, thanks for *that* reminder," Fleet said.

CHAPTER SEVENTY-FOUR

NORTHERN CALIFORNIA, NEAR MT. SHASTA. SEPTEMBER 4

I RESTED, my back against a large rock, working to catch my breath. Annie joined me and sat down, huffing hard. She looked to be in great shape, and had kept up with me just fine, but at this high altitude, the climb had to be really hurting her. It didn't feel that good to me, and I was used to this high altitude.

She pulled out her water and downed some, then handed the plastic bottle to me. I took a drink and handed it back.

"You all right?" I whispered.

"Give me a half minute and I'll be fine," she whispered back.

From here on in, we had to be ready to move in any direction on an instant's notice. We weren't more than three hundred yards below Steven's home. And we had thirty minutes to climb that three hundred yards and get ready.

Annie and I had agreed that if either one of us ended up facing Steven alone, and he made any move, we would just shoot him, and she would clear it up later.

With that, I agreed completely. I had no intention of facing him any more than I would face down an angry bear in the wilderness.

We just needed to do whatever it took to slow down his escape.

Since there was really no preparation that we dared make for fear of alerting him in some manner, we decided to go early the next morning, before Steven moved out to kill more people, me included.

Mike had a helicopter that he had bought from one of the local Vegas news stations, and at four that morning told three of his best men they were going on a little mission, but didn't tell them where.

I had left Carson's home at a little after four as well in one of Mike's special limousines, picked up Annie at her place, and then headed for the airport. We were taking no chances that Steven had people watching me, or both of us. My jet dropped us both off in Redding and then went on north to wait in Portland for the call to return.

I rented a car in Redding and we drove just over two hours north and east to where we figured would be the easiest and safest place to leave the car. From there, we had gone in on foot, doing our best to avoid any of Steven's security systems.

There had only been two fairly obvious ones that I had seen, and we had managed to go around both without losing too much time. But I had no idea if he knew we were out here or not. I sure hoped not. He was a sniper. We wouldn't even know what hit us.

We had had three hours to make Steven's place from where we left the car, meaning we would arrive at the manufactured home by two if it worked out right, and we had read the maps correctly.

It was now one-thirty. We were doing fine. I just hoped the rest of the crew were as well.

At one, Mike's team, in the helicopter, planned to move north to a staging place just eight minutes flight time from Steven's property.

It would be from there, at exactly 2 p.m. that Mike would alert the authorities as to Steven's home.

All of them.

So, from two until eight minutes after two, it was up to us to slow Steven down in any way we saw fit.

And, as Annie had said, "Preferably without getting killed."

I looked up the hill. I could only see a small patch of the home through the trees and over the rocks, and no sign of any window.

I didn't want to get into any line of sight from any window.

I studied all the trees ahead of me, looking for any cameras. I couldn't see anything, or even motion sensors. More than likely, deer would trigger them too often to have them down here, but I had no doubt he had them in the immediate area around his home. I didn't plan on getting that close. I figured we didn't need to.

I had one walkie-talkie with a very short range, and I hadn't turned it on.

And I had a pistol with two extra magazines and Annie had her standard pistol.

Annie had been surprised when she had learned I was a damn good shot, and practiced regularly during the summers, both with a pistol and rifles, even though I never hunted. The practice always just relaxed me. And being from Idaho, handling a gun was sort of expected. I just hoped we wouldn't get into a gunfight, but if the situation warranted, we both had the ammunition we needed to keep him pinned down while help came.

It was one of our options.

"You ready?" I whispered to Annie.

She took one more drink, put the bottle away, and then stood. "I am."

She looked a little pale, but she was strong enough to make the last three hundred yards. This was all going to be over with fairly quickly, one way or another.

"We're going slow from here. Stay close to me and watch your footing."

She nodded.

It took me twenty minutes to pick my way up the hillside, staying behind any cover I could find.

Annie stayed with me like a shadow.

About fifty yards down the road from the manufactured home, we finally crested the hill. We lay in the dirt and took turns just poking our heads up enough to get a lay of the land.

The home had been placed in such a way that the front door and windows faced the other side of the ridge, where I knew the remains were of the dam Steven and his father had built. Why anyone would want a view of their worst mistake and biggest tragedy was beyond me.

The ridge had been flattened, more than likely back during the construction of the dam, and there was almost no cover besides some boulders along the edges, a few dry weeds, and a large, recent-model Ford pickup sitting in front of the house. From what I could tell, it seemed to be his only means of transportation.

"Only one car," Annie whispered, ducking back beside me after taking a moment to look things over.

"That's Steven's mistake number one," I said, then checked my watch. "If I can get close enough, a few flat tires might really slow him down. You stay in this position and I'll work my way down along this side to get closer to the truck. That way we'll have him bracketed."

"Stay close to cover," she whispered.

"You do the same," I said.

"Planning to," she said.

There were still ten minutes until the entire world started in this direction.

I eased back away from the ridgeline and moved as carefully as I could along the steep hill, working to get closer.

I finally went back up to the edge about fifty paces from the Ford. That was as close as I dared get.

I couldn't see Annie's position from where I was so I couldn't signal her that I was ready.

I again glanced at my watch.

Four minutes.

All we could do now was wait. As a professional poker player, I was real good at waiting.

The next four minutes were the longest wait I had ever had.

CHAPTER SEVENTY-FIVE

NORTHERN CALIFORNIA, NEAR MT. SHASTA. SEPTEMBER 4

STEVEN HARRISON stared at his computer screen, not believing what he was seeing. Not only had the FBI been alerted to his home's location, but the California Highway Patrol and the local police down in the valley.

"God damn it all to hell! How the hell did they find me?"

He slammed his fist on the top of the computer, then took a deep breath and made himself think.

He had planned for this.

It would take a while for the Feds to arrive, but the local police would have the roads closed off in less than fifteen minutes, and if there was a cop car close, or one of the helicopters standing by or already in the air, he had less than ten minutes.

He swore at the computer, shut it off, then grabbed a big industrial-sized magnet and set it on top of the hard drive.

He had planned this escape a lot while in jail and then over the last few months, but had hoped he would never have to use it.

Too bad. He had liked it here.

He took a large can of gas from the utility room and sloshed the contents on the drapes and chairs and computer. If they were coming for him, why not give them a big signal fire to direct them?

He grabbed the duffel bag beside the door that contained money and some basic supplies he might need. Then he took the keys off the mantel over the fireplace and put all six in his pocket. He couldn't let those go up in flames, not after all the work he'd done to get them.

His plan was to take the truck down the road about a half mile to a side logging road and ditch it in a small cave there, then take a motorcycle he had stashed there and get to another cave down a trail about four miles away.

No one knew about that cave, not even the engineers that originally did the rock surveys of the area. He could hide in there for a week, since he had enough food and water stored there. Then he could work his way over land toward the Nevada and Southern Oregon borders, and eventually back to Las Vegas.

It would take some time, but at this point, time was on his side.

At the front door, he paused, lit a match, then tossed the match in the direction of the soaked couch.

The fire caught quickly, barely giving him time to slam the front door closed.

He turned to move to the truck and stopped cold.

Doc Hill was standing about fifty paces away, a gun in his hand.

And he was smiling.

CHAPTER SEVENTY-SIX

NORTHERN CALIFORNIA NEAR MT. SHASTA. SEPTEMBER 4

I LOVED THE LOOK on Steven's face when he turned and saw me. I wished I had a camera to share that Kodak moment.

He paused for just an instant, then moved away from the door and down off the porch as behind him his home started to burn. He must have spread around something to help the fire along because it was already roaring.

"How did you get here?" he demanded as he headed toward his truck, acting as if I was just someone he expected to meet on the street.

"Just came to play out your last hand," I said. "Wish I had brought marshmallows, though. I didn't know we'd have a campfire."

Steven sneered and kept moving. "I have to admit," he said, "you're good. Having you in this game was this wonderful extra bonus I got when I killed your father."

I stepped away from the edge and stood in the middle of the road about twenty paces in front the truck. "You in a hurry to get somewhere? Expecting company for this cookout?"

My message was clear. He would have to go over me to leave.

I had no doubt that right now Annie was cussing under her breath at me. We were supposed to have stayed in cover, not stand up and walk toward the killer like a bad western movie.

"No company," Steven said. "I just have a few errands to run, people to kill."

He reached for the truck door and I shot out the passenger front tire. Then quickly I put another shot into the driver's side front tire right near him.

Luckily for him, I was a good shot.

He jumped back, stumbled, and went down, dropping the bag and swearing.

He grabbed a good-sized rock as he got to his feet and turned to face me.

Annie came up out of cover along the ridge and came forward slowly off to my left.

"I hear that rocks were your father's weapon of choice for murdering people," I said. "Like father, like son, huh?"

"I am nothing like my father," Steven said, almost spitting out the words. "He was pathetic and weak."

"Yeah," I said, nodding. "I have to agree with that. He liked to threaten family and friends of his enemies, not face them and kill them like you do. Of course, you didn't face any of those people you killed with that mess there, did you?"

I indicated the ruins of the dam below him.

He turned bright red. He dropped the rock, grabbed his bag, and started to fish in it, more than likely for a gun.

Before I could act, Annie shot him in the leg.

Steven spun, the bag flying off to one side as he fell.

Then he came up into a sitting position, spitting dirt.

"That had to hurt," I said.

His leg was bleeding badly as he climbed to a standing position, balanced on his one good leg. He growled at me and Annie as she got closer, then started toward his bag.

This time I was the first to act. I put a shot into the dirt between him and the bag.

He kept going, so Annie and I both shot again into the dirt in front of him, the message clear.

Touch that bag and get shot again.

He turned and started hopping toward the edge of the road on the dam side.

I had no idea where he thought he might go. More than likely down a trail there. The burning house was blocking any escape along the ridge, and Annie and I had the other way down the road blocked. The only thing on the dam side of the house was a rock cliff.

"You know," I said, moving along parallel to him, "that running is damn hard on one leg. And to be honest, it looks kind of silly."

He kept hopping along, his leg bleeding, leaving a red-and-black trail in the dry dirt.

I followed him, keeping a safe distance.

At the edge of the rock cliff, he looked both ways.

I stopped about fifteen paces away, making sure to stay out of his reach.

Annie moved around to block his retreat, her gun constantly aimed at Steven.

He glanced at Annie, then turned to face me, as in the distance the sound of a helicopter cut through the silence of the mountain air. His eyes were full of panic and fear.

"Hear that?" I asked. "It's your ride. Why don't you just sit down and put your hand on your leg to slow down the bleeding?"

His pants leg was completely soaked dark red. Annie must have hit something important, because at this rate, he wasn't going to last long.

He glared at me, his mean dark eyes cold and angry. "Seems this game is yours. I'm out of chips. Time for me to walk away."

"Hop away," I said.

He turned toward the remains of the dam he had built and started down a narrow trail there, trying to hop along the thin rock ledge.

I couldn't have stopped him if I had wanted to, which I didn't.

It took less than ten seconds before his foot slipped, he lost his grip, and he went over backwards.

The fall was about sixty feet to a rock ledge where he hit and bounced, then came to rest with his neck and back in a very awkward and unnatural position.

"Watch that first step," I said, far, far too late.

Annie actually laughed at my lame joke.

CHAPTER SEVENTY-SEVEN

MIKE'S HELICOPTER came in fast and hard. It landed about a hundred yards down the road from where we stood, kicking up clouds of dust and filling the air with the fantastically loud sound.

Annie and I had moved farther away from the burning building as things inside started exploding, more than likely ammunition and propane tanks. The dust cloud from the chopper washed over me. I turned away to keep the sand and dirt out of my eyes.

Mike was first out of the helicopter, his gun drawn, moving fast toward us through the dust cloud as the helicopter shut down.

"All clear!" I shouted over the sound and through the choking dust.

He kept running until he was beside us.

By the time he reached us, the helicopter's engines had shut down and the blades were slowing, letting some of the dust settle.

Behind us, a massive explosion sent flames even higher into the sky as the house became completely engulfed.

"Steven," Annie said to Mike over the noise. She pointed over the edge.

All three of us moved closer to the edge, looking down.

"He dead before or after the fall?" Mike asked, smiling at me.

"After," I said. "Annie shot him in the leg, but the fall was his idea. I tried to talk him out of it."

"Why?" Mike said, shaking his head.

"At the time, I was asking myself that same question."

Mike turned and went back to stand down his men who had spread out from the helicopter like a trained crew of Marines.

I handed Annie my pistol. "I'm betting this needs to be taken, since I did fire shots."

Annie nodded and took my gun. She checked it, then put it in the back of her belt. "Well, where do you think the keys are?"

"My guess is either in the bag or on his body," I said. "I'll check the body. It's going to take mountain rescue to get that body off that ledge, though."

"You can get down there?" she asked, glancing over the edge again.

"Sure can. I'm part mountain goat, or did I forget to tell you that?"

"No comment on that," she said, shaking her head and turning to look in the bag.

I didn't tell her I had seen a couple of pretty good trails down the side besides the one Steven had tried. And one of them passed right close to the ledge Steven had landed on.

Carefully, in the hot afternoon, with the burning house sending up a gigantic plume of gray and black smoke, I worked my way down the hot rocks. I was sweating more by the time I got to the body than I had been up on top.

"Nothing in the bag but a lot of money, a gun, and some food," Annie yelled down to me as I reached the ledge.

I was glad that there had been a gun in that bag when Annie shot him. Better all the way around.

I signaled I'd heard her, then knelt beside the body.

No matter how many times I had been around death, it never got easier. The smell of the blood and bowels always choked my nose and gave me nightmares for a week. I had no doubt good old Steven's body would do the same, since the big black flies were already being drawn to the splattered blood.

I patted the outside of his pockets, then worked my hand into his front pants pocket, trying not to get any blood on me.

I found six keys, all like Carson's, only with different numbers on them.

I stared at them for a moment in the hot sun, not really feeling anything either way, then put them in my pants pocket and stood. I glanced back up at Annie and Mike who were staring down at me like I was at the bottom of a very deep pool.

"Got them," I shouted.

Annie gave me a thumbs-up signal and a smile.

"Just in time," Mike shouted back. "I got reports of two more helicopters coming in fast. One is FBI."

"Be right up," I said with one last glance at Steven's body.

There was still one more hand to play. One more player in this game.

Chapter Seventy-Eight

THE BACK ROOM at Mike's business looked like a nightmarish cross between a gunsmith's shop, a locksmith, a computer store, and a used-car lot. And it was huge. The space filled most of a small warehouse tucked off the old Boulder Highway, the small front office being what the customers saw, the back being only what Mike and his employees saw.

Around the high ceiling was a storage area with ladders up to it.

We were in the very back of the huge space. From the looks of it, not many customers got back here, and for good reason. The place smelled of oil and old computers and was almost cold because the air-conditioning was set so high. Parts of different equipment lay everywhere in the clutter. But I had a hunch Mike knew exactly where everything was.

Ace and I and Annie stood in one corner of the big warehouse, near a work bench covered and surrounded by thousands of key blanks. Mike was sitting on the only stool in front of the bench, his massive shoulders hunched over, studying the seven keys I had brought him.

He had them in order by number and was examining every one of them. We stood in silence around him while he worked. There was no way I was going to let those keys out of my sight with anyone, no matter how much I trusted the person.

The afternoon and evening of the day Steven died had been one continuous interview for me. I must have gone over what happened on that ridgeline two dozen times for five different agencies. When I had my turn with the FBI, I didn't ask about Heather, and none of the agents talking with me ventured any information. I doubted she worked for them anymore, after what had happened on her watch.

Yesterday had been even more interviews, but thankfully, the story the press got was a simple one.

Working together, different law enforcement agencies, with the lead of the Las Vegas Police Department, had taken down the man who killed Paul Hanson and others.

My name was kept out of the story.

Thankfully, Annie's name was held out as well, on her request.

From the moment we got on my plane yesterday evening to come back to Vegas, she had been smiling, almost bubbling, and today her smile was even brighter.

So was mine I was sure. Last night, for the first night in a long time, I actually slept almost soundly, even though this wasn't over.

"So," Mike said, looking up from the keys, "you want me to make you copies of the two missing keys?"

"I do," I said. "I'm assuming it's possible."

"You're lucky, it is. The changes in the keying patterns vary in a distinct pattern from key-to-key. You're missing key #9 and key #6, so I can figure them out."

"How long?" I asked.

"How about a half hour?"

I nodded.

"You know these are bank keys. I'm not supposed to make copies."

Annie laughed. "You need a court order?"

"Oh, hell no," Mike said. "Just wanted to make sure you all knew what we were doing was illegal."

"Just make them look like the others," I said. "Right down to the numbers scratched in."

And for the next half hour we watched Mike create the two missing keys that were going to help us open a record to a very nasty night a long time ago.

A night that had cost me my father.

CHAPTER SEVENTY-NINE

WASHINGTON, D.C. SEPTEMBER 8

TEN IN THE MORNING. Heather Voight, dressed in her jogging shorts, a sports bra, and a thin shirt, left her apartment in the Hillcrest Heights area, cut across the street between cars, went north one block, and then into the park.

It had been another long, almost sleepless night. She was on paid leave until the hearing about her actions and conduct. She had no doubt she would be fired. It was only a matter of time. And with Paul dead, she doubted the President would lift a finger to help her. Even if he wanted to, she doubted he could. She was betting he blamed her, even though the entire mess was his fault.

She was just glad that Doc and the Las Vegas Police Department had run Steven to ground and killed the bastard. At least she didn't have to think about going after him on her own. Now all she had to do was deal with the nightmares of Paul's head exploding as she was talking to him.

She got onto the jogging path, dropped into her normal running pace, and tried to just *not think*.

Around her, the air was thick and warm, and no doubt the day was going to be even warmer. Maybe one of the last real summer days of the year.

She was going to miss summer.

She was going to miss her job. She had no idea what she would do next. Nothing seemed interesting to her.

As she entered a grove of tall trees at the half mile mark, feeling the relief of the shade, Doc Hill and Detective Annie Lott stepped out from behind the trunk of a large tree.

Her first thought was that it couldn't be them.

Not here.

But yet there they were.

She slowed to a walk about ten feet away. "You're a long way from a poker table. What the hell are you doing out here?"

"Came to talk to you," Doc Hill said, smiling.

"We need your help," Detective Lott said.

Heather laughed. "Didn't you hear? I'm on paid leave until they can fire me."

"We know," Doc said. "That's why we figured you could actually help us get to the man who was behind Paul's death."

"You already killed that scum," she said. "Or at least that's what I heard."

"We think Steven was just the hired gun," Doc said.

He was no longer smiling.

The simple sentence took her breath away and made her legs weak.

She moved over toward a bench under a tree. For the first time since Paul's death, she tried to think like an agent. If what Doc had said was true, even more people might die before this was over.

Doc started to say something more, but she just held up her hand for him to not say anything.

"Stay right there," she ordered.

Then she moved around them in a complete circle, walking slowly as if walking off a cramp in her thigh, but actually looking for any signs that she had been followed, or that they had been.

Or that anyone had a listening device on them.

Middle of the morning, a number of mothers with young children were out for a stroll, a few other joggers coming along the path, but no one else.

For the moment, they seemed clear.

She came back to them and nodded. "We walk and talk and keep your voice low and your head down when speaking."

Both of them nodded.

"What do you need from me?" she asked as they got back to the path. Her stomach was twisting just like it had the night Paul was killed. This nightmare couldn't be continuing, could it? Was that possible?

"A trip to Seattle," Doc Hill said.

Heather didn't need to ask any more. She knew about the box and the keys. She didn't know what was in there, but she knew it was explosive for the President. And had been deadly for Paul and others.

She nodded. "When?"

"Doing anything this afternoon?" Doc asked.

She looked at him. He was deadly serious, of that she had no doubt. "Actually, I think I'm free. My hearing isn't for two days."

He told her how to get to his plane at the airport. "We can talk safely on the plane."

"Give me an hour, plus or minus considering the traffic."

"We'll be there," Doc said.

With that, she turned and went to a fast jog, headed for home, a quick shower, and another trip west.

She knew exactly who they were talking about, and if the President really was behind Steven, then she would do everything in her power to bring the bastard to his knees.

She owed Paul that much.

CHAPTER EIGHTY

SEATTLE, WASHINGTON. SEPTEMBER 8

WE MADE IT BACK to Seattle in almost record speed, and by the time we were ready to leave the plane for the three limousines and the panel truck waiting outside, it was the middle of the afternoon Pacific Time.

It had been a long day on the plane, going back and forth across the country.

Annie and Mike and I had left Las Vegas for Washington, D.C., at midnight for the four-hour flight east, and we had all tried to sleep some on the plane.

At one point, while the three of us were talking, Annie had curled up against me and fallen asleep. Having her there like that, relaxed and comfortable, had been one of the nicest feelings I had had in years. I really wanted this entire mess over, mostly to have us all really safe again, but also to find out if there really could be something between Annie and me.

On the way to Seattle, Heather had been surprised to learn that Mike had been tailing us, blocking any kind of electronic surveillance while we talked to her. He had been in a special van he had rented.

"You're good," she had said to him. "I didn't spot you."

"So are you, Agent Voight," he said, smiling at her. "You interested in a job?"

She also smiled. "I just might be, depending on how this turns out."

Annie looked at me after that conversation and smiled. The connection between them was clear to anyone watching. Even I could see it, and I was known for not seeing that sort of thing at times.

Now that we were on the ground in Seattle, my biggest worry was that the President, or someone working for the President would have the bank watched. I was almost sure that he did in some fashion or another.

My hope was we could get in and out without him hearing about it. As long as he knew we didn't have the contents of that box, the safer we were for the moment.

Fleet had called ahead and talked with the bank manager about the bank's facilities. It had a private copy machine that good customers could use for a fee. I planned on using it.

We just had to make sure that no one inside the bank alerted anyone outside the bank that the box was being accessed. That was Mike's job. He didn't tell me how he planned on accomplishing that. All he said when I asked was, "Complicated. Just trust me."

With only a few muttered "Good lucks," we all climbed into our perspective limousines and Mike into his van.

The time was 3 p.m.

It took me a half hour to get on my disguise, with the help of a professional makeup artist named Carol from Mike's team. Annie and Heather were on their own with their disguises, and they had to change cars along the way as well.

The keys were secured in my pocket, and I had a phony paunch strapped on. I had some wrinkles applied to my eyes, and a gray-haired wig, along with a gray moustache. I wore an expensive suit and carried a briefcase in one hand and an expensive walking stick in the other. For a very short time, I was going to be Benson James, one of the signers on the box.

Fleet would be standing by a few blocks away with top legal help in case I got into trouble.

I climbed out of the limo at exactly fifteen minutes until four, right on our scheduled time.

I pretended to limp slightly, using the walking stick, as I made my way up the short flight of stairs and into the old bank. It had been a fixture in the Seattle area for almost a hundred years, with its high ceilings and marble floors and pillars. The place felt just cold to me, and I couldn't imagine why anyone would bank in a building that felt more like a mausoleum than a place to do business.

I moved to the counter for signing in for the safe-deposit boxes.

The clerk was a young woman with a pristine look and a small wedding ring on her finger. She had to be very new on the job. Not too new, I hoped, that she had to have the bank manager's permission for things like this.

She looked at my request, then at my ID, then said, "That's a special box, sir. It takes nine keys."

"I have all nine," I said, patting my vest pocket like that was where I had put them.

"Good," she said, having me sign Benson James' name.

She checked it against a signature card while I stood and worried, without looking like I was worried. I had practiced that damn signature for hours and hours.

She nodded, then said, "This way, sir."

She unlocked a big gate, let me pass, then re-locked it.

I was steps away from finding out what had killed my father and a bunch of other good men, and when that gate clicked shut behind me, all I wanted to do was bolt.

It was too much like a jail cell, and I was breaking far too many laws.

CHAPTER EIGHTY-ONE

THE YOUNG WOMAN put the bank's key into its slot in the wide and very old-looking box.

"Just insert the keys one at a time and turn them," she said.

With her watching, I took out the keys and inserted #1 and turned it. It clicked solidly.

She nodded and said nothing.

I guess that was what it was supposed to do.

I went down the line to #6 without a problem, but that sixth key was the one that Mike had made, the one that worried me the most.

I inserted it and it caught for a fraction of a second, then also clicked.

I forced myself to breathe.

The last three keys fit just fine and I pulled out the covered, heavy box.

"You can take any room in there," she said, pointing to where the privacy rooms were for the box holders.

"I will need to copy some private documents," I said. "Do you have a machine in the bank I could use? I'd prefer not to take them out of the bank." I knew the bank had the copier, but that was what Fleet had told me to say.

"Of course," she said, smiling. "Just bring out the documents you would like to have copied and I'll show you to the machine and how to use it."

"You've been very kind," I said, hefting the box and going into one of the private booths.

I set the closed box on the desk and stared at it. I had no desire to open this, to see what really had happened back in 1982, what had cost me my father when I was only six years old, but I had to.

I just hoped I was the first one to get here.

I lifted the lid.

Inside, on top of a very thin pile of paper, was a signed document with nine signatures describing the events of the night, including how R.A. Scott, Nyland Harrison, and Jeff Taylor killed Kevin DeFoe with rocks after he was caught cheating. The note said they had no intention of killing him, just stopping him from running away down the trail.

Such a stupid thing to do. Chances were Taylor would have been hurt or killed anyway, running on that trail in the middle of the night, if they hadn't stopped him.

There, on the signed paper, as I expected, were Dolan Chase's and Paul Hanson's names, as well as my father's name.

There was a small, hand-drawn map of the area around R.A. Scott's house showing the airstrip, the river, and a mark showing exactly where they had buried Kevin DeFoe's body.

There were also four pictures. Two graphic shots of Kevin DeFoe's body that I didn't linger over, another two of the men involved in different group shots.

My father and Dolan Chase were in both pictures. They did not look happy.

I felt sick just looking at it. Not because of the graphic nature of the pictures of DeFoe, but of what these papers in this box had caused. Far too many people had already died because of these six pieces of paper.

I opened my briefcase and put the documents and photos into the case, inside a manila envelope.

It seemed so light, so small, for something so powerful and dangerous.

I closed the lid on the box, leaving it empty, then stopped and made myself breathe.

There had been no surprises.

Just simple evidence of a single moment in 1982 echoing down through time, destroying lives as it went.

And to make sure it had no more effect on my family and friends, I had to finish playing out this last hand.

I put the box back and took the keys, then called for the woman.

She took her key from the slot above the special box, then showed me to the copy machine.

It took me less than three minutes to make two copies of everything, including the pictures. I put each set into its own manila envelope. And with the documents out of the box, I also put three pages of phone records that Mike had retrieved from Steven Harrison's private phone, showing that Dolan Chase and Paul Hanson had called him from their own private lines over a dozen times, from before my father's death to the day Paul was killed.

It didn't take a genius to put together what had happened. Steven had called the President and his chief of staff, offering to round up all the keys in exchange for something in return. From that call onward, it had only been the President or Paul who called Steven.

It was now all together, the documents from 1982 and the phone records from the last three weeks. Three separate envelopes with the exact same thing in them. One envelope had only originals. I planned on keeping that one.

I thanked the young bank woman, told her I had decided to take the documents with me after all, and that I wouldn't need to get back in the box.

Then I went to stand in line for a teller.

Stepping into line just ahead of me was Heather Voight in a very effective disguise of an overweight housewife in a plaid dress. I almost didn't recognize her, even though she was right where she was supposed to be.

I handed her an envelope and she put it in her large purse without so much as a nod.

I stood there for a moment until Heather went up to an open window to ask a bogus question, then I turned away and went to a work counter.

A moment later Annie came into the bank, also in a disguise. Instead of brown hair, she had on a blonde wig, a tight blue dress that showed off her wonderful body, and red lipstick. The look just wasn't her.

She stood next to me at the workstation and opened a briefcase in front of her.

"Any problems?" she asked.

I slipped her an envelope as I said, "None, except trying not to smile at your disguise."

She put the envelope into her briefcase as if it belonged to her. "Not funny," she said.

But I could tell she was also trying not to laugh.

"See you back in Las Vegas," I said. "Watch your back."

She nodded and said nothing.

I turned and headed for the front door, the original documents in my briefcase.

Outside, the fresh air and warm September afternoon calmed me down. Mike was in a van down the street and he gave me a thumbs-up as I glanced in his direction.

So far, all was clear.

The FBI now had a copy of everything.

The Las Vegas Police Department now had a copy of everything.

We now had the best hands in this game that we could get, considering we were playing against the most powerful man in the world.

CHAPTER EIGHTY-TWO

LAS VEGAS, NEVADA. SEPTEMBER 9

SINCE I HAD the President's private phone number from the phone logs of Steven's phone calls, I didn't bother to go through the White House switchboard. But I did wait until later in the evening, Washington, D.C., time, to make sure he was back in his residence.

With a quick call to Annie's phone number at the police station, Heather signaled she had made it back to Washington. More than likely, she had already talked to the people she needed to talk to. When she had suggested she give her boss the papers, I had at first thought it was a bad idea.

"If my boss knows what happened with Paul, and has seen the documents, including the phone records, I will be a great deal safer. And more than likely retain my status once he learns how he and I were both used by Paul and the President outside of my normal line of duties. Director Smith is a friend of the President, but he doesn't like being used."

I had agreed. And I hadn't asked where she would hide the envelope.

Annie had made it safely back to Las Vegas by commercial airline and this morning had put the papers in a bank safe-deposit box with her name and her captain's name on it. If anything happened to her, her captain was instructed to go get the papers and release them to the press.

I had my set also well protected, slipped between the photo and the backing board of the large picture of me and my father in Carson's bedroom.

Ace, Fleet, and my mother knew it was there, sealed and stamped and already addressed to a friend of mine on the *Las Vegas Sun* newspaper.

For the phone call with the President, I had Mike make sure the call could not be traced or recorded in any fashion on my side. And I used a cell phone that Mike said he had bought from a small-time pickpocket earlier that evening, and that would be destroyed ten minutes after I used it. I had no doubt it was freshly stolen, but I didn't ask and Mike didn't say.

The President answered with an abrupt, "Yes?"

"Doc Hill, sir," I said. "I hope I'm not calling too late."

There was a pause on the other end. I clearly had surprised him.

"Not at all. What can I do for you?"

"I have some items I'm sure you would like to own, for old time's sake. Call them a connection with my father."

For a moment I wanted him to think I was willing to give him the keys. To see if he knew we had already been to the bank.

"What would you like for this connection?" he asked.

He didn't know. Good. That meant I needed to tell him.

"I've been to the box in Seattle and emptied it, sir," I said, pulling the rug out from under him.

Silence.

"Yes," he finally said.

"Understand, sir, that there are three full sets of the documents, plus copies of Steven's private phone calls to this line with you."

He inhaled hard, but said nothing, so I went on.

"All are in safekeeping with instructions to release to the press and law enforcement agencies if anything happens to me, my family, my friends."

After a moment he said, "I understand." His voice was just about as cold as I had ever heard a voice be.

"I would like to meet." I said. "You, me, your wife, Detective Annie Lott from the Las Vegas Police Department, and FBI Agent Heather Voight. A private, unrecorded meeting."

"I'm afraid Agent Voight is no longer in good standing with the bureau," he said.

"I think you may be mistaken, sir. You might want to check with her superiors."

Silence again.

"She is in custody of a set of the documents, sir. I felt it was only right to include her, since she was working for you when her boyfriend was killed. Don't you?"

Silence again.

This President did not have a reputation of being silent, yet I seemed to leave him speechless a great deal.

Finally he said, "I will be in San Francisco in three days. I would be glad to meet there at that time. My secretary will call your home tomorrow and set it all up."

"That will be fine," I said.

And then for the second time, I hung up on the President of the United States.

Chapter Eighty-Three

THE BUILDINGS of San Francisco flashed past the limousine's windows as we headed in from the airport toward the President's hotel.

"I could get used to this," Annie said, leaning back against me and putting her head on my shoulder.

"So you like the private planes, limos, all that?"

"You bet," she said, kissing me on the cheek. "What woman wouldn't?"

Over the last three days, while we waited for this meeting, our relationship had gone to the next level, for lack of a better way of calling it.

Annie had called it "Sex like rabbits in heat."

I just called it the next level.

And, I had to admit, it was a great level.

For years, I didn't think I dared have a long-term relationship because of what my father had done to my mother. Some sort of strange thinking that it was hereditary or something that stupid. But actually, my father had stayed with my mother as best he could under the circumstances. They

343

had spent years in a very strange relationship, yet still loved each other and remained faithful to each other. The more I thought about that, the more amazed I became.

My mother and I had finally had the "discussion" I had been putting off. We had spent an afternoon with me yelling at her sometimes, her in tears at times. But mostly we just talked about what had happened, why she and Carson had made the decisions they had made, and why they hadn't told me when I became an adult.

I don't know if I would ever get past every bit of the anger at her and Carson and Ace, but I was going to try. I couldn't see any reason to not do so.

And now, maybe, just maybe, with a woman as smart as Annie, I could make something work with a relationship. I was sure going to play the hands to find out.

"Why the luxury all the time?" Annie asked, looking up at me. "You know, this doesn't seem your style. You strike me as more of the covered wagon kind of guy."

"Wait until you see my house in Boise," I said. "You'll think a covered wagon looks good."

She laughed, then leaned against me and watched the city pass outside.

I could tell she was worried about the coming meeting. So was I. This wasn't going to be easy on anyone involved.

At the hotel, after a number of security checks on different levels of the hotel, we were finally allowed to go upstairs, all the way to the top suite.

The President met us as we got off the elevator. His wife, Penny, was behind him. She looked tired and very, very worried. She had a right to be both.

Heather joined us from a side room and stepped into the presidential suite as we did, closing the door behind us all.

"Doc," the President said. "It's a pleasure finally meeting you. I've followed your career since you started. Carson was very proud of you."

He wasn't really smiling, but he at least shook my hand. Clearly the man was a politician right to the last gasp.

"Thank you, Mr. President," I said. "This is Detective Annie Lott of the Las Vegas police."

"Princeton grad, future great poker player," the President said to Annie. "Glad to meet you."

The President extended his hand, and Annie shook it. "Thank you, sir," she said. "I'm sorry this is under such trying circumstances."

The President nodded, then glanced at his wife before moving into the middle of the big suite and taking a seat at a large dining room table, indicating that Annie and I should do the same. His wife sat beside him, but didn't touch him.

Heather remained standing off to one side, her back to the door.

I took out of my pocket all nine keys and placed them in front of the President. They rattled on the table.

"Two of them match yours and Paul's, of course."

The man just stared at them as if he had seen a ghost. I imagined he had. Those keys were a ghost that had haunted his nightmares for decades.

The First Lady looked pale, as if she were about to faint. She couldn't seem to take her eyes off the keys. Clearly, he had told her. But I had no idea if she had known all along, like Ace and my mother had. Or was just learning about this mess the last few days. It would go a lot easier on her if she had always known.

"I have the originals of all the documents," I said. "Agent Voight has copies and Detective Lott has copies, all ready to go to the press and authorities, all well hidden and protected if something happens to any of us."

The President waived my statement aside. "I understand your threats. What do you want?"

"Your resignation," I said. "Nothing more."

CHAPTER EIGHTY-FOUR

"WHY WOULD YOU WANT HIS RESIGNATION?" his wife asked, clearly shocked.

The President sat back, his eyes glazed.

"For the good of the country, if no other reason," Annie said. "For the good of his party, for the memory of all the men in that game that are now dead. If we release those documents, the next year will be a living nightmare, and you will be impeached anyway I'm sure."

"Why in the world did you think you could work with Steven Harrison?" I asked, not hiding the disgust in my voice.

The President came back as if I had slapped him.

"I didn't work with him!" he shouted, coming up out of his chair at me across the table. He was a very powerful man and I could feel his anger.

It was very, very real.

His wife put a hand on his arm and after a moment of glaring at me, he sat back.

346

I waited for an answer to my question, the tension in the room almost suffocating.

"He called me on my private line," the President said, his voice low. "Taunted me, told me he was starting to round up the keys. Dared me to try to stop him."

"The bastard thought it was all a big game," the President's wife said.

The President nodded. "Steven said my key would be the last one, the biggest prize."

"So why did you call him so many times?" Annie asked.

"To try to stop him, to offer him money, offer him other things, anything to get him to stop killing my old friends," the President said, his voice fading. "He always just laughed. God, I hated that laugh."

I remembered Steven's smirking laugh from the game at R.A.'s cabin. The guy's insanity and feeling of superiority clearly made everything and everyone around him just funny.

The President seemed to shrink in on himself and his wife touched his arm gently for support.

"Don't you understand," he said, "in this job, my hands were tied by the very fact that I was in that game in 1982. Paul and I considered reporting it as a threat to the Secret Service, but we were afraid of the investigation getting leaked. All we decided we could do, and barely that, was talk to our friend, FBI Director Smith. The Director and Paul decided to send Agent Voight to try to stop him and protect you and the others."

The President looked over at Heather. "By the time Paul went to Vegas, we were starting to panic. Steven was ahead of us at every turn, and getting close to all the keys, and if someone like him got the information you have, he could have done a fantastic amount of damage."

He glanced at me, then back at Heather. "Don't you understand? That's why I sent Paul to help you. That's why I called Steven that day to tell him about the documents in R.A.'s home safe, to have him walk into your trap."

He took a deep breath. "But as it ended up, all I did was kill my best friend."

"And you didn't send Special Forces men to stop Nyland from running at the game I set up?" I asked.

The President actually laughed, but there was no humor in the laugh. "Oh, sure, I can just call any branch of the military to go do personal favors for me. Those men that night were Steven's buddies from his days in the Army. Both ended up dead, killed by Steven. Their bodies were found yesterday in Idaho above Sun Valley. I just heard about it this morning."

I glanced over at Heather. She had said nothing. She just stood there staring at the President.

I sat back and tried to think.

I had been convinced that the President had been working with Steven. It was no wonder there had been no one watching us at the bank, no threats in the last three days, nothing. Maybe, just maybe, he hadn't been directing Steven in the first place.

"Sir," I said, "with this murder cover-up in your past, what made you think you could become the President? Didn't you realize that someone would use it against you?"

The President laughed. "Son, don't you play the hands that are dealt you? I didn't plan to become President. I just got on the crest of a really big wave and let others push."

I glanced at Annie, then back at Heather. Both of them seemed to be in deep thought. I wanted to believe the President, that he too had been working to stop Steven. The facts seemed to fit that, but the phone records also fit the other theory, that he had tried to use Steven to round up the keys to protect his career.

I needed more information.

"Sir, can you tell me what happened that night in 1982?" I asked. "Who really made the threats against the families?"

"Mostly Nyland, but eventually a few others joined him on that," the President said. He looked directly at me. "Carson wanted nothing to do with it, and neither did I. But Carson was the most vocal. Neither of us would help bury that damn cheater's body. It was Nyland and R.A. and Jeff Taylor who had killed him, they buried him."

"Tell him," the President's wife said when her husband stopped for a moment and seemed to get lost in the past. "In case he doesn't know. He was too young to remember."

The President looked at me. "Your mother was beaten and in the hospital before we left R.A.'s the next morning. Carson talked to her over a short-wave radio. He got so angry, I thought he was going to tear Nyland apart. It was R.A. who stopped him."

The President took a deep breath, glanced at his wife for support, then went on. "Nyland said that the next person would be killed, not just beaten, and it would be you, Doc. And then someone each of us cared for. That pretty much convinced us all to go along with them. I couldn't risk the life of my Penny," he said, touching his wife's hand.

The First Lady looked at me. "And your father couldn't risk your life any more either, or your mother's. That was why he left."

"This has been our biggest nightmare for all these years," the President said, "just as it was your father's and mother's."

I sat and thought as silence filled the big room. He had given me the same story as the others, no different. He was as much a victim to Nyland, and Steven as the rest were.

And now we were finishing the game that Steven had started by asking him to resign. And I wanted nothing to do with Steven's sick game. I just wanted it over.

"I'd like a moment to talk with Detective Lott and Agent Voight," I said.

"Please," the President said. "Take your time." He chuckled to himself. "I don't think I have anything that might be more important than this."

The First Lady put her head on the President's shoulder as Annie and I stood and moved back to the door to talk to Heather.

As we got close, Heather whispered, "He's a good man, and a good president. I believe him. I would not be respecting all the work Paul did if I asked him to resign now."

I nodded.

"Annie?"

"I agree with Heather. All my police instincts tell me he wasn't involved with Steven, other than how he said. He was used. And right now, we're still being used by a dead man and I don't much like it."

Neither did I. "So we take back our demand?" I asked. "And we destroy the paperwork, all of it?"

"We do," Heather said.

Annie nodded.

We turned back to the table. This time Heather joined us, sitting down next to Annie.

"We have changed our minds," I said. "We would like to retract our demand that your resign."

Now the President looked puzzled and the First Lady let out a deep breath of relief.

Before he could say anything, I kept going, "When we leave here and return home, we will destroy all copies of everything. There will be no more evidence of that game in 1982."

"Just ugly memories," Heather said.

The First Lady stared at me.

The President opened his mouth, then closed it, then opened it again. No words came out.

"I loved Paul," Heather said. "I know you did as well, as he loved you. You need to stay here, finish his work, fight the fights he wanted you to fight, the reason he pushed you into this job."

From the look in the President's eyes, I would never doubt that we had made the right decision.

CHAPTER EIGHTY-FIVE

LAS VEGAS, NEVADA. SEPTEMBER 14

THE EARLY MORNING was cool for this time of the year in Vegas, with the temperatures getting all the way down to the low seventies. It was still a little too warm for a fire in the fireplace, but I didn't care. Mother turned up the air-conditioning as I started a fire in Carson's fireplace.

Annie had come over. She had the envelope I had given her from the bank. She had sealed it and never looked at it. She said she didn't need those images in her head.

When I had come up with the idea of a special burning ceremony, I had called Heather. She had told me she was about to go get the documents from Director Smith and destroy them. I told her my plan and she got the time off work. I sent my plane for her. Mike went along for the ride and to keep her company on the way back.

So now there were seven of us in the living room of Carson's home, plus there were soon to be two special guests.

Ace and my mother sat on one couch. Annie and I had the other. Fleet had a chair, and Mike and Heather were manning a special video hook-up beside Carson's big television, working together like they belonged together. I had no doubt that Heather was going to be spending a lot of time in Las Vegas in the future. It would take her some time to get over Paul, but I had no doubt Mike would help her in any way he could.

"You ready?" Mike asked.

"As ever," I said.

Mike signaled he had a connection. We all faced the camera sitting on top of the big television.

"All together now," I said, "Good Morning, Mr. President."

There was a very familiar laugh from the television as the image cleared and we were facing the President and the First Lady. They both looked years younger than just a few days ago and were smiling.

"Good morning, everyone," he said, smiling.

I stood and held up my envelope. "Before we cook in here from this fire, let's get this over with. These are the originals that had rested in that damned box in Seattle since 1982."

I held them up, then tossed them into the fireplace.

Everyone cheered. I think the President was the loudest.

Annie stood. "My copies, sir. Please don't tell anyone I'm destroying evidence of a crime. It could be bad on my poker career."

Everyone laughed, then cheered as she tossed the envelope into the fire and we watched it catch and burn quickly.

Heather moved toward the fireplace. She looked at me, then at Annie. "Thank you both for tracking down and killing the bastard who shot Paul."

All I could do was nod.

"My pleasure," Annie said.

Heather turned to the camera. "And thank you, Mr. President, for continuing the work you and Paul started. It's all I ask. It's all he would have wanted."

With that, she tossed her envelope into the fire as we all cheered.

I couldn't imagine the weight that was lifting from the President's shoulders. As President, he didn't need any extra. He had enough.

"Thank you," the First Lady said, "for finally ending this nightmare."

On the couch, my mother and Ace were both just smiling and nodding.

"Yes, thank you," the President said. "I can't imagine how I could ever repay you all for this."

"A larger Social Security check would be nice," Ace said.

"Honestly," I said after the laughter stopped, "just do the best job you can in there. And come and play some cards some time."

"Yeah," Ace said. "We're always looking for some fresh blood with money."

"I just might take you up on that," the President said, smiling. "Thank you."

The screen went dark.

With that, the game was over.

At least it was over for as long as the President kept his word. There was an old saying. *Never trust a poker player. He'll lie to your face and take your money with a smile.*

The President was a poker player and a politician, the worst combination. I believed him, but I didn't trust him.

Annie stood and went to stir the ashes, to make sure every scrap was burnt.

I watched her as she dug at the flames with a rod. I had discovered over the last few weeks that I liked watching her no matter what she was doing.

I liked arguing with her, kissing her, just being with her. That felt new and different to me.

My mother went back into her room.

Heather and Mike worked to gather up his equipment and then started taking it out to his truck.

Ace and Fleet began talking about an investment property in Boise and went into the kitchen, leaving me and Annie pretty much alone.

She kept stirring the fire.

I said nothing.

Then, after a moment, she glanced up at me with a puzzled look on her face. "You didn't..." she whispered.

I only shrugged.

She smiled, then shook her head, clearly understanding.

She went back to stirring the ashes, making sure every scrap was gone.

She knew I hadn't burnt the originals from the ashes and paper in the fire. There were no actual remains of photos in there, just paper. I had those originals stashed in a very safe place, where they would only be found if I died. I had no plans of telling anyone where they were. Not even Annie.

I hoped to live at least as long as the President was in office, then I would destroy them myself.

I had a hunch the President knew as well that I hadn't destroyed everything. He wasn't stupid, and he knew I was a poker player.

He understood that I wouldn't just hand over the game to him. As long as he kept his promise and left everyone alone, that's how this game would end up.

Even.

A chopped pot, with both of us taking the prize we each wanted.

"So, what would you like to do now?" I asked Annie.

"Honestly," she said, standing, "go down to the Bellagio, sit in a hot poker game and try to take as much money from as many people as I can."

"And forget about the President and being a cop?" I asked, smiling at her.

"Absolutely," she said. "Forget about everything. I just want to play cards. Let the world take care of itself for a day or so."

"No wild bunny sex?" I asked, trying to keep a straight face.

"Afterwards," she said. "Afterwards."

"Spoken like a true poker player."

USA TODAY BEST-SELLING AUTHOR

DEAN WESLEY
SMITH

KILL
GAME

A COLD POKER GANG NOVEL

If you liked this Doc Hill thriller, you might also like the
Cold Poker Gang mysteries, in which Doc Hill, Annie,
Fleet and the gang also appear. Following is a sample
chapter from the first book in that series, *Kill Game*,
which is available from your favorite bookseller.

CHAPTER ONE

_____

THE IDEA JIM HAD on a warm early-summer evening was to find the rumored place for afterhours dancing called "The Path." Jim had just graduated high school, the proud class of 1992. He was headed next year to Stanford, full academic ride, and he was really looking forward to getting out of the desert in a couple months. He had been born and raised here and was excited about living somewhere else. Anywhere, actually.

Jim stood barely five-nine, had long brown hair, and a moustache he was doing his best to grow and mostly failing.

Sharon, his girlfriend over the last six months, also now graduated, wasn't happy he was going so far away. She had been offered a scholarship at UNLV and had taken it. So between them there was a tension of the coming split.

Sharon was actually taller than Jim, with long blonde hair and skinny legs that seemed to always be stuffed into jeans a size too small. She had also done some light modeling and as she aged, she just got better looking.

Jim had no idea what she saw in him, but they always had such a good time together. They had two hobbies: Dancing and having sex in every place they could imagine or risk.

Tonight they were thinking of doing both at the same time. They had heard how really crowded the dance floor at "The Path" could be. Sharon had suggested, with a smile, that it might be fun to try a little "fooling around" on the floor while dancing.

Jim was game if she was. With Sharon, he would try just about anything. Logic often never played a part.

So they parked down on Paradise Road, about two blocks from the club, and headed down the sidewalk along the row of low warehouses, holding hands and laughing, the coming separation only a distant thing to ignore on such a wonderful spring night.

The club had an entrance off an alley into a large warehouse, but until two days ago, on Sharon's birthday, both of them hadn't been eighteen and old enough to get in, so they hadn't tried to find it.

Paradise had street lights and even though the area felt rough, both of them were native to the city and knew this really wasn't a bad area. They were as safe as they could be at midnight in Las Vegas.

Cars lined the street on both sides, so they knew they were in the right area even though they didn't know exactly where the club was. And between traffic on the street, if they listened hard, they could hear the pounding beat of the music echoing through the one-story buildings of the area.

"Maybe it's down here?" Sharon asked, pulling Jim into the first alley they came to.

Jim could tell at once they were in the wrong place.

And then the smell hit them.

The putrid smell of something rotting in the heat. It was a cloying smell that seemed to make the air thicker than it actually was, and fill every sense. It turned his stomach instantly. He knew it was a dead person instantly. He had smelled that before. He had no idea how police who worked around dead bodies ever got used to the smell.

"What is that?" Sharon asked, stopping and covering her mouth and nose. After a moment she started to back toward the street, her eyes round and her skin pale.

Jim stood his ground. He had been with two friends last year up on Lake Mead when they found a floater near the shore. He knew that smell. Someone had died.

But there was no body in the alley. Just walls of warehouses. Not even garbage cans.

He stepped toward one wall and the smell decreased.

"Jim, get out of there," Sharon said from the sidewalk behind him.

He motioned to her that he would be right there, then stepped toward the other wall. Originally a white stucco wall, it was now stained with years of grime and lack of paint that he could see even in the dark shadows.

And the smell got much worse.

There was no door in the wall, just a nearby high window that was cracked slightly.

Someone was dead in that room beyond that window.

He turned and went back to Sharon, taking her hand. They went around to the front of the building, took down the address, then said, "We have a phone call to make."

He could see a pay phone a block away on the outside wall of a closed grocery store, so he started off in that direction.

"I thought we were going dancing?" Sharon asked, scrambling along in her high heels, working to keep up with his fast strides.

"We are," he said. "But we have to call the police first."

"Why?" she asked.

"That smell," he said.

"You are going to report a smell to the police?" she asked. "It was bad, but not a criminal offense I'm sure."

"I wouldn't be so sure of that," Jim said, letting go of her hand as they reached the phone and he started digging into his pocket for change.

"What do you mean?" Sharon asked, looking worried. There was one thing he really liked about Sharon. She was smart and knew he was smart, so they trusted each other on a lot of things.

"I've smelled that smell before," he said, as he dropped the coin into the phone and pushed zero for operator."

He glanced back at her puzzled expression.

"Near the body I found up at Lake Mead."

She put her hand over her mouth and even in the strange lights of the street, he could see she had lost most of her tan very suddenly.

The operator answered and he was connected to the police. He gave them his name, his location, and the address of the building.

Then he said clearly, "I want to report a dead body."

ABOUT THE AUTHOR

USA TODAY BESTSELLING AUTHOR Dean Wesley Smith published more than a hundred novels in thirty years and hundreds and hundreds of short stories across many genres.

He wrote a couple dozen *Star Trek* novels, the only two original *Men in Black* novels, Spider-Man and X-Men novels, plus novels set in gaming and television worlds. He wrote novels under dozens of pen names in the worlds of comic books and movies, including novelizations of a dozen films, from *The Final Fantasy* to *Steel* to *Rundown.*

He now writes his own original fiction under just the one name, Dean Wesley Smith. In addition to his upcoming novel releases, his monthly magazine called *Smith's Monthly* premiered October 1, 2013, filled entirely with his original novels and stories.

Dean also worked as an editor and publisher, first at Pulphouse Publishing, then for *VB Tech Journal,* then for Pocket Books. He now plays a role as an executive editor for the original anthology series *Fiction River.*

For more information about his work, go to www.deanwesleysmith.com, www.smithsmonthly.com or www.fictionriver.com.

www.ingramcontent.com/pod-product-compliance
Lightning Source LLC
Chambersburg PA
CBHW022143010726
47493CB00002B/319